Shee,
Your spirit brings by-
so much joy in my
and around my business.
I thank you for what you
represent for me. Have a
great read!

Gay
04-23-23

WHEN A ZOMBIE TASTES SALT

The story of a servant girl in Haiti

ELSY DINVIL

Erèz's name is the Creole pronunciation for her given name, Heureuse, and "heureuse" is a French adjective that means "happy."

Editors:
Eva Fitzsimons
Honda Cevallos

ISBN: 978-1-66788-500-1

Self-Published in the United States

1st Edition

Dedication

This book is lovingly dedicated to my late mother who survived years of abuse as a restavèk (child slave). It is also dedicated to all the current child slaves in Haiti who dream of being free someday, yet are trapped in this horrific system of slavery disguised as servanthood. To my Haitian brothers and sisters who also witnessed the devastating psychological scars left upon our mothers and fathers from the aftermath of years of serving as restavèks and who also inherited the generational trauma they passed down to us, many hugs to you.

FOREWORD

My mother was a resilient woman who worked hard her entire life. When my sisters and I were growing up, she was a quiet storm in our house, and had the final say in every major decision in our lives. Her confidence and steadfastness were the results of years of patient work by a man who was able to love her for who she was: a human being. That man was my father, Luc Dinvil, who saw beyond my mother's background, financial status, and insecurities. Most importantly, my father could see past the shattering effects of a childhood that stripped my mother of her basic human dignity and deprived her of joy and happiness. With his love, kindness, and gentle persistence, my father strengthened my mother's mental health and built her back up. He helped her discover her innate gifts, put her on the pedestal she was born to be on, and supported her in the incredible matriarchal role of our family.

In 2017, I traveled back to Haiti with the purpose of digging and sifting through the details of my mother's childhood story. When I arrived, the level of my mother's dementia had progressed to the point that it was difficult to obtain the significant information I was seeking. I desperately wished I had asked her about her young life years prior.

It was exceedingly painful to witness my once vivacious and vibrant mother in such a deteriorated state. My heart broke when didn't recognize who I was, even after I planted a big fat kiss on her warm familiar cheek. She looked at me and smiled as if I was a stranger. After about fifteen minutes of me staring at her in shock, I heard her say, "When did you land?" A little relieved, I knew it had finally clicked for her that it was her very own daughter standing in front of her.

My mother loved perfumes and scented white talc powder. When I spoke to her before my trip, she had requested some toiletries. I made sure to bring them all, carefully selecting them just for her. I had packed perfumes, a watch, scented white talc powder, deodorant, casual sandals, muumuus to wear around the house, and dressy clothes and shoes to wear to church. As I pulled each of these items from my flowery black-and-white suitcase, she had the unabashed expression of a child who was receiving every single one of her most desired toys for Christmas. She took each article from me, all the while maintaining the widest childlike smile on her face as she repeated, "Thank you, my daughter. Thank God, I didn't abort you!"

After a few moments of this, I just wanted to be alone and cry, but I didn't feel it was right to do so in front of my sister who had been caring for our mother for over two years. Furthermore, I didn't want to deny my mother any shred of the innocent joy she was experiencing. Although my sister had prepared a room for me to sleep in, that night I chose to sleep next to my mother. I was brought back to times long-past as I realized some things hadn't changed since I'd seen her last, years ago. I watched her familiar routine as she brushed her teeth over the small aluminum bucket in front of her bed, holding an aluminum cup in one hand and brushing her teeth with the other. After brushing her teeth, she knelt in front of her bed and prayed incoherent prayers that only God Himself could understand.

I couldn't hold on to my tears any longer, and I wept in the pitch darkness of that night as it truly dawned on me that she wasn't going to be with us for much longer. She died seven months after that visit, and my heart was broken. The pain of losing her remains extremely palpable even today. I had every intention to take care of her in ways she never could have imagined, but unfortunately, her time had come before my best laid plans came to pass.

When A Zombie Tastes Salt is a compilation of bits, pieces, and fragments of my mother's life story. When my sisters and I were growing up, my mother wished to recount stories of her childhood as a restavèk; however, we wanted no part in hearing the gruesome details of the pain she endured and survived as a child. Had we been strong enough to listen to her share her story, the lines written in this book would likely be very different. The major periods of my mother's life as depicted in this book would more accurately embody her true life's story. The events she lived through would be represented with more authenticity, but instead, I filled in the cracks with fictitious characters as needed from my observation of the Haitian culture as a whole to add depth to the story and make it a more complete picture.

Many characters in the book are in fact very real. Man Féfé, Mèt Féfé, Misyé Noël, and Bòs Latou are all people as real as you and I. I met many of them, though not all. Man Rebecca, for example, died before I could meet her, but I know my mother held her in very high regard and often spoke of her fondly. During my visit to my mother before she passed away, she asked me several times if I had seen Man Rebecca. The impact Man Rebecca had on my mother was deeply meaningful to her even in her final days on this earth.

I grew up around many of the characters portrayed in these pages. Though some are not named directly, pieces of them are represented in the story; for example, Tant Aséli, who was my oldest sister's godmother. To this day, I retain many tender memories of my sisters and I stopping by Tant Aséli's house after church to kiss her on the cheeks. Often, after we kissed Tant Aséli goodbye, she gave my youngest sister and I dous pistach (peanut butter fudge) wrapped in pieces of brown paper to take home with us. I can still recall her gorgeous light-skinned children with their long beautiful curly mulatto hair. Even the parrot mentioned in the book was part of my childhood. My mother often joked about the jako (parrot) when it rained because the only time the bird saw fit to speak was when it started raining by announcing, "Madame, rain, rain, rain."

My knowledge of the culture as a born and raised Haitian helped me complete the narrative of the story. I also waded through research to find details about Haiti in the 1930s, '40s, and '50s. Unfortunately, detailed historical information about the city of my birth, Jérémie, is still exceptionally scarce. As you read this book, take the historical information presented with a grain of salt. If you are curious about Haiti during the era I write about, I would encourage you to conduct independent research before drawing any definite conclusions about the country's history during those years.

You will also notice that I put a lot of emphasis on the words "peasant" or "peasant-like." This is largely because citizens residing in the Haitian countryside are still discriminated against by Haitians living in the city. They are regarded as lesser-than because of their demeanor, their command of the Creole language, their obvious limited knowledge of the French language, the way they dress, and their overall mannerisms. I wanted to clearly portray the differences between life in the city and life in the countryside in Haiti. Additionally,

I wanted to illustrate the subtle societal divisions within these classes in the Haitian culture. My mother was born one of those peasants, but she was able to overcome countless obstacles throughout her life. One of her greatest personal accomplishments was to learn to read and write in her fifties. Her perseverance in life serves as a tremendous motivation and inspiration for me.

While I hope you will enjoy this book, I realize that the subject matter is intense and sometimes graphic. It is not a simple or easy thing to learn that so many children in the world of today still live in brutal and appalling conditions just as my mother did more than eighty years ago, but I strongly believe that it is critical to shed light on the horrific practice of Haitian children being enslaved and abused in this system that is still very active in today's Haitian culture. In fact, much of modern Haitian society still normalizes this system.

CHAPTER 1
Nan Maché

Wednesdays were maché, or flea market day, and Erèz never ceased to be fascinated and mesmerized by the large trucks as they rolled by, painted in bright colors. They came early in the morning from the larger surrounding cities. Many of them arrived at the maché from downtown Jérémie, as well as cities like Beaumont, Marfranc, Chambellan, Latibollière, Prévilé, and occasionally even from Les Cayes, the fourth largest city of Haiti. Transfixed, Erèz watched the trucks one by one as they pulled in with loud music blaring. The drivers showed their own excitement as they blasted their horn in perfect rhythm to the beat of the music. It was a game of musical klaxons, and Erèz wondered if they had rehearsed so they could nail the rhythm ever so perfectly each time. Her eyes glanced to the tops of the trucks to see what they were bringing in. She could see the brown skin of the African yams, the yellows and greens of plantains, and a multitude of burlap sacks that were stuffed with charcoal.

The maché was an endless cacophony of sound. Erèz's small ears got filled at once with the many voices of merchants and customers negotiating back and forth over the price of goods; the occasional loud bang of a motorcycle muffler; and the oinking pigs and bleating goats as farmers made their way through the bustling crowd looking to sell their fine animals. Above all, she could also hear the voices of the town's representatives speaking to the crowd through a blue-and-white megaphone, announcing what new legislation was being passed.

The youngest of three children, Erèz was the only one that her mother took to the maché. Her oldest sister, Maria (nicknamed Yaya) and Ilèyis, her brother, usually left early in the morning with her father to work on the farm and to take to pasture the few goats the family owned. Instead of leaving Erèz all alone in their small bamboo straw house, her mother took her to the maché.

Every week, Erèz's mother loaded a small packet of wood scraps on her head after carefully securing a twokèt to protect her scalp. A twokèt is a Haitian Creole word for a doughnut-shaped support made of dry banana leaves and folded in a circle, which was then placed on one's head under the heavy load. Though she did enjoy the exciting sights and sounds of the maché, Erèz's little heart was saddened as she would have much preferred to attend school. At eight years old, Erèz had not yet spent a single day in school.

When some of her friends went to school in the morning, they often waved goodbye with a friendly "Sak pasé Erèz? Na wè pita tandé" ("What's up Erèz? We will see you later, yes?"). She would wave back, but sometimes her eyes filled with tears because she couldn't join them. Her mother tried to soothe her by telling her that lajan an preské kont (the money for her school) was almost together. Knowing how badly Erèz wished to go to school, it weighed on her mother's heart to see her daughter suffer that much.

Erèz imagined scenarios of her little friends in their classroom with their crisp pleated blue and white skirts, and wished she could be learning right alongside them. When these thoughts struck her, she sang the cheerful songs her friends taught her, ones they played to during recess. She dreamed often of that day she would step into a schoolyard, and longed for the morning that she would kiss her mother goodbye and join her group of friends walking to school. All would be excited for the day, but Erèz would be especially eager and enthusiastic to learn to read and write. She had pictured this scene in her head countless times since she was five years old. Three years later, she still lived in that dream.

At the flea market, one could also find the Madan Saras. Erèz greatly admired those hard-working women. Those were the entrepreneurs who attended the maché every Wednesday, their trays brimming with an endless supply of household goods. Fragrant soaps, scented deodorant, snowy baby powder, underwear for adults and children alike, not to mention all manner of fresh produce from their gardens. Beyond that, the Madan Saras were pillars of their homes, neighborhoods, and communities. Often, they were the main providers for their children, and made it their responsibility to watch over the children of others while treating them as their own. Their strength, determination, and resilience impressed Erèz deeply and impacted her to her core.

Erèz often dreamed that some day she too would become one of those clever and strong Madan Saras who spent their days bargaining with countless deal-seeking customers. She envisioned herself in a future where she would be literate, independent, and an absolute master bargainer with the haggling shoppers that would come her way. Sometimes, the Madan Saras brought their little girls with them to the maché instead of sending them to school on maché day. Though Erèz was not nearly as well-dressed as those little girls, and their mothers were much wealthier than her parents, they played together nonetheless. Of course, there still were some parents who would never allow their kids to play with her because of her raggedy clothes. They noticed the faded colors and tiny holes that peppered her garments, signs that she obviously came from a poor family who couldn't afford much. Those snobby city women automatically assumed that Erèz would be a bad influence on their kids, and that she would teach them peasant-like mannerisms. Those ladies prevented all interactions between their kids and her. In Erèz's heart, she understood the unspoken rules and maintained her distance from that group of kids, but regardless of the discrimination she dealt with, she happily played with many little girls her age when her mother didn't need her help too heavily during the day at the maché.

Being at the maché was also a time that Erèz could see the wealthier children who lived in the area pass by in their blue-and-white or red-and-white plaid shirts. As the little girls went by, Erèz imagined what the letter A might look like and made up an image in her head. Erèz couldn't escape the reminders that she was unable to go to school like other children. Her mother was aware of this and made sure to never comment on how beautiful the little girls were in front of Erèz. They always looked so perfect with their well-combed hair, probably moisturized with Haitian castor oil, and the beautiful ribbons and barrettes adorning their hair.

While Erèz prized the time she spent seeing the sights and running around playing at the flea market, what she truly loved most of all were the delicious treats her mother gave her during those weekly trips the day of the maché. At the start of the day, Erèz's mother always treated her to a fresh grated coconut bar, or a grilled peanut bar, or even just grilled peanuts. At the end of the day, Erèz was offered some type of fritay which was some form of fried deliciousness. Plantains, dumplings, chicken, slices of sweet potatoes, or pork belly could all be part of fritay. Her mother was rarely able to buy much with the money from her sales, but she always managed at the very least to buy two pieces of hot fried plantains for Erèz to enjoy before the ten-mile journey back to their house.

At the end of the maché day on Wednesdays, Erèz's mother purchased household items that were difficult to find at home in Guinaudée using the money that she had earned from the sale of the wood scraps and charcoal. Even when they were available in Guinaudée, her mother preferred buying them for cheaper at the maché. Erèz usually helped her mother out on their way back to the house by carrying on her head a recycled burlap sack with the few household items that her mother could afford folded at the bottom. A piece of Rosita soap for laundry, which was done by hand at the Guinaudée River some Saturdays; a recycled sixteen-ounce plastic bottle filled with kerosene, tightly secured; a mesh for the kerosene lamp; some olive oil that barely filled half of an eight-ounce plastic bottle; and a few pieces of pen ralé, buttery bread for her father to dip in his coffee in the morning. This constituted the shopping in the maché for the week. Occasionally, people in their neighborhood would ask Erèz's mother to do them a favor and buy specific items they needed like castor oil, or brown sugar, and she would pack them in the same burlap sack with her goods before placing it on top of Erèz's head.

Erèz and her mother spoke about anything and everything on their way back to the house. One question that Erèz always asked without fail was if the money was almost ready so she could attend school next October, when the school year began. Erèz was always assured that her mother was saving money for her tuition, and that it was almost ready.

CHAPTER 2
Guinaudée

Guinaudée was one of the small villages located in the country-side of Jérémie, the third largest city in Haiti. Guinaudée was known for its greenery and vast, sprawling landscapes. It was filled with coconut and mango trees, and an abundance of plantains, breadfruits, sweet potatoes, and African yams.

When Erèz was a child, everybody knew each other in the village. The little foot-carved alleys that made up the streets didn't have names, but every adult knew where every family lived and each child's name. Adults cared for children that weren't their own, reprimanding them when they caused trouble. The village was essentially one big family, and everyone wanted every child to be well-behaved and cared for. Neighbors were also known to share and exchange what they har-vested from their farms, and people commonly traded sweet and sour oranges, limes, avocados, pomelos, soursops, quenepas, tamarinds, and mangos. People passing in front of their neighbors' houses waved a bonjou (good morning) or bonswa (good afternoon). They asked each other if they'd had a good evening the night before and inquired after each other's children. It was a serene and peaceful place populated with some of the kindest and most generous people one could ever find.

Erèz's house sat in a valley. If one was to travel the main road, Erèz's family's tiny house could be spotted with its small entrance door. From the road, one could see the flimsy tins that made up the roof of the house and the pieces of old carton boxes that Erèz's father had placed close to the front door to support the mud wall that could crumble at the slightest disturbance. If one took the time to look further, they might also notice a second little house. This served as the kitchen, where Erèz and her mother often spent time together preparing and cooking the family's dinner. Contrary to the tin roof of the two-room house in the front, the kitchen's roof was tightly covered with large dry coconut branches that served as the perfect defense against the hot sun and prevented the crickets and cockroaches from crawling through or flying at night, but didn't provide much protection against rain. If it had rained during the day, the beautiful orangish-ginger dirt in the yard became very muddy. Some mornings, it became so gooey and slippery that at least one family member would slide and fall. If it was an adult that fell, the kids always had a good laugh because seeing an adult tumble and fall was always a hilarious sight for them.

Moving further down the road, a traveler could see Erèz's closest neighbor's banana and plantain gardens. Those flourished beautifully and served as a long fence between the two yards. By those thriving trees was a tiny pond where the frogs hopped and splashed about. At night, anyone in the neighborhood could hear them chirping, croaking, or even whistling through the deep darkness of the night. Erèz was terrified of the cheerful little frogs and hated them. While other children spent gleeful afternoons running and chasing each other through the vast banana tree maze, Erèz never ventured through the trees even when the sun shined the brightest, fearing a frog might jump on her out of the blue.

The neighbor who owned the vast banana tree garden and pond was Mèt Robèto. He was the principal at the National Primary School of Guinaudée, the only national school for the whole village besides the private Catholic school, Immaculate Conception School. Everyone called him "Mèt" or "Master" in Creole out of respect for his profession as an educator and title as a school principal. His name was really Roberto, but most people skipped the "r" in the middle and pronounced it "Mèt Robèto." Mèt Robèto was considered one of the most influential and respected leaders in the village. People of the village often sought out his advice when they found themselves in challenging situations or needed assistance with something. Erèz's family benefited from his kindness. He had written numerous letters in French for Erèz's parents when they wanted to reach out to Erèz's mother's cousin, Cecilia, who lived in the capital, Port-Au-Prince. There, on Mèt Robèto's front porch, Erèz's mother and father sat on a little wooden bench explaining what they wanted to tell Cecilia. Mèt Robèto sat behind his well-loved wooden desk and carefully took in every Creole word to translate their thoughts into his best French.

CHAPTER 3
Tant Lucienne

Not too far from Erèz's parents' house was the house of Erèz's best friend, Marie-Jeanne. Marie-Jeanne's one-room house was even tinier than Erèz's. The walls were made of dried coconut branches, and the roof was covered with dried banana leaves. Tant Lucienne or Aunt Lucienne was Marie-Jeanne's grandmother, and she was a fixture inside the home. She sat in her weathered rocking chair all day, always carefully observing the world around her. At eighty-plus years old, Aunt Lucienne's body could only do so much after the years of raising six children alone. Her knees ached and she rarely left her trusty rocking chair except to use the latrine that had been dug in the backyard. Both Erèz and Marie-Jeanne worried about Tant Lucienne's old knees giving out on her if she squatted for just one minute too long while pooping. Would she fall backward into that deep and possibly endless hole full of poop? Miraculously, she always made it back to the rocking chair. She was almost always out of breath from the endeavor, but survived it each time. Upon her rocking chair hung her precious rosary. It had been a wedding gift from way back in the days of her youth. Although all that was left on the delicate thread were just a few beads and the crucifix tip, it was her dearest possession. This rosary never left her side even as she laid herself down to sleep in the only bed in the house.

When Aunt Lucienne prayed, rolling what was left of beads in her old rosary, as much as one tried, not a soul could hear what she was softly muttering to Saint Peter, the Patron Saint of Guinaudée and all the other saints she knew, plus Mary, the Mother of Jesus; her Heavenly Father; her brother, Jesus; and the Holy Spirit. Everyone knew that Tant Lucienne mumbled the prayers under her breath on purpose. This kept the only activity that gave so much comfort to her soul intimate while she dealt with the many unspoken psychological burdens from her past that haunted her and her slow physical state.

Every Friday evening, Marie-Jeanne's mother undid the two long braids at each side of Tant Lucienne's head. Her salt-and-pepper hair was beautiful. Even at her age, her head was full of long, thick curly hair. Marie-Jeanne's mother scratched Tant Lucienne's scalp using the end of the comb with the smaller set of teeth to remove dandruff. She then carefully moisturized her scalp with fresh Haitian castor oil. She delicately parted her thick hair in very small sections, dipped the index finger of her right hand in the heavily used tin can half-full of oil, and she then made sure to cover each and every strand of hair with the oil. Anyone who caught sight of Tant Lucienne after having her hair braided on Friday evening always teased her by saying that "Grandma is looking more like a teenager." Her cheerful grin indicated that she appreciated the teasing and compliments without saying a word. All her life, Tant Lucienne was a woman of very few words. Despite six of her front teeth missing, Tant Lucienne gladly accepted the compliments with the widest smile on her face, unveiling decayed gums and dark spaces between her remaining teeth. These Fridays with her freshly moisturized scalp gave Tant Lucienne her only opportunity during the week to socialize with young women in the neighborhood.

CHAPTER 4
Marie-Jeanne's Mother

Marie-Jeanne's mother made grated coconut bars to sell for a living. She woke up very early in the morning to make coffee for Tant Lucienne. Some days, she also made cerasee tea by picking up some fresh cerasee leaves or branches on her way to the house from the school where she sold her bars. Cerasee tea and the plant it came from were known to cleanse the body, strengthen the immune system, and heal a hundred and one sicknesses, including fever. Adults in the neighborhood made cerasee tea to wake up their digestive systems before eating breakfast. Before she took off in the morning, Marie-Jeanne's mother also cooked bread soup with spinach for little eight-month-old Patrick—her youngest child, Marie-Jeanne's little brother. She then used their only pot to sanitize a couple of baby bottles by boiling them in hot water and then made up two bottles to leave at the house so that Marie-Jeanne could feed her baby brother.

Those bottles were carefully prepared by mixing two tablespoons of dried cow's milk with water and kept in a stainless-steel pot that a friend had gifted her when Marie-Jeanne was born eight years ago.

Marie-Jeanne's mother sold her coconut bars in front of the Immaculate Conception Catholic school. She loaded her tray on her head over the twòkèt, made the sign of the cross as a good Catholic believer, and with a confident smile told Tant Lucienne, "kay la sou kont ou wi, manman," ("the house is in your hands, mother") To Marie-Jeanne, who always woke up with her mother to help with Patrick and any other task that needed tending in the early hours, she said, "Take care of your little brother, okay!"

As she walked away, Marie-Jeanne and Tant Lucienne could already hear her cheerfully greet every female vendor she encountered. "How are you doing my dear friend?" or "Good morning, dear friend!" was heard until she had finally walked too far for them to hear her enthusiastic greetings. Some vendors were heading to Jérémie, others were selling produce from their farms right in front of their yards, others were heading to a flea market in another village close by.

Marie-Jeanne's mother usually arrived at school no later than seven-thirty so that the students with enough money could purchase coconut bars as they entered the schoolyard. She also sold to a second wave of students during recess at ten o'clock in the morning. Sometimes she sold out of the tablèt kokoyé and sometimes she didn't. When she didn't, she remained in front of the school with the other vendors until the end of the school day at one o'clock, hoping that the last wave of students would buy a piece of tablèt kokoyé to munch on their way home.

The sugar cane vendor in front of the school, Edwa (the Creole pronunciation of "Edouard"), loved spending the day making jokes and entertaining his fellow vendors. Everyone enjoyed being around him, including Marie-Jeanne's mother and even the majority of the students. When Edwa was around selling, no one felt the time passing by because they were too busy laughing at his jokes and engrossed in the wild tales he told.

On her way back to the house, Marie-Jeanne's mother always stopped at Madan Jean Claude's boutik (little shop). She picked up just enough brown sugar, little pieces of broken cinnamon sticks, and star anise to make a new batch of tablèt kokoyé for the next school day. When it came to the coconuts, Bòs Dieuvène regularly brought a dozen of them for her every Sunday morning for the school week. When she ran out, she asked anyone who knew Bòs Dieuvène to tell him to bring some more for her. She took an abònman with him and paid him for the coconut once a month.

Abònman is a Creole word meaning an agreement made between a vendor and their customers that the vendor will regularly deliver a fixed amount of products for a predetermined amount of money on a specific day or date. Both parties decide on the payment terms and the day the customer will make the lump sum payment for what they purchase. Marie-Jeanne's mother and Bòs Dieuvène agreed on a once-a-month payment. People can take an abònman on almost anything they want, but this type of agreement is most commonly used between farmers and their customers for cow's milk. The basic payment term for this type of abònman is also once a month.

In Haitian Creole, the title "Bòs" is put in front of men's names out of respect. These men can either be farmers, carpenters, mechanics, or practice some sort of technical or manual work for a living. These men might also be elders in the community who didn't pursue higher education. Men with higher education are usually addressed as *Monsieur* in French or *Misyé* in Creole. Men who are lawyers or teachers are addressed as *Maître* in French or *Mèt* in Creole.

Until Marie-Jeanne's mother returned to the house, Marie-Jeanne acted like a mother to Bébé Patrick. Just like Erèz, Marie-Jeanne didn't go to school because her mother couldn't afford it. She changed little Patrick's bamboo cotton or batiste fabric diapers when necessary and fed him the milk or bread soup that her mother had prepared before she left in the morning. When he was sick and cried non-stop, Marie-Jeanne held him all day long to console him and made him feel better. She always sang this Creole song to calm him when he cried:

Dodo ti pitit manman

Dodo ti pitit manman

Si ou pa dodo

Dyab la va manjé w

Si ou pa dodo

Dyab la va manjé w

Sleep little baby of the mother

Sleep little baby of the mother

If you don't fall asleep

The devil will eat you

If you don't fall asleep

The devil will eat you

That song always lulled Bébé Patrick to sleep even if he woke up shortly after.

CHAPTER 5
A Fowl Journey

When Erèz wasn't too busy helping her mother in the house or the yard, she asked for her mother's permission to go play with Marie-Jeanne.

On her way to Marie-Jeanne's house, Erèz was always scared of one particular chicken that roamed the neighborhood with her little chicks. That chicken was always ready to jump at anyone to grant them a big peck on their arms, feet, or anywhere she managed to land. Sometimes, when the chicken was unable to jump at someone who got too close to her chicks, she would give them a run for their money by chasing them as far as she could. People nicknamed the chicken Piman Bouk, which means Scotch bonnet pepper in Creole. It was a very fitting name considering how feisty and protective she was of her little chicks.

For some reason, no matter how careful Erèz was to stay away from the chicken, Piman Bouk always chased her. Sometimes, as Erèz ran for her life away from the enraged chicken, she would fall and scrape herself: her arms, a toe or two, shins, knees, and even her lips were not left unscathed. Sometimes, the safety pin that held together her old flip-flops would come loose, forcing her to quickly remove the shoes and run barefoot as she cried at top of her lungs so that any adult nearby might come rescue her from the chicken's wrath.

On the days that the chicken chased Erèz before she was half-way to her friend's house, she was too fearful to attempt heading back to Marie-Jeanne's house a second time. When she was too close to Marie-Jeanne's house to dart back to her own house, she found herself flying into Marie-Jeanne's parents' one-size-fits-all living-room-plus-bedroom, trembling with fear. This made it very difficult for Erèz to slow down on time to avoid slamming herself into the small table in the center of the room. Sometimes that resulted in some rib pain or other injuries, but for her, all of that was preferable to the wrath of the chicken. Sometimes, the irate chicken was nowhere to be found on Erèz's path to Marie-Jeanne's house. Instead, Erèz would encounter one of Bòs Marcel's pigs sniffing the ground in the hopes of finding some food. Other times, she found a couple of pigs in mud puddles after the rain, swimming and playing happily while wagging their tails out of joy. The pigs were much friendlier than the chicken as all they cared about was enjoying their strolls and ignoring humans.

On the days that Erèz made it safely to Marie-Jeanne's house, she often found Marie-Jeanne sitting on the edge of the porch with Tant Lucienne, who held her rosary and mumbled her prayers. She always greeted Tant Lucienne with "Bonjou Tant Lucienne." Of course, this was only if Erèz got there before noon. If it was in the afternoon, Erèz would say, "Bonswa Tant Lucienne." Tant Lucienne always responded warmly with "How are you, my daughter?" That was what was so beautiful about the village of Guinaudée. Every little girl was every adult's pitit fiy, or daughter, and every little boy was every adult's pitit gason, or son, and they genuinely meant it. Every adult watched after the wellbeing of every child, and the parents never had to worry about someone hurting their kids.

If Marie-Jeanne's mother was around when Erèz went over, if she had time, Erèz was in for a special treatment. Marie-Jeanne's mother would have Erèz sit on the ground in front of her, grease her scalp with some of her Haitian castor oil, and braid her hair. When Erèz returned to her house, her mother was always impressed with the new hairstyle that Marie-Jeanne's mother gave her. Erèz's hair was so long and puffy that anyone combing and braiding her hair would have plenty of options to play with.

Because Marie-Jeanne was often busy with little Patrick, most of the time that Erèz came over they couldn't play freely. Instead, they talked and laughed while Tant Lucienne listened pensively. Occasionally, Tant Lucienne chimed in to talk about her life when she was a young girl. She talked about her parents who trained her to be very disciplined and a hard worker. She talked often about her aunt, Tant Sylvie, who took her into her house when she was a young child and her parents couldn't take care of her. She loved Tant Sylvie, who had always been good to her and never mistreated her. Even when Tant Sylvie didn't treat her the same as her own kids, she still made sure to buy her a uniform every year, and sent her to the school for restavèks in the afternoons.

Some days, Tant Lucienne was very quiet when Erèz showed up. After the bonjou or bonswa to Tant Lucienne, Erèz sat there, sometimes tickling Bébé Patrick if he was awake. Patrick recognized Erèz and often smiled at her when she showed up, displaying his little pink gums in anticipation of the fun baby games Erèz would play with him. Other times, Marie-Jeanne held him on one arm as she sat with Erèz playing oslè. Oslè is a game played with five goat knuckles or five rocks by throwing one in the air and collecting one, two, three, or four on the ground. They played for hours until Marie-Jeanne's mother came back in the afternoon. When she came home, Erèz knew it was time for her to head back to her house, as Marie-Jeanne would be busy helping her mother grate coconut to make the coconut bars for the following day.

Saturday afternoons were different, however. On Saturday afternoons, when Erèz and Marie-Jeanne came back with their mothers from hand-washing clothes by the river, Marie-Jeanne got her big break for the week and played all afternoon with Erèz, worry-free from caring for Bébé Patrick until it was time for both of them to go to bed. For some reason on Saturdays, when all the adults were around, the angry chicken and her chicks could rarely be spotted. The chicken knew to stay away; otherwise, she would be in trouble, with many people chasing her away all at once if she attempted one of her overly protective attacks on one of the kids.

Marie-Jeanne and Erèz jumped rope, raced each other barefooted up and down the graveled slant near the main road, and played lago kaché (hide-and-seek). When they played lago kaché, Erèz never ventured by the banana-tree maze for fear one of the frogs would jump on her. Marie-Jeanne also knew not to waste her time looking for her there. When they didn't play lago kaché , they sat on Erèz's favorite glossy rock to play hand-slap for hours. As they played, they sang random songs they'd been singing since they were babies or spontaneously created some in Creole with catchy rhythms and rhymes inspired by the natural music and sound of their palms slapping each other. Other times, they held tightly on each other's hands while standing, pulled away from each other and extended their bodies backward to spin around as fast as they could on their little bare feet. They would only stop when they got extremely dizzy and the earth spun too quickly beneath them, and then the only option was to throw their skinny bodies on the ground, both out of breath.

Occasionally, Erèz's parents tiré kont (told stories) out in the open air on Saturday evenings as the bright stars and shining moon stood still, listening silently in all their splendor, observing and sucking in the genuine joy of the moment, like two uninvited guests to a laughter feast waiting for the host to signal them to join in. Those Saturday-night joke-telling sessions always happened on the left side of Erèz's house while Erèz and Marie-Jeanne both listened carefully and created analogies from what they understood in their young minds. Other times, the adults burst out laughing at a joke with double-meaning that Erèz and Marie-Jeanne's young minds couldn't comprehend. They both laughed anyway, not at the joke per se, but rather at the funny way the adults hysterically laughed non-stop while holding their bellies, twisting their bodies from side to side, and trying to catch their breaths from the joyful pain of laughter.

Sometimes, Ilèyis and Yaya would chime in as well, taking turns at telling jokes. Marie-Jeanne's mother, holding little Patrick on one hip, would join them later after greasing her hair with Haitian castor oil and braiding it for the week. She always washed her hair on Saturdays while she bathed and swam in the river, using fresh flowers from hibiscus trees that she picked up on the way there. After all, the clothes she just hand-washed would take a while to dry over the gravel and rocks by the riverside. When she finally got to the house from the river, she perfectly greased her scalp and curly hair strand by strand with Haitian castor oil, and then braided it. The neighborhood party would be complete when she finally headed over to the group after her haircare ritual. In the darkness of the night, a neighborhood chorus formed. Loud laughter echoed and joined together as other groups of families gathered and had their own joke-telling sessions in their front or back yards.

CHAPTER 6
Restavèk

Restavèk is a Creole word that derived from two French words: "rester" and "avec." The word "rester" means "stay," and the word "avec" means "with." When someone who lives in the countryside cannot take care of their small children, instead of watching them waste away from malnourishment, they look for a middle-class or rich family who lives in a city that can take the child on as a servant. Some of these families treat these kids as their own, some mistreat them, and others just treat them like mere slaves, working them like machinery or equipment. Some are struck in the head. Some are slammed against walls. Some are hit with fresh branches. Some are hit with the rigwaz. A rigwaz is a braided stick made with two strands of cow's skin. Others are beaten with a matinèt, a wooden stick with three straps of leather attached to it, meaning that the restavèk receives three hits in just one blow of the matinèt.

Tant Lucienne had heard stories about kids being mistreated in the homes of rich people in the city, and although she had had a very good time being a restavèk at Tant Sylvie's house, she decided long ago to work hard to raise her children instead of giving them away, and that was exactly what she did. Though she couldn't offer them the world, at least they did not run the risk of falling into a cruel household as restavèks. Erèz listened to that piece of Tant Lucienne's life story many times and she was always intrigued by Tant Lucienne's time living in the city when she was young.

Erèz occasionally dreamed about being a restavèk in the home of someone in the city. She generally brushed off the idea, knowing that her parents didn't know too many people in the city; although, truth be told, her parents did sometimes speak of a few wealthy family members that supposedly belonged to a very high economic class in Jérémie. Of course, Erèz couldn't imagine that such big aristocrats would take her in. It probably wouldn't work out as they'd likely become quickly frustrated and displeased with the frequency of her parents' visits to see their beloved daughter.

CHAPTER 7
Piwouli

On Saturday mornings when she had enough money, Marie-Jeanne's mother sometimes commuted the sixteen miles to Jérémie on foot to go buy her ingredients in bulk. She would inform Erèz's mother early in the week that she would be going to Jérémie in case she wanted to send some provisions down to her cousin, Rachelle. Erèz's mother would often send African yams and sugar cane to Rachelle because those tended to be very expensive in the city. She would also ask Marie-Jeanne's mother to let Rachelle know that she sent her good tidings and wished her a good morning when delivered the fresh goods to her.

Marie-Jeanne's mother left very early in the morning on those Saturdays. She ran up the hill from her house instead of walking so that her back and knees didn't hurt, using the momentum so she didn't slide back down with the heavy load that she carried over her head. Plus, when she ran, there was a lesser chance that small rocks could get stuck in her plastic sandals. Once on the road, she greeted the Madan Saras also heading to Jérémie, baskets filled with fresh produce from their farms on their heads, and they conversed and laughed about anything and everything most of the way to the city.

Erèz's godmother's son, Ti Roro, would occasionally be in the group of people heading to Jérémie, walking behind his mother's donkey. He closely followed his mother who usually carried a large bamboo tray on her head filled with all sorts of goods like plantains, oranges, pomelos, avocados, and fresh green soursops. On the side of the tray were reused bottles filled with fresh cow's milk strategically tipped in such a way that the milk didn't drip. Ti Roro's big task was to get the donkey to walk at a faster pace by commanding it with his little voice as loud as he could, "ech ech" (pronounced exactly as the letter H) while hitting the donkey's bottom with a branch or with a rigwaz, which forced the donkey to move faster.

Ti Roro's mother, Madan Polo, was Erèz's godmother and that made him Erèz's godbrother. When Erèz was in the yard that early in the morning, Madan Polo would project her voice from the road calling out to Erèz, "How are you, my goddaughter?"

Erèz would reply as loudly as she could with her little peasant voice and accent, "Good morning, godmother. I am not doing too bad."

"I will make sure to bring you a lollipop later," Madan Polo promised as she continued heading her way. Erèz would dream all day long about enjoying her lollipop, known as piwouli in Haiti, and her godmother never forgot the promises that she made to her goddaughter.

Upon her return from Jérémie, Madan Polo would call Erèz from the main road to come get her piwouli. Erèz loved the sound of unwrapping the clear plastic around her piwouli to get to the treat inside. She then took her time to enjoy her piwouli as she let her little tongue wander over every delicious bit of it. She did everything she could to make her piwouli last as long as possible; slower licks, shorter licks, and anything else she could to savor it. When she finished, she already started dreaming of the next Saturday in the near future that her godmother might go to downtown Jérémie and gift her another piwouli on her way back.

CHAPTER 8
Erèz At Home

When Erèz's mother had time in the evening, she lovingly braided Erèz's long, beautiful dark curly hair with two thick French braids on either side of her head. Her mother usually sat on a tall straw chair while Erèz sat in front of her, straddling a smaller chair made from the same material. Erèz cherished and valued those moments spent having her hair braided. Sometimes, it took a week or longer before her mother found the time to braid her hair again.

Water at Erèz's house was a precious resource. When the water level became too low, it was usually Yaya who traveled the three miles to fetch the water necessary to fill the krich, a large pitcher used to hold water. On the day that Yaya had to fill the krich, she didn't leave with her papa to work on the farm like usual because many trips needed to be made in order to obtain the necessary amount of water for the family. Despite carrying a gallon in each hand, it took hours. Eventually, when Yaya got older, she learned to balance a large bucket on her head filled with water, and then it only took her three to four trips to fill the krich.

Erèz's father often slept after his long day of hard work in the farm he rented. He didn't own the farm, but wished he did, and he had to pay the rent every six months. The rent dried up almost all his revenue and he was constantly preoccupied with how he was going to make ends meet.

While he slumbered, Yaya usually occupied herself with a needle, mending and darning her old clothes. She was ten years older than Erèz and often acted like her second mother. It was not unusual for Yaya to reprimand Erèz or spank her with the palm of her hand when Erèz dared to disobey her orders. If the offense was especially egregious, Yaya took a short trip to the fence to pull a small tree branch for whipping her sister's little bottom.

Although Erèz couldn't play with her teenage sister, she did have numerous friends in the neighborhood; however, even that time playing dwindled. As she grew older, Erèz's little friends started having too much homework from school, leaving them less time to spend together jumping rope, playing hide-and-seek, and regaling each other with jests and stories as they did during the summer months.

Erèz's brother, Ilèyis, was an incredibly quiet boy. As she sat in front of her mother getting her hair braided, Erèz sometimes wondered what her brother was thinking about. He just stared at the tin roof peppered with tiny holes, lost in his imagination. When it was raining, Ilèyis moved his floor mat with its flannel sheet to a dry corner to retreat into his mind again. His mother usually placed a couple of repurposed one-gallon tin paint containers on the floor to collect the raindrops. At first, the rain drops thudded loudly in the cans. As the tin containers filled up, the sound of raindrops landing in the water softened, making a dull, sweet sound. Erèz counted each drop with her fingers just for the fun of it.

Some nights, when the rest of the family came together for their evening meal, Erèz laid on the large, glossy rock in front of the house. This was her favorite rock, and she loved this shiny polished space that was all her own. While her father, Yaya, and Ilèyis recounted the events of their day inside, Erèz's imagination carried her to different lives and situations as she stared at the night sky from her beloved rock. From where she laid, she fantasized about what her first day of school would feel like. In the movie playing in her imagination, she saw herself stepping into the school yard as smiling teachers greeted her and welcomed her to her very first school year. She wondered if she would be the tallest student in her class, because she might have to start from the very beginning with the five-year-olds. That image of herself being the oldest of her class didn't bother her at all.

In Erèz's mind, she ran her fingers across the spines and edges of her brand-new books. While holding her breath, she could imagine the exact smell of the pages as she leafed through each book. Sometimes she would find a small chalky rock nearby, and use it to make mark-ings on her shiny rock. She pretended that just like her friends in the neighborhood, she was studying and writing. With school comes recess, of course, and she pictured herself wearing a bright and starchy blue-and-white plaid skirt as she ran and played with her friends in the schoolyard, the teachers watching them and smiling.

She imagined the delicious lunch that would be served to her and her classmates. The students were instructed to bring their bowls and spoons for this midday feast. She remembered one of the girls describ-ing a banquet of hot cornmeal, bean purée, sautéed mashed eggplant, and other savory vegetables. Of course, she couldn't forget the smoked herring, the main animal protein the teachers served right after every recess. Each student eagerly stood in line under the hot sun, waiting for their share. From her glossy rock, Erèz visualized herself standing among them, holding her own aluminum bowl.

In another vision, she imagined herself as an adult. She was all grown up and counted herself among the Madan Saras, negotiating at the maché every Wednesday. She was smart, well-educated, and successfully sold her top-quality products. Nobody could negotiate quite like her as she rehearsed the scenario in her mind. Other times, while she laid on her favorite rock, she prayed to Saint Mary, the Mother of Jesus, just as she was taught by her Catholic mother. She prayed that a miracle would happen for her parents so that they would have enough money to send her to school. In her prayers to Saint Mary, she often prayed for a book. She would gladly take any book, old or new, and it wouldn't matter at all. She also prayed for a *Ti Malice*, the reading primer that the teachers used to teach the students the alphabet and assign their homework for the next day.

CHAPTER 9
Zétrènn

Zétrènn is a Creole word used to describe the gifts that people exchange during the New Year festivities. Traditionally, when Haitian children were sent to kiss their godparents on the cheeks for Christmas, New Year, or for Epiphany on January sixth, the children came bearing bountiful baskets.

Parents, especially the ones who owned a farm, sent their children with baskets full of freshly harvested goods. Those baskets were often filled with African yams, sweet potatoes, and freshly pulled carrots. Some parents added fresh fruits, including oranges and pineapples. When they could afford it, the parents also sent the rooster from their coop! All this was gifted and presented by the children with kisses on the cheeks and warm wishes for a happy New Year, or as it is in French, Bonne Année.

Godparents expected that their goddaughters and godsons arrived dressed up in their very finest Christmas and New Year's clothing to wish the godparents a Bonne Année. In turn, the godparents presented each of the children with little gifts wrapped in beautiful Christmas-themed paper. In the countryside where Erèz grew up, the godparents were not quite as formal and did not wrap the gifts in fancy paper. They simply placed the gifts in a plastic bag or a brown paper bag. When Erèz turned six years old, she received the biggest surprise as her beloved godfather handed her a plastic bag and told her with the biggest, sweetest smile on his face, "Bònn ané, fiyòll!" ("Happy New Year, goddaughter!") She could barely contain her excitement, but still managed to reply with great reverence, "Mèsi wi parenn," ("Thank you yes, godfather.") When Erèz peered into the bag, she could hardly believe her eyes. Her kind godfather had outdone himself. Inside the bag was a brand-new pair of pink flip-flops for her to wear around the house, a pair of black shoes for special occasions, and a lovely flowery green dress.

Erèz knew her mother would keep that particular dress in the black plastic bag under her bed where she kept everyone's special occasion clothing, as well as all the important papers like the family birth certificates. Her new dress would be added to that bag with her father's handsome black suit and her mother's floral print dress. It was the special dress that her mother only wore when visiting her aunt and cousin in Jérémie or when she was attending Easter Mass at the Saint Peter Catholic Church three miles down the road.

Erèz excitedly kissed her godfather goodbye on both cheeks and could barely contain herself on the way home.

Like most of her little friends, Erèz spent her days mostly barefoot. Not a shoe was to be seen as they chased each other, jumped rope, and played all kinds of games. At night, after she rinsed the ruddy dirt from her slender dark-chocolate body, she would scrub her feet clean and wear the treasured flip-flops her godfather had given her. Even several years later when one of the flip-flops developed a hole at the bottom, and the Y-shaped strap had to be held in place by a safety pin, she continued to dearly cherish her flip-flops because they had been a gift from her godfather.

CHAPTER 10
Opportunities

One day, during a passing conversation, Rachelle, Erèz's mother's cousin, made mention that their other cousin, Man Féfé, was looking for a little maid to help with tasks around her luxury home in Jérémie. She thought Erèz might be the perfect fit as she was still at a tender enough age to be inclined to obey all that she was told instead of being a little too rebellious toward the lady of the house. Needing time to herself to consider what would be best for Erèz's future, her mother went to the maché by herself that week. On the way there, she wept at the thought of giving up her youngest little girl to her well-established cousin. Despite her sorrow and tears, she reminded herself that she must do whatever was necessary to give her youngest baby girl the best opportunity for a bright future. If she selfishly kept Erèz in the village, she would never be able to learn how to read and write. If Erèz remained analphabet, unable to read and write, there was no chance she would ever accomplish her great ambition and dream to become a Madan Sara, or to help take care of her and her husband in their older days.

That evening, she spoke to her husband about taking Erèz to Jérémie. They were both very aware that they could barely take care of her and feed her, let alone pay school tuition. With great unhappiness, they both agreed that sending her away would afford their young daughter many more opportunities than keeping her in the countryside.

The following Monday was especially hot, and Erèz was venting the wood fire in the backyard with an old straw hat while her mother peeled the plantains. The weather that afternoon was far more humid than they were used to in mid-July. Erez's mother noticed they were both dripping with giant droplets of sweats. She observed little rivers of sweat flowing down the side of Erèz's face and falling to the ground as she waved the straw hat with her long slender arms. The hole that ripped at the bottom of Erèz's faded old blouse that she was wearing became even larger after the recent wash by the side of the river.

Erèz's mother was about to say something about the dress, but a considerable commotion halted her as she opened her mouth. The screams of a little girl pierced the air and then Mèt Robèto's voice shouting followed. The little girl darted by with Mèt Robèto's two dogs in hot pursuit followed closely by Mèt Robèto, who waved his arms in an attempt to catch the dogs' attention before they bit her, all the while bellowing at them to head back to the house and leave her alone.

Apparently, the little girl had been singing and dancing as she walked by. The dogs perceived her bouncing as annoying, and jumped from where they were laying on the front porch to chase her. When the dogs finally calmed down, Erèz and her mother overheard Mèt

Robèto saying loudly to the little girl as she went her way, still crying and trembling from the shock of being chased by two dogs, "Sing on key next time and work on your dancing skills so that the dogs can become your friends!" This event was not soon forgotten and made the entire neighborhood laugh.

Later, on that humid Monday, Erèz's mother filled their little cauldron with water and placed it on the wood fire in the middle of the three big rocks. She called for Erèz to bring the half-gallon clay container that was used to keep sea salt. There was little salt left, but she rinsed the salt out from the bottom of the container and added it to the water. She waited for the water to boil before adding the plantains. Once the plantains were placed in the boiling water, Erèz's mother covered the pot with fresh leaves that she had cut from one of Mèt Robèto's plantain trees in the back. As Erèz's mother began preparing a piece of smoked herring, she started speaking rapidly.

"Your father and I have agreed to take you to Jérémie to the house of my cousin, Man Féfé. There is no hope for you here in Guinaudée. I know you would like to learn how to read and write, and your papa and I cannot provide that for you. I want to make sure that you are going to make your manman proud. You have to understand, though, that the worst thing that can happen is for her to send for me to come get you. This is your only chance, Erèz. Don't mess this up!"

Erèz didn't believe her ears. She managed to answer, "Yes, mother."

"Now, when an adult is talking to you, you are supposed to reply 'wi, Misyé, ("yes, Mister") or 'wi, Ma Tant ("yes auntie"). If they want you to address them differently, they will tell you, and you are expected to obey. Do you hear me?"

Wide-eyed, Erèz repeated, "Yes, mother."

Without skipping a beat, Erèz's mother continued, "When you are walking by where one or two adults are talking, remember to hold the bottom of your dress so that it doesn't touch any of them. Do you hear me?"

Erèz's mother quickly demonstrated what she was telling her by holding both sides of her skirt and folding them right between her legs.

Erèz nodded quickly and emphatically, "Yes mother!"

Erèz's mother was not quite finished, "You know that we don't use toothpaste often. When you arrive to Man Féfé's house, you might not be able to use the corn chaff or pieces of charcoal we use here to clean your teeth. I am sure she will give you some toothpaste. You need to make sure to thank her properly and say 'mèsi ma tant,' for everything that she gives you."

"Yes, mother!"

"You are never to look an adult in the eyes. This is very disrespectful. Look to the ground when an adult is talking with you. Do you understand?"

"Yes, mother..."

"Will you remember how to scrub a pot?"

"Yes, mother."

Erèz's manman narrowed her eyes a bit and decided to test her daughter, "Can you explain to me how?"

"I will wet some leftover ashes, dampen the corn husk, grab some wet ashes, and start scrubbing." To prove she knew what she was talking about, Erèz mimed the procedure with her hands for her mother.

Erèz's manman couldn't help but smile at her daughter, "Yes, that's it. And can you tell me how you are going to wash the dishes?"

The young girl thought for a moment and said, "I will fill two bowls with water and scrub each cup and plate with fresh lemongrass and rinse them twice." Again, Erèz pretended to perform the task for her mother through the air, wrinkling her nose a bit when she was scrubbing the hardest.

Her mother tried to hide the smile that was pulling on the corners of her mouth, "Yes, that's good. Alright, I am going to get your dresses ready, but we cannot take the one you are wearing with us to the city."

Erèz looked down at her dress, nodded, and sighed, "Yes, man-man," in agreement.

"I will come see you often. I will bring you oranges, soursop, quenepa, and some of Marie-Jeanne's mother's coconut bars."

"Yes, mother," she said, and her eyes lit up at the thought of frequent visits and treats.

Just when Erèz thought her mother was finished, her mother suddenly remembered, "Do not forget, you are a little girl, and no matter what, you are absolutely not to burst into loud laughs. That is not what a well-behaved girl does. Do you hear me?"

Erèz almost laughed at that particular advice from her mother, but caught herself halfway. That wasn't a good idea. Instead, she politely responded once again, "Yes, mother."

Erèz soon discovered that she had very little time left with her family. Saturday of that week, the plan was for both to commute to Jérémie where Erèz was going to be a restavèk to Man Féfé and her family. Erèz spent the remainder of the week saying goodbye to her godmother and godfather and spending as much time as possible with Marie-Jeanne, Baby Patrick, and Tant Lucienne.

The visit to Erèz's godmother and godfather's house went a little bit longer than she expected. Reality truly began to set in when they each gave her twenty-five Haitian cents and blessed her saying, "May God protect you." It dawned on her that she would not see them for a very long time, and she knew she would miss them. When she got back to the house, Erèz leaned against her front door balancing on one foot as the other wiggled nervously. Erèz realized it was probably going to be a long time before she would see any of the people she held dear in her life. She knew for a fact she was going to miss Marie-Jeanne and running around the maché every Wednesday, and playing with little girlfriends her age. She teared up a little, but her small face involuntarily lit up as she remembered that she was finally going to go to school in just a few months, in October. She imagined herself in the same blue-and-white uniform she admired seeing so much on the girls passing through the maché on their way from school or on the main road from the front porch of her house.

CHAPTER 11
Goodbye

The night before Erèz's Saturday morning departure, she went to say au revoir to Mèt Robèto, Marie-Jeanne, Marie-Jeanne's mother, and Tant Lucienne. She knew in her heart that it would be a while before she would be able to come back to Guinaudée to see them. That idea scared her, but the idea of going to school in just three months, in October, overwhelmed her with much more joy.

Tant Lucienne blessed her and said, "Make us proud!"

Marie-Jeanne's mother grabbed Erèz's right hand and directed her to the back of the house where she warned in hushed tones:

"Don't talk to any boys. They are good for nothing!"

She then opened Erèz's tiny hands and placed fifty cents in her palms as a goodbye gift. She closed Erèz's fingers over them and whispered, trying hard to hold her tears, "Go with peace, my daughter."

When Erèz got back to the front of the house, Marie-Jeanne was waiting for her. They both wanted to cry, but Marie-Jeanne turned her face away from Erèz so that she couldn't see the tears streaming down her face.

When Marie-Jeanne finally turned around to look straight into Erèz's eyes, she said, "Don't forget me when you get to the city!"

Erèz's eyes brimmed with tears as they both held tightly onto each other's hands, and she replied, "We will see each other again."

When they released each other's hands, they realized their grips had been tighter than they had thought as both their hands hurt. Erèz turned around without saying a word and headed to her house. She stole a glance back to see Marie-Jeanne standing in the same place sadly watching her dearest friend leave.

During that night, Erèz didn't sleep much although her mother warned her the trip would be long and painful on her little feet. She was simply too excited that she was going to finally sleep on a bed, listen to a radio, live in a house with electricity, and watch bikes and cars speeding up and down her auntie's street. The images of her soon-to-be new life raced non-stop through her mind all night and she was too restless to fall asleep. She was going to finally drink water straight from the backyard of the new house, wear new shoes and new dresses and, yes, shiny new flip-flops! The best thought of all involved her wearing her brand-new crisp uniform to attend school in October, just three months away. Oh, that got her so excited!

Erèz woke up very tired, but even lack of sleep couldn't take away from the excitement of starting her new life in the city of Jérémie. Her mother had purchased a new safety pin to hold the bottom of her already broken flip-flops together for the trip. They planned for Erèz to make the journey wearing the flip-flops, and then change into her special-occasion shoes when they arrived downtown. Erèz and her mother left very early that Saturday morning as their walk to the city of Jérémie would be three hours long.

In her right hand, Erèz held an old plastic bag containing the pair of black shoes and the dress that her godfather had given her two years ago. She also brought the most presentable of the little dresses that she often wore around the house, for the only other one she owned had too many holes to take to the city.

On Erèz's mother's head was a basket filled with fresh plantains, African yams, a few oranges and ripe bananas, and pieces of sugar cane to take to Man Féfé and to Rachelle, who had initially suggested giving Erèz away to her as a servant.

Erèz's mother spent the entire trip fighting with her conflicted feelings. She knew she couldn't give Erèz any opportunities by keeping her in Guinaudée. At times, she could barely feed her and that was obvious in how frail Erèz's body was and by the redness beginning to show in her hair. The proof was right in front of her that her daughter was not getting the nutrients a child her age needed to sustain her body and grow, but despite all that, she wondered if she was doing the right thing by giving her away as a restavèk and questioned how she was going to cope with losing her youngest daughter.

They greeted everyone they met on their way in the darkness of the early hours of the morning. Erèz's mother didn't give too much explanation as to where exactly they were headed. When friends on the road asked her if they were going to Jérémie, she answered in her regular high-pitched peasant-like voice with a cordial "wi," but didn't elaborate further.

As usual, Erèz's mother walked barefoot. She didn't want to ruin her only black plastic pair of sandals on the rocks that covered the road. The cracks and calluses on both of her feet indicated she was a veteran barefoot-walker who was used to the rocky streets. Her toes even opened and looked more like chicken feet. She looked more comfortable walking barefoot than the few times she wore shoes.

That morning, she had carefully folded her black plastic sandals in a worn piece of fabric stained by the red dirt from the yard and placed them underneath the banana leaves that lined her basket of provisions. Erèz's mother's feet always carried some red dirt in the cracks no matter how long she scrubbed them against a rock. She always carried some water to wash her feet when she was about to get to the city, and that morning was no different.

As soon as Erèz and her mother arrived at Kafou Bak, where the main national guard station of the City of Jérémie was, Erèz became excited, but also a little nervous. This was her first time seeing formal service men in their sharp uniforms carrying guns and pistols and vigilantly observing the three-stop road.

American troops were still present in Haiti in mid 1934, and on that morning in mid-July, one American guard was among the Haitian soldiers in the station. That was Erèz's first time seeing a blan, a white person, with blue eyes and curly hair. Little did she know that her mother's cousin, who would soon become her master, was also a mulatto with light skin and equally light-skinned children. She was going to spend the next ten years of her life serving those mulattos with their light skin and long, sleek hair. As Erèz stared at the national guard station, she realized she was trembling a bit as she faced her new reality. In the mere two hours since she'd left her house and all that had been familiar to her for the past eight years, she had already taken so much in.

As she stood there watching the soldiers, and especially the strange white one, her mother took the basket from her head, put it on the ground, and pulled the pair of black plastic sandals from underneath the banana leaves. Erèz started noticing all the fancy cars driving by, full of well-dressed people. She had seen big trucks loaded with people and merchandise pull into the maché on Wednesdays, but her eyes had never witnessed this type of opulence and affluence. She felt rather small at the sight of so much wealth on display, and compared it to the simple life she'd known in Guinaudée. For a moment, she felt a little bit of guilt for having been so excited to leave home, although she still found comfort at the thought of going to school.

Since it was the weekend, those wealthy city residents were heading to one of the beaches close to the city of Jérémie, or perhaps driving to nearby farms to choose the goat, rooster, cow, or pig that would be butchered for their parties and social gatherings that Saturday evening or on Sunday for an elaborate dinner. Some of the men driving their shiny convertibles had their wives next to them in the passenger seats. Those women appeared as happy as could be, laughing as they held onto their big straw hats, large white ribbons flowing in the wind.

As soon as Erèz's mother was done scrubbing and rinsing the red dirt and dust off her feet, she put on the black plastic sandals and loaded the basket back on her head to continue their journey. They were now only thirty minutes from downtown Jérémie. The big waves of the blue ocean came and went and ran alongside them for about ten minutes on the left side of the road. As Erèz watched fishermen on the little boats untangling their nets, she fantasized about returning to this beautiful beach area with the cousins who were about to welcome her.

When they arrived at anba la vil Jérémie (downtown Jérémie), the street was packed with women who were out early to purchase fresh ingredients for the Saturday soup, known as bouillon. Their baskets were loaded with crabs, goat feet, goat heads, cow intestines, shrimps, beef bones, watercress, taro roots, plantains, African yams, carrots, and collard greens, as well as other provisions for Sunday's meal.

The ladies acted very proper, and their clothes were impeccably pressed and pleated. Their composure and countenance were nothing like the ladies in the village of Guinaudée. Unlike Madan Robèto, Marie-Jeanne's mother, and Erèz's godmother, who greeted everyone they met on their way, those women said a resigned "bonjour" only to the people they knew and ignored the rest. The atmosphere in the city of Jérémie differed from Guinaudée, where people would holler loudly from the end of the road to greet each other with the friendly and familiar "Sak pasé?" ("How are you doing?") Erèz's mother knew how to walk through the crowd, and Erèz followed her closely while holding tightly to the black plastic bag that contained her two little dresses and her pair of shoes. The safety pins on her flip-flop popped many times during the walk and her mother stopped each time to fix it. At one point, Erèz's mother pulled out the extra safety pin just in case the old one had given up.

When they arrived at Man Rachelle's house, Erèz's mother gave her sugar cane, mangos, avocados, and African yams from her basket. She also asked for her permission to go to the backyard and get Erèz cleaned up before they both headed to Man Féfé's house. Man Rachelle had running water in her basin. The water was crystal-clear and so fresh compared to the water from the river in Guinaudée, which was cloudy at times. They drank some of the fresh water from the palms of their cupped hands. Erèz's mother rinsed her feet and black plastic sandals one more time, and dried them with the piece of rag stained with the ruddy Guinaudée dirt.

Erèz's mother then rinsed her daughter's face, both of her little arms, and scrubbed her feet. She folded Erèz's flip-flops in the same rag she kept her old sandals and said, "I am going to save these for you." Erèz nodded her head in obedience, but knew there wasn't much wear left in these flip-flops, especially after that long commute from Guinaudée to the city of Jérémie. Her mother then pulled out Erèz's black shoes and little white socks from the basket she carried on her head. The socks had been cleaned, but the stains from the orangish-red mud easily revealed they were the only ones she had. The elastic holding the buckles in each shoe was almost completely broken, but Erèz's mother dressed Erèz with as much care as she could, hoping to make the best impression possible on her rich cousin, Man Féfé.

After they cleansed themselves, Man Rachelle invited them in for a cup of very sweet coffee with evaporated milk and two pieces of Haitian buttery bread. Erèz had only eaten buttery bread when her godmother would, on rare occasions, bring her a piece from downtown Jérémie. The little buttery bread from her godmother added an extra dose of excitement each and every time she surprised Erèz with one, and it always came as an unexpected treat alongside the lollipop wrapped in plastic. Erèz and her mother enjoyed the warm breakfast, but Erèz especially enjoyed sipping her creamy and extra sweet coffee.

Erèz's cousin told her as she ate, "Now that you are in the city, you need to be a good girl because Guinaudée doesn't have much to offer you." Erèz nodded while keeping her head down out of respect for her cousin.

Man Rachelle continued telling her mother, "Thank you for this wonderful harvest! I will cook the yam in today's soup."

"You're welcome," smiled Erèz's mother.

"Madame Féfé is expecting you," Man Rachelle continued. It was clear from her tone of voice and the pronunciation of the words she carefully chose that it took great effort for her to converse fully in

Creole. She mumbled, and her facial expressions revealed her frustration with herself as she struggled to pick the right Creole words to communicate with her peasant cousin.

On that note, Erèz's mother loaded the basket back on her head to continue the journey to Man Féfé's house. The two cousins didn't live too far from each other. As they drew closer, Erèz's mother choked up, wiping her tears away quickly so as not to show Erèz how devastated she was to be giving up her little girl.

Erèz, on the other hand, was already thinking about school. She imagined herself wearing her plaid shirt and navy-blue pleated skirt. She would be just like the students in Guinaudée and the ones passing through the maché on Wednesdays. In just three months, her dreams would finally come true. It even occurred to her that in the city of Jérémie she would be able to buy as many lollipops as she wished instead of waiting for one from her godmother on Saturday evenings.

Erèz's mother composed herself and said with a knot in her throat, "Don't touch what doesn't belong to you!"

Erèz responded, "No, mother."

Her mother continued, "Don't comment in conversations you have nothing to do with! Keep your dignity! Know that people can give you all sorts of names, but it's all better than being called a thief!"

Erèz nodded emphatically with her head as she uttered, "Yes, mother." This was a lot of pressure being put on a little girl's eight-year-old mind! Not only was there the urging of her mother who wanted her to be on her best behavior, but there was also the overwhelming nature of this new big city with the motorcycles, the fancy cars, and the light-skinned ladies walking in high-heeled shoes speaking perfect French that Erèz could barely understand. She felt so little and quite inferior. This was all so different from what she had known her entire life. It was such a whirlwind to see the countless cars whizzing by and to try to make sense of the many streets crisscrossing each other. This was nothing like her little house in Guinaudée, with its small yard of red dirt from where she ran up the low, rocky hill to get to the main road. In just a few short hours, all this new highlife had appeared, and it intimidated her. Only the idea of going to school three months from now made her a little braver.

After they left her cousin Rachelle's house, Erèz's mother held onto her hand and Erèz felt the tightness of her grip as they got closer to the house that Erèz would call home for ten years.

CHAPTER 12
An Uncertain Welcome

When they finally arrived at Man Féfé's house, the porch's floor was still wet, and the smell of the deodorized water they used to scrub the clay bricks that cemented the floors was very fragrant. The towering brown double doors, made from solid iron, were opened just enough for someone to peek in and see what was happening inside the house.

Erèz and her mother watched through the opening between the doors as Man Féfé and her husband, Mèt Féfé, ate their scrumptious breakfast. Erèz and her mother observed them for a good ten minutes before saying anything that would disturb them. It was odd that the couple didn't feel the stare of the two at their door. When Erèz's mother suspected their hunger had subsided a bit, she called from the porch, "Bonjou!" in her peasant-like intonation.

Man Féfé's eyes darted toward them. Forcing herself to speak in Creole instead of the French she normally expressed herself in when speaking to her rich friends, she said, "Oh, it's you! Come through the side of the house."

While she usually rushed to greet her visiting rich friends at those big brown doors, she didn't show the same eagerness toward her cousin, Erèz's mother, and Erèz. After all, even though Erèz and her mother were family members, they were also dirt poor, and thus not worthy of much attention in her eyes. She received Erèz and her mother like anyone living in the city would receive poor or broke family members belonging to the peasant class.

Even when Erèz's mother would bring her fresh provisions from Guinaudée for Christmas, which included a plethora of freshly harvested African yams, sweet potatoes, pieces of sugar cane, mangoes, pineapples, soursops, sour oranges, plantains, green figs, and sweet oranges, she still treated Erèz's mother like a low-class peasant despite being somewhat grateful for the gifts. Man Féfé never invited her to come inside the house or walk through the living room when she came to town from Guinaudée, but instead received her on the little bench under the tamarind tree in the backyard. There, she or the maid served leftover coffee to Erèz's mother in a battered old cup alongside a piece of bread deemed unworthy to be eaten at the breakfast table. Hospitality routines for family members from the countryside ended at that. Of course, company of a much higher class had the luxury of being able to walk freely through the house from the front to the back door, passing through the living room and dining room while hollering Man Féfé's name and laughing out loud. Company from a higher social class in the city of Jérémie also took a seat in the living room, and got served freshly brewed coffee and delicacies from an expensive silver tray by Man Féfé herself and rarely by the maid, because she didn't want the maid to bring embarrassment to her and her family with her peasant-like demeanor.

Conversations between Man Féfé and Erèz's mother were always superficial and too often demeaning. Man Féfé inquired after the family back in Guinaudée and commented about how skinny and pale Erèz's mother's face was. She talked just enough to sound friendly, while in her heart, she couldn't wait for her to leave.

When Erèz and her mother made it to the backyard through the little alley on the side of the house, a woman who appeared to be the maid told them that Madame would come talk to them after she finished her breakfast. The face of the maid didn't appear very welcoming. As she passed them to go scrub the pot under the tamarind tree, Erèz and her mother exchanged glances as if they communicated about how extremely tired and frustrated she looked. The maid didn't mutter another word as she made it obvious that she didn't wish to entertain conversation from the two peasant strangers. She silently passed them as she headed to the kitchen.

At this point, Erèz's mother couldn't help herself and let loose, in her high-pitched peasant voice, a "Bonjou, my daughter."

"Bonjou madam," replied the maid in Creole, as she continued heading into the house, even shorter than she sounded the first time that she spoke to them.

Mother and daughter both stood there waiting. At one point, Erèz's mother unloaded her bamboo tray, laid it on the ground, and removed her twokèt. Erèz continued to cling tightly to the old plastic bag holding her belongings. She started feeling very unsure about living in such an hostile and unwelcoming environment, and her only comfort at that moment was to hold onto the most precious things she owned, the dresses that her godfather gifted her two years ago.

They waited on Man Féfé for close to an hour before she graced them with her presence in the backyard. She purposefully chose to make them wait to ensure they understood she had better things to do than entertain peasant visitors, even when they were family members. She would never have dreamed of treating her friends who were highly socially ranked this way, but this hypocrisy was considered normal. In fact, a friend from the city would have been immediately greeted with an extravagant display of warmth and kisses on both cheeks.

Man Féfé carefully walked down the steep steps from the back door of the house in her high heels to where Erèz and her mother were standing. From the way she walked with her back so straight, one could tell that woman had likely never worn flat shoes in her life. Pink sponge rollers peeked from underneath the floral print wrap on her head. She said to them with a glance at Erèz, "Is that the girl? How come she is so skinny?"

From that comment, Erèz's mother knew her cousin was disappointed, but there was nothing she could do about Erèz's physical appearance and humbly responded, "You know how it goes, Man Féfé."

Man Féfé continued with her harsh criticism of Erèz, shaking her head, "But just look at her skinny long legs…" That was the moment when Erèz knew in her little heart that she wasn't as welcome at Man Féfé's house as she thought she was going to be. She started to wonder if Madame would even find her worthy to be sent to school in October. That thought frightened her, but she chose to be hopeful.

"What's your name again?" And, with that question, she fully captured Erèz's attention, bringing her back to reality. Erèz responded quickly with her name.

"Ah, I forgot," Man Féfé responded. She thanked Erèz's mother for the provisions and asked for Erèz's belongings. Erèz's mother pointed to the little plastic bag that Erèz was still holding tightly.

Madame's eyes widened with surprise at how few belongings Erèz had brought, and she said, "Well, I suppose I can see what I can find from the girls' rooms that they don't wear anymore."

They continued to converse, and Erèz's mother implored her to keep Erèz safe for her and train her well. She said she had already warned Erèz to behave, stay out of adults' conversations, and to keep her hands off of what doesn't belong to her.

She finished her semi-planned speech by saying, "In time, I am sure you will be happy you have taken Erèz in your home. She really is a good girl and very hard little worker. You'll see that she's very obedient and quick to learn!"

Man Féfé listened pensively as if each word that Erèz's mother said weighed heavily on her, as if she wasn't yet sure if Erèz was truly a good fit for her five-person family. Erèz's mother finished her speech and stood there looking hopeful that Erèz would indeed be able to stay. Man Féfé said casually, "Alright. No problem." Erèz's mother sighed audibly in relief and proceeded to thank her cousin profusely for agreeing to take her daughter in under her roof in the city of Jérémie.

At this point, Erèz's little belly rumbled. It had been hours since she and her mother had had the coffee and bread at Man Rachelle's house, and the day's journey had been a very long one with the travel by foot from Guinaudée. Erèz knew from a very young age how to contain her hunger, but that didn't stop her mother and Madame from hearing her tummy rumbling.

"Let me see if there is anything left for you two to eat." She went back up the steep stairs with the same elegance that she had walked down. She returned holding a plate with breakfast that had been left unfinished by someone else, perhaps one of her own children. There was also a lone piece of bread that someone had taken a bite of already.

Seeing the maid going about her business, Man Féfé asked, "Andrea, is there any more coffee?"

"Non, Madame," said Andrea. Man Féfé commanded her to bring Erèz and her mother two cups of water, specifying to bring the water in plastic cups instead of glass ones.

Andrea rinsed the soap foam from her hands and headed toward the steep steps that led to the door of the kitchen, which was attached to the house. She came back with two plastic cups filled with water. It was obvious Andrea had used the oldest and ugliest cups dedicated to the least important visitors like vendors, handymen, or very poor peasant family members from Guinaudée.

Erèz's mother folded half of the scrambled eggs with smoked herring, bell peppers, and onions into half of the old piece of bread and handed it to Erèz. She ate the rest herself with the crooked old fork, also reserved for lower class visitors. Once they were finished with their meal and water, Erèz's mother knew it was time to say goodbye.

Yet from the treatment Erèz had just received from Man Féfé, Erèz's mother remained undecided about leaving her dear daughter with her cousin. Reluctantly, she also remembered Erèz would have many more opportunities in the city of Jérémie than in Guinaudée. In her heart, she thought of this as a test of faith and believed she was handing her daughter to Manman Mari, Mary the Mother of Jesus. She said to herself, "God knows everything."

She got up and said to Erèz, "I am going to go. Behave. I'll come see you in three months."

Erèz could hardly utter a word because everything was all happening so fast. She nodded yes with her head as she replied like any peasant girl would, "Yes, Mother."

Erèz watched her mother make her way to the steep steps leading to the alley. Erèz heard her mother say, "Make me proud." Then, as if in a bad dream, Erèz's eyes filled with tears that clouded her vision as she watched her mother begin to disappear from sight up the stairs.

Her mother glanced back toward her direction once again to say, "Don't cry, my daughter!" and just like that she was gone and Erèz found herself alone in her new world.

CHAPTER 13
A New Identity

Erèz clutched even tighter to the plastic bag that contained her very few valuables. She stood there realizing that leaving her at her cousin's house was the biggest mistake her mother could ever make. Of course, she couldn't debate her fate with her mother since the adults in her life had the last say. She already promised her mother that she would be on her best behavior and make her proud, and she was committed in her little mind to obey head-down to everything she was told to do in the new house. In the midst of that all uncertainty, visualizing herself in the blue plaid shirt and well-pressed pleated skirt for school lit a bit of hope in her heart.

Lost in her little daydream, she suddenly felt someone slap her extremely hard on her face. It felt as if the slap had peeled the skin right off of that side of her cheek. Erèz realized that she wasn't lost in her daydream anymore and that Man Féfé had actually slapped her not ten minutes after her mother had walked away. With that slap, Erèz's fears were confirmed. Every sense in her tiny body that had screamed at her that she was not going to be welcomed at Man Féfé's house had been on point all along.

As she snapped back from her daydream to this harsh new reality, her mother's cousin stood imposing in front of her and stated in an even and authoritative voice, "If you don't stop your tears, I am going to give you something to really cry about."

With that said, Erèz wiped the tears off her face, agreeing that she didn't want to be hit again with a similar blow or a harder one. She remained in place, wondering if her face was swelling from the powerful, unexpected slap.

A shuffle and noise from the rubbly pieces of wood that covered the drain in the little alley on the side of the house announced that someone was coming down the steps. Bòs Cyprien walked down the steps with a wooden tray covered in fresh green banana leaves. The stain on the leaves and the smell indicated to Erèz that Bòs Cyprien was carrying a freshly slaughtered goat. The four feet of the goat tied together were showing on one side of the tray, and Erèz was all too familiar with that smell from her time at the Wednesday maché under the blazing hot sun.

Man Féfé looked contemptuously at Bòs Cyprien and said, "What took you so long? Thanks to you dragging your feet on the roads, the bouillon won't be ready until six o'clock today."

Bòs Cyprien looked a bit troubled, knowing Madame wasn't one to easily forgive and forget anyone's mishaps. He engaged in a long explanation trying to vindicate himself and remain on the good side of Madame, but he knew he was not going to be taken seriously, forgiven easily, or won over Madame's hardheaded ways when dealing with her servants or anyone from the lower class.

The true reason why Bòs Cyprien came late from buying the goat that Saturday was because the farmer wasn't home when he arrived at his house at six o'clock that morning. He waited three hours before the farmer showed up and by the time the goat was slaughtered, skinned, eviscerated, and cleaned, it was almost noon. Since Madame's thoughts were considered facts, she wouldn't listen to the truth that getting to the house late wasn't totally Bòs Cyprien's fault. The fact remained that the bouillon would be ready at around six o'clock that Saturday instead of the usual twelve-thirty or one o'clock.

After Madame berated Bòs Cyprien, and Bòs Cyprien noticed that he could finally talk without getting her angry and agitated, he decided to change the subject.

"Is that the girl?" He asked in Creole, pointing toward Erèz while trying to be as proper as he could be in speaking to Madame.

"Yes," Madame replied in Creole with a French accent.

Bòs Cyprien unintentionally humiliated Erèz by asking incredulously, "Why is she so skinny?"

Madame rolled her eyes at the question. It was obvious that Erèz came from the countryside of Guinaudée, and her family was too poor to properly feed her and provide for her. Instead, she responded in her Haitian-French accent, "Why are you asking me? Ask her yourself."

Madame then looked back at Erèz and said, "Get out of my sight!"

Erèz, still holding on to the little worn plastic bag, didn't know where to go or what to do. She had no idea where to go in the house or what exactly Madame wanted her to do at that moment. As she stood there dazed, trying to figure out what to do next, she realized one of her teeth had loosened from the violent slap she received from Madame earlier.

She knew better not to mumble a word or show any sign of pain or malaise as that would likely attract a full whipping or beating. She tried taking a step forward and that was when she realized the sole of her right foot was still very sensitive if not swollen from where the safety pin had been poking her relentlessly during the long journey from Guinaudée to Jérémie.

As Erèz looked down at her foot, she overheard her cousin say, "One could easily mistake her for a zombie." On that quite mean note, Man Féfé turned to head back up the steps. On her way up, she angrily hollered with authority for Andrea to come get the goat's head, feet, and intestines to further clean and flash rinse them, and then marinate them for the bouillon that Saturday.

Bouillon, which is spelled bouyon in Creole, is a popular soup that is mostly cooked on Saturdays in Haiti. The purpose of cooking bouyon is to replenish the body with plenty of nutrients after a week of hard work. It is also made when someone is ill to help strengthen their body.

The ingredients in the bouillon are countless: African yams, taro roots, watercress, leafy greens of all kinds, carrots, leeks, green onions, onions, oil, butter, potatoes, green plantains, and more. Arguably, all Haitians love bouyon, and they especially love the buttery handmade dumplings in this soup which are made of flour, water, salt, olive oil, and butter. The dumplings can be shaped in different sizes and forms. Chewing on the gummy texture of a boiled dumpling in between spoonfuls of hot bouyon is the best feeling on earth.

In just two hours, Erèz had lost her identity as a little girl. It all happened so quickly that she couldn't keep up with all the changes, and her mind was racing.

She could barely accept the fact that she was not going to see her mother again until three months later, in October. Her self-esteem was completely crushed as this was the first time she became aware that her skinny appearance was simply not good enough for the city of Jérémie. She was never made aware that having long skinny legs might be a sign of malnourishment even when her mother lovingly teased her out of endearment by calling her pyé long (long legs) instead of by her name. Her mother's intent was never to make her feel less than or make her feel bad about herself in the way that Bòs Cyprien and Madame, her cousin, just did.

In just two hours Erèz had gone from a beloved daughter to a:

1) Child servant

2) Restavèk

3) Sentaniz

4) Zombie, and a

5) Vaut rien

All synonyms for the peasant child given away by her parents in hopes of finding a better future in the home of a wealthy family living in the city.

Erèz was no longer everybody's little girl. In fact, she was nobody's little girl now. Instead of having a lot of mothers and fathers in the community of Guinaudée watch over her, she was completely alone and lost in a world full of uncertainty.

CHAPTER 14
Andrea

Andrea didn't say much, and Erèz was certain she must not be a friendly person. Little did she know Andrea was going to become a second mother to her.

Andrea came back under the tamarind tree with all the goat's parts that Madame wanted cleaned and added to the bouyon. She started a fire with pieces of wood kept close to the tree for that purpose. In between the three rocks that served as pillars to support the pot, she littered pieces of newspaper that the Monsieur of the house had already read. She placed a good amount of wood pieces and wood scraps on top of the newspaper kindling, and then she lit a couple of matches carefully in the center of the little mountain she had created to properly nurse the fire.

Erèz stood there observing, and the fire started right away. She could tell Andrea was an expert at starting wood fires. As soon as the fire started crackling, Andrea placed the pot over the fire. This particular pot was covered with an outer layer of thick dark residue that had become the official coating, as if the pot was enameled that way. Later, Erèz noticed that Andrea scrubbed the interior of the pot with a piece of coconut husk and a handful of fresh, powdery ashes. These two elements made the inside of the pot shine like new.

Andrea added a handful of coarse salt, sour orange peel, and lime peel to the water in the pot. While waiting for the water to boil, she proceeded to clean the goat meat for the bouyon. Erèz recalled that her mother only used sour orange and salt in the water when she flash-rinsed her goat meat to sustain the smell of the goat. Andrea continued cleaning and ignored Erèz standing there.

"Do you want to help me?" Andrea asked after awhile.

Erèz quietly nodded and responded, "Yes," in a soft tone.

"What do you have in that bag that is so precious?" Andrea asked, glancing over at Erèz's plastic bag.

"My dresses."

"Why don't you remove your shoes? In this house, they are going to put you to work. You won't have time to be pretty, girlie."

Erèz had already concluded that in her mind, and she nodded in agreement.

"Put your bag behind the tree and we'll see where Madame wants you to keep your belongings. Do you have a pair of sandals to wear?"

Erèz shook her head no, and explained that her only other pair had fallen apart on the journey over, and her mother had taken them back to Guinaudée with her.

"Okay, I will ask Madame if the girls have any old shoes they want to pass down to you."

Andrea remained focused on cleaning the meat with her head down, rushing to get the bouyon going. When she finally looked up to talk to Erèz, she noticed her small face was completely swollen. With more sadness than Erèz expected to hear in her voice, Andrea quietly said, "Madame should not have done that to you. As soon as I am done marinating that meat, I am going to take care of your little cheeks."

"Yes, auntie."

For a moment, they both remained silent.

"Do you know how to use a mortar and pestle to crush ingredients for the épis?" Andrea eventually asked. *Épis in Creole means marinade, and Haitians make a fresh marinade every day to cook the protein for their main meal.*

Erèz nodded eagerly, "Yes, auntie."

"Okay, my daughter."

Crushing the ingredients for the épis was Erèz's favorite thing to do while her mother was cooking back home in the countryside of Guinaudée. Andrea handed the mortar and pestle to Erèz who immediately and expertly started crushing the green onions, garlic cloves, black peppercorns, coarse salt, parsley, and cloves.

The ingredients were mashed in no time and that pleased Andrea, who proceeded to chop the goat's feet into various pieces using a machete on top of a glossy rock. As she chopped the goat's feet, Erèz asked her if it was possible to save the two oslè in the back feet of the goat for her.

"I can be very careful in keeping the oslè intact, but sometimes Sherline collects them also." Erèz was disheartened, but she didn't have any choice. Andrea continued to scrub the meat with fresh pieces of sour orange and rinse it in another pot filled with clean water.

Erèz found the big basin filled with clean running water fascinating. This was worlds different from back home in Guinaudée where her sister Yaya walked miles to retrieve clean water from the river. The running water at Madame's was crystal clear, and when it overflowed, it ran on a cemented slant that dripped all the way to the backside of the house onto the road leading to the cemetery located just a few hundred feet up the street.

With Erèz's help, Andrea got the meat marinated and the bouyon cooking in no time. She found herself smiling as she worked on the bouyon because Erèz was surprisingly helpful and handy.

As the pot of bouyon boiled, she warmed up some water with some salt and pulled Erèz off to the side to gently pat her face with a piece of white scrap fabric from Madame's sewing stash. She repeated the pats and whenever Andrea thought the water was too hot, she blew on the wet fabric so that she didn't burn Erèz's already swollen face. Andrea handed her a plastic cup containing water and two Saridon pills for her to take. Erèz obeyed and drank as if Andrea was her real mother.

As she swallowed the pills, Madame spotted them and yelled loudly, "You don't have anything better to do?"

Erèz's heart sank even more as it was obvious Madame was intent on seeing her suffer. When it came to the loose tooth, Andrea told her that she would have to deal with that on her own. She warned her that Madame wouldn't care to send her to the clinic to see the dentist.

For three weeks, Erèz suffered tremendously with the loose tooth that Madame dislocated with the slap. She rubbed her tongue repeatedly over that tooth every night as she tried to sleep, hoping she would be able to get it loose to a point where she could remove it with her hand. After what seemed an eternity, she was finally able to remove the tooth. She bled in the middle of the night once she pulled it, but she was happy that finally she was able to find some type of relief.

"You are going to have to learn quickly in this house. If not, you won't survive. Little girls don't last long here," Andrea told her gravely.

The bouyon was ready around two-thirty.

"Do you know how to set up a table?" Andrea inquired. That was the first time Erèz heard the term mété kouvè (set the table) in Creole. She shook her head no, but Andrea told her she was going to teach her. By this time Madame confined herself upstairs, and Erèz felt quite relieved that she wasn't around.

Andrea explained to her that in order to serve the bouyon, she needed to place a plate underneath the big bowl. This plate would be used to discard the bones after the person was finished eating the meat off them or sucking on them. One spoon would be placed on the right side of the plate. From a china cabinet filled with beautiful glasses, fancy plates and bowls, and expensive silverware, Andrea removed a fine white tablecloth. Upon that cloth, Andrea completed the rest of the setup as Erèz tried to memorize the many steps of properly setting the table. When Andrea had finished, Erèz was certain that she had never seen such a gorgeous table display, even in her wildest dreams.

Andrea prepared a refreshing cold limeade and placed it in a large glass pot in the middle of the table. Just enough ice cubes floated on top to keep the juice cold, but not too much to dilute the delicious flavor of the limeade. She carefully sliced fresh green limes to garnish the top.

Andrea poured some limeade for Erèz to drink in one of the old plastic cups, knowing all too well that Madame would not have wanted her to have any of it. Erèz soon learned that when Madame was around, Andrea wasn't as friendly toward her. If she showed too much affection for Erèz, she knew she risked being fired or reprimanded for being too distracted from her duties. In fact, when Madame was around, Andrea pretended to be almost as mean as Madame. Erèz played the game well with Andrea. For her part, Erèz strived to perfectly complete all the tasks Andrea set for her so that Madame could applaud Andrea for a job well done.

Later that day, Erèz learned another lesson on how differently people were treated in her new world. At dinnertime, it became quickly obvious that not everyone was treated equally in this classist society. She realized she would never have the opportunity to sit at the table and eat with the rich people she was serving.

Rich families ate on fine china with shining silverware. They gossiped, laughed, and told jokes at the table. Servants were often deemed unworthy of names and went by "female adult servant," "man servant," or "little girl servant." These nameless servants sat in the backyard in the baking heat to eat their food from old broken aluminum bowls. If they were lucky, they were able to drink whatever was left of the day's fruit juice from old plastic cups. They didn't have gleaming silverware, but instead used crooked old aluminum spoons and forks.

Erèz waited for her portion of dinner on Andrea's little bench under the tamarind tree, thinking about Guinaudée, Yaya, and Ilèyis. She allowed herself to wonder about her father coming back from those long hours under the sun working on somebody else's farm for pennies on the dollar to keep them afloat. She thought of Marie-Jeanne and Bébé Patrick. She recalled all the conversations she'd had with Tant Lucienne, sitting on the porch as Marie-Jeanne fed little Patrick.

She remembered all the fun they'd had under the bright light of the moon with their closest neighbors on Saturday nights. She recalled her solitary nights on the big glossy rock counting the stars, clueless and careless of the world outside of Guinaudée. In her daydream, she saw Ti Roro holding his small tree branch, walking behind the donkey loaded with fresh vegetables from his parents' farm as his mother—Erèz's godmother—walked in front of him, waving hello to everyone she knew.

Erèz thought about the sweet lollipops wrapped in crackly cellophane that her godmother usually brought her on Saturday evenings from Jérémie. Erèz's godmother knew her favorite lollipop flavor was cherry, and she tried to make sure she always brought her that flavor every time she returned from the city.

Andrea placed one little piece of bone in Erèz's bouyon and did the same in Bòs Cyprien's bowl. Andrea ate what remained of the bouyon right from the bottom of the pot where she had saved herself a nice piece of bone from the goat's head. She sucked on the piece of bone for what seemed an eternity. She only placed the bone down when she felt the family was done eating their dinner at the table. Andrea rushed to collect all the silverware, plates, and the glass jar half-filled with the limeade. Bòs Cyprien smiled knowing that she didn't like sweet juices much; most would go straight into his old aluminum cup that he always kept outside just for this reason.

Though Andrea spent most of her day at Madame's house, she did not actually live there. As a single mother to two children, she left every evening to go care for them and spend the night at her own house. She came to work every morning at seven o'clock and left at six o'clock in the evening. That first night, Erèz dreaded the moment Andrea would have to leave and be completely alone in this house with this new family.

"Do you know how to do dishes?" Andrea asked her as she scrubbed. Erèz nodded in the affirmative as she rinsed a greasy plate. Andrea stopped scrubbing for a moment to look at Erèz, and said, "You are a nice little girl, you know that?"

With that compliment, Erèz genuinely smiled from ear to ear for the first time the entire day. She didn't allow herself to forget to politely respond with the "Yes, auntie," to Andrea's question, with the demeanor of a respectful girl from the countryside. The joy was short lived as she remembered that in just a couple of hours, Andrea would be gone and she was going to spend the evening all alone.

They finished doing the dishes, and Andrea started scrubbing the pots by grabbing handfuls of fresh ashes from the woodfire where she had cooked the bouyon earlier. After scrubbing the pots, Andrea washed them quickly in a soapy solution with an astonishing amount of foam. Erèz was amazed at the sheer abundance. Her own mother was always careful to use just enough to get a plate or two clean. When Erèz did the dishes or scrubbed the pots back in Guinaudée, the first wash with the ashes sufficed.

With her head down, she continued to chat with Andrea as they worked on cleaning the dishes together. Instead of laying the clean dishes on a fresh banana leaf on the ground like Erèz's mother used to do back in Guinaudée, Andrea used a bamboo basket. Erèz paid attention to each step of the process as carefully as possible so as not to forget. She wanted to avoid any chance of receiving another painful blow to the face later on. The reminder to make no mistakes and to perfectly complete any tasks that were given to her was constant in Erèz's mind as the side of her face still burned and remained swollen.

CHAPTER 15
Bòs Cyprien

Bòs Cyprien was the gason lakou. Translated word for word, this means "boy of the yard." He oversaw everything that had to do with taking care of the exterior of the house, and at night, as everyone slept, he also assumed the role of bodyguard, vigilantly stepping out in the yard and patrolling to keep everyone safe. From time to time, Bòs Cyprien's loud and boisterous laughs could be heard across the yard. He often straddled the wall that served as a fence between the house and the little street leading to the cemetery. The cement at the top of the wall was set with broken bottles to prevent thieves from jumping in the backyard, but Bòs Cyprien always managed to find the perfect spot where the glass would not cut him. One mishap could easily result in severely slicing his foot or leg, but it never happened. From this perch, Bòs Cyprien chatted with this friend or that friend as they passed by on the road.

When he wasn't too busy, that was what he enjoyed doing. He sat on top of that wall facing the Catholic church watching people going up and down the street. Occasionally, Bòs Cyprien let out appreciative whistles upon seeing certain ladies walking by who caught his eye. Most of the ladies just ignored him and continued on their way, but some were bold enough to respond to his advances and flirtations. Erèz learned a lot about Bòs Cyprien in this way. For example, once she overheard him speak with deep sadness about his wife who had suddenly passed away about a year ago. Sometimes, he would open up about his son who was crippled and lived in a little town an hour away called Calas.

One afternoon, Bòs Cyprien engaged in a very lively argument with one of his best friends, Bòs Arnold, about a piece of land that he wished to purchase close to his mother's house in Calas. Bòs Arnold wanted to hear none of it as he desperately tried to convince Bòs Cyprien to stay as far away as possible from this deal. Apparently, that particular family selling the piece of land served evil voodoo spirits that might be sent against Bòs Cyprien and hurt what little family he had left. Alas, it was too late to back out of the deal as Bòs Cyprien revealed to Bòs Arnold that he had already put down money on the land. He truly wanted to start a farm and hire someone in Calas to take care of it. They both agreed a farm would be profitable, but the conversation concluded with Bòs Arnold wiggling his index finger up at Bòs Cyprien saying, "Don't say I didn't warn you!"

Bòs Cyprien remained there lost in his thoughts about the conversation he'd just had. Should he move forward with the purchase of the land, or should he count the down payment as lost money? Was it true that the family he was purchasing the land from was involved in voodoo? Would those potentially powerful spirits harm his family, or were they just rumors that Bòs Arnold foolishly believed? Of course, Erèz didn't know the answer to any of these questions any more than Bòs Cyprien did, but she definitely knew that Bòs Cyprien was preoccupied.

CHAPTER 16
A Trip Into Town

Erèz continued to have nightmares about the angry chicken that used to chase her on her way to Marie-Jeanne's house. She thought to herself that she would rather have many angry chickens chase her than remain at Madame's house. Erèz knew that even if she had a thousand mean chickens chasing her in Guinaudée, numerous adults would come to her rescue and save her from being pecked. That was how it worked in Guinaudée. Here, there was nobody to rescue her from Madame's unexpected cruelty.

She knew she needed to grow up quickly in order to live up to Madame's standards and meet her rigid expectations. Instead of tying up a bunch of coconut or palm leaves together to sweep the dirt ground back in Guinaudée, Erèz needed to master using a broom quickly. Andrea taught Erèz how to use a broom for the first time in her life, but it was still uncomfortable for her to hold the broomstick, let alone use it effectively to correctly sweep the backyard. As she prayed hard that Madame wouldn't hit her with another blow to the face for something as simple as not being able to hold a broomstick correctly, her thoughts got interrupted by Bòs Cyprien's voice.

"Where are you from, little girl?"

"Guinaudée, tonton," Erèz replied as every little girl from the countryside of Haiti would to a male adult, addressing him as tonton, or "uncle."

"I haven't been to Guinaudée." Bòs Cyprien continued. "Is your father still alive?"

Erèz replied, "Wi, tonton,"

Bòs Cyprien continued, "It's not easy living here. Try hard so that they don't send you back. Little servants don't last long here."

With that comment, Erèz's heart started beating extremely fast as if Madame had just slapped her again. She imagined all the terrible things that could happen. Life wasn't going to be easy, living in that house.

Erèz tried holding on to the ray of hope that her dream of going to school in October would be realized, but it was difficult now that she lived in constant fear of being physically abused. Even so, she didn't want to be sent back because going back to Guinaudée would be proof that she had disappointed her mother, her father, and her whole community.

Erèz recalled the last conversation Mèt Robèto had had with her when her mother made her say goodbye to him. Mèt Robèto told her that learning how to read and write would save her from poverty and that was the sure way she could become the smart Madan Sara she always dreamed she could be. She could then return to Guinaudée with enough money to help her dad redo the roof of the house. All of the last goodbye conversations with the adults in Erèz's life in Guinaudée ended on the words, "Make us proud!," which pressured Erèz to excel no matter what.

After reflecting on Bòs Cyprien's warning about little girls not lasting too long at Man Féfé's house, Erèz vowed that afternoon to make all the adults who raised her back in Guinaudée proud. No matter how often she got hit or slapped, no matter how much she had to cry, she took it upon herself to suffer so that she could please her immediate and extended family in Guinaudée. As she was lost in her thoughts, thinking about all she had to learn so that Bòs Cyprien's prophecy of not lasting long didn't come to pass, she jumped when Madame, her cousin, opened the door to the backyard.

"Where is that skinny little zombie?" Man Féfé shouted, referring to Erèz and pretending not to see her sitting at the bottom of the stairs.

Bòs Cyprien pointed with his nose toward Erèz's direction. Madame pretended as if she was pained to speak Creole instead of French, "Come here, ti fiy."

The condescending and sardonic way she said "ti fiy" made Erèz nervous, but she walked toward Madame. When Erèz was close enough, she placed money in Erèz's hand and said, "Go buy bread for supper tonight from Madan Dikrépen's house."

Erèz responded, "Wi, ma tant," out of respect for Man Féfé, not realizing that addressing her that way would prove to be a huge mistake.

Suddenly, Madame grabbed and squeezed her left ear as hard as she could and whispered, "If you call me auntie one more time, I'll whip your bottom so hard you won't be able to sit down for a week."

On that note, scared and terrified, Erèz quickly replied, "Yes, Madame!"

That demand was just to feed her ego and turlututu ways.

Turlututu is a French term that translates into someone's extravagant ways of carrying themselves to show their superiority over other people. Someone who uses big words with great intention when they talk acts as a turlututu. In the Haitian culture, for example, a Haitian who pretends not being able to express themselves in Creole and prefers speaking French to people who cannot comprehend French and only speak Creole just to feel important acts as a turlututu. Someone who seemed bothered by raw Creole terminologies can be viewed as a turlututu.

As Erèz's ear burned and stung from Madame's pinch, she recollected herself and held the bottom of the dress she was wearing with her hands between her legs as her mother had taught her. Madame looked at her incredulously, and she said in Creole, "Look at how this foolish little zombie stands."

Erèz felt miserable, knowing that she was being called a zombie instead of her given name. The term "zombie" had a very bad connotation in the Guinaudée community. She couldn't deny that zombies did in fact walk with their heads down, and although her mother had instructed her not to look adults straight in the eyes as a sign of respect, she very well knew she was nowhere near being a zombie.

She wasn't a dead person brought back to life to serve the whims of the living. She wasn't a mindless, senseless husk. She was a person, a girl that everyone considered sweet, kind, and obedient to adults. She was devastated by this new identity created by Madame, but there was nothing Erèz could do other than obediently respond to her demands, no matter what was requested of her. Now, her destiny was all tied to serving Madame's family in the city of Jérémie. As Madame continued to look at her with disdain, it dawned on Erèz that maybe she *was* a little zombie-like. Erèz held her head down, afraid to look Madame straight in the eyes. She didn't dare to make any noise, fearing her other ear would be assailed next. A couple of tears rolled down her cheeks, but fortunately Madame didn't notice.

Erèz took the medium-sized basket from Madame's hands and headed toward the little alley that led to the street, not even knowing where Madan Dikrépen's store was.

As she made the last step that took her directly onto the busy street, she attempted to cross without looking both ways. A lady across the street shouted at her, "Look where you're going! If you're not careful to look both ways, one of these cars will hit you, little zombie!"

Surprisingly, a car stopped just in time to avoid hitting and possibly killing Erèz on the spot. That near brush with death while crossing the street shocked her terribly as that was the very first time in her entire existence that she attempted crossing a busy street. She was shaken from the experience and took a moment to calm down.

The driver screamed loudly enough for people on both sides to hear, "What are you doing mountain girl? Go back where you belong! It's better for everyone!"

Once she saw no cars coming, Erèz ran across the street as fast as her long skinny legs would carry her. She heard passersby heartily laughing at what the driver had said, and she became even more embarrassed. She now knew she looked different from everyone else here, and stood out as a little peasant in her demeanor. People in the city of Jérémie didn't appreciate peasants much, and that would not help her at all as she tried adjusting to the city life.

She went up and down the street that afternoon completely lost, confused, and self-conscious. She was unable to locate any house at the bottom of the hill that looked like a store that sold bread. The same lady who yelled at Erèz when the car had almost hit her earlier noticed her wandering aimlessly back and forth and laughed at her.

She called loudly from across the street, "Did they send you, little girl?" In the true meaning of that phrase in Creole, the lady was very clearly implying that a bad spirit might have sent Erèz from the mountains to the street of Mònn Jibilé to disturb the entire community and create mayhem.

With all the strength left in her frail body, Erèz responded in her small voice, "Non, ma tant." That brought more laughter upon her.

As she headed back down the street looking for Madan Dikrépen's house, she almost bumped into a little girl servant who, just like her, was also carrying a basket. Hers, however, was full of fresh hot bread. She had obviously come from Madan Dikrépen's house as the smell of the bread permeated from underneath the colorful cotton kitchen cloth covering the basket.

The girl didn't even wait for Erèz to speak when she said brightly in Creole, "Are you looking for Madan Dikrépen's house? Here it is!" She pointed toward the second house from where they stood.

Erèz gratefully said in her little peasant voice, "Thank you. What's your name?"

"Marianne," the girl responded sweetly and waited expectantly for Erèz to share her name.

Erèz pointed at herself and said, "Erèz."

Marianne smiled at her and gave her a shy wave as she turned to leave, skipping a bit as she went.

Erèz didn't realize she had to go through a little dark alley just like the one on the side of Madame, her cousin's house, to get to the back of the house where she would buy the bread. When she finally got there, Madan Dikrépen was busy pulling freshly baked bread from the brick oven with the help of her workers, and quickly putting more rolls in the oven to be baked.

A group of customers waited for French bread, and Erèz joined them, patiently waiting her turn. Everyone who was there noticed she was new.

One lady asked her, "Where do you come from, little girl?"

"Guinaudée, ma tant," Erèz responded politely. To her surprise, everyone burst into laughter. She had no idea why her response would elicit such a reaction.

The lady continued with her questions to make fun of Erèz and bring more merriment to the group waiting for their bread, "Who do you belong to, little girl?"

Erèz responded, "Renise wi, ma tant," referring to her mother's name.

The small crowd laughed even louder as the woman, who was now almost out of breath, continued with her questioning, "Where do you live, little girl?"

Erèz humbly replied, despite the embarrassment she felt on the inside of her, "At Madame Féfé's house."

"Oh, at Madame Féfé's house?" The lady paused, and then a little more seriously continued, "You're not going to stay there for long," confirming what Bòs Cyprien said earlier. The lady then went on to make as many comments as she could about Madame. It was clear to Erèz the lady loved to gossip.

"Madame Féfé doesn't wear her panties just for wearing them," the lady said at one point. *This phrase is used in Haitian Creole to describe a Haitian woman who always means business. She is strong and independent, willing to take on challenges, and not afraid to stand up for herself.* With that particular comment, the crowd remained silent, suggesting that everyone was in agreement and aware of Man Féfé's reputation.

Erèz quietly stood in the same spot. By now, it was close to an hour and fifteen minutes since she had left the house. The idea crossed her mind that Madame would probably be angry at her, but there was nothing she could do other than wait for the bread. She observed Madan Dikrépen working with the three men. She methodically kneaded the dough by pulling and folding it repeatedly. A man periodically checked on the bread in the hot brick oven, removing the loaves just as they were perfect. When Madan Dikrépen noticed the look on the man's face that let her know that a round of bread was ready to be removed from the oven, she walked over to verify. Indeed it was ready, and she pulled one of the long wooden peels to remove the hot bread with perfect crispy yellow-orangish crust.

At the first glance of the bread, Erèz's tummy rumbled as she recalled Marie-Jeanne's uncle bringing the exact same types of bread from Port-au-Prince. Marie-Jeanne's mother always wrapped a couple of those breads in a piece of brown paper to send to Erèz's mother. She looked forward to eating a piece at the bottom of the stairs in the backyard tonight while counting the stars under the bright sky of the city of Jérémie.

When it came her turn to get her bread, she handed the money to Madan Dikrépen. It surprised her how wet the two gourdes from Madame, her cousin, had become. She didn't realize that the hand that was holding the gourdes was sweaty out of nervousness from all the teasing and ridiculing she suffered all day.

Madan Dikrépen looked at Erèz with a bit of disgust as she gingerly took the two wet gourdes using just the tip of her thumb and index finger. She placed them on the edge of the table full of hot bread so they could air dry before adding them to the stack of money she kept in a well-used thirty-two-ounce tin can.

After placing the bread in the basket, Madan Dikrépen told Erèz, "Tell Madame, I said hello. Let her know I will be making fresh peanut butter tomorrow."

Erèz replied "Wi, ma tant."

Erèz took the basket of bread and headed back to the little dark alley leading to the main street of Mònn Jibilé. On her way back, she considered the countless times she almost got killed by a car, got lost looking for Madan Dikrépen's house, was ridiculed by a group of city people, and waited for what seemed like hours for the bread to be baked.

As she stood there reflecting outside of Madan Dikrépen's house, a young man on a bicycle, who seemed to appear out of thin air, swerved to miss her but still managed to side swipe her with great force.

She found herself face down on the ground. Before Erèz could even think of herself and her condition, she desperately looked around for the basket of bread. It was a foot away from her on the street, but fortunately it remained intact and all the bread remained safe as it had been tightly wrapped in paper and cloth. She felt a huge sense of relief.

To her surprise, this young man behaved gentlemanly toward her instead of addressing her the way most people today had. He hopped off his bike and helped Erèz off the ground, saying to her in Creole, "Forgive me, little girl! I tried avoiding you, but I didn't see you step out until it was too late."

Later on, Erèz would learn that the young man's name was Dodo, though his real name was Dominique. He was deeply in love with Carline, the oldest daughter of Madame. Dodo would later ask Erèz to give love letters to Carline for him whenever he bumped into her on the streets. Dominique and Carline's clandestine relationship was kept hidden from both Madame and her husband, Mèt Féfé.

Perhaps part of why Dodo was so kind to Erèz was because his heart and soul were still full of joy from catching a glimpse of Carline from her window upstairs. Upon seeing her beautiful face in the window of her room, he waved from his bike and quietly uttered, "I love you." The sweetest sight was that of Carline silently mouthing back that she loved him too as her eyes followed him down the road happily riding his bike.

By the time she was close to Madame's house, Erèz's left elbow and pinky toe had been bleeding quite a bit from the collision. Regardless, she gathered enough strength and pride within herself to pat herself on the back because despite the pain she felt all over her body, she was still very much alive. She limped to the little dark alley of the house and reached to open the back door to place the basket of bread on the table. Unknown to her, Madame had spotted her coming up the road and carefully hidden herself by the wall against the main back entrance. There, she waited patiently to hit her with a matinèt.

A matinèt in a Haitian household has three strands of leather attached to a piece of wood. It is used to beat little servants or even the family's own children as punishment. Sometimes the little servants committed some error or disobeyed, but sometimes they did not. They were at the mercy of the adults, who arbitrarily decided when something done by the little servants was enough to trigger a beating. Each strand of the matinèt regularly measures around twelve to eighteen inches, and the piece of wood that serves as the handle is eight to ten inches.

As Erèz set the basket of fresh bread on the table, she felt the matinèt strike her little back in three different spots. That was what one might call Erèz's official baptism with the matinèt as she had never been punished with one until now. When Yaya would punish her back in Guinaudée, she used just one fresh branch. When Yaya's branch hit her little legs, Erèz only felt one hit instead of three. Before Erèz knew it or had time to turn away from the table, Madame hit her a second time in the back with the three-stranded matinèt. Madame hit Erèz a third, fourth, fifth, and sixth time. On the seventh hit, Erèz let out a piercing scream from pain she could no longer contain.

Madame, her cousin, coldly told her, "If you scream again, I am going to give you something to cry about." She then proceeded to hit Erèz several more times on her back. Erèz kept from making any sound as best she could. She felt something warm dripping down her back, and then down her leg. It was blood. The skin on her tiny little back was splitting under the repetitive hits of the matinèt.

When Madame finally noticed it was serious enough that Erèz's back was bleeding, she stopped and said in Creole, "When I send you somewhere, be quick about it. I am not going to let you make a fool of me in my own house."

Erèz was barely able to reply, "Wi, ma tant."

Madame viciously pulled Erèz by the ears to face her and calmly said, "I am not your aunt."

Erèz, nearly hyperventilating from trying not to make any sounds during the pulling of her ears, heard a woman's voice from the street saying in French, "How are we doing? What are you feeding the people tonight?"

Erèz recognized that voice immediately. It was the voice of the lady who had made fun of her all afternoon from across the street.

Madame replied in French, "On est là, Mo." Mo was the sweet nickname everyone on the street called her. The lady's name was actually Gertrude, but since she was married to Mèt Maurice and now used her husband's first name as her first name as well. She was addressed as Madame Maurice in French, Madan Moris in Haitian Creole, or simply as Mo by her closest friends.

Madame turned sharply to Erèz and said, "Get out of my sight."

Mo, close enough now to see Erèz, laughed and said, "Oh, look at that! I didn't know that little zombie lived here."

Erèz's back continued to bleed as she left both ladies to gossip about her, with Mo recounting to Madame all that went on earlier. Madame laughed as she heard about Erèz wandering up and down the street looking for Madan Dikrépen's house. Erèz felt quite ashamed as if she had greatly disappointed her whole family back in Guinaudée with that first serious matinèt beating. Before long, her body was shivering under an intense fever from the beating.

At that point, on her very first day in the city of Jérémie, she had a sore foot, a bleeding back, a bloodied elbow, possibly a broken pinky toe, a loose tooth, and the side of her right face was still swollen from Madame's first slap. All she could do was to sit at the bottom of the stairs, crying softly out of shame and pain.

CHAPTER 17
Alone

At some point that evening, Bòs Cyprien happened upon Erèz, and he remained there pensively for a moment, shaking his head at how cruel and sadistic Madame had been. He didn't say a word and headed inside the house.

Every Saturday, Bòs Cyprien brought warm konparèt, a delicious biscotti-like delicacy, for Mèt Féfé to enjoy with his hot chocolate for supper. Mèt Féfé loved dipping his konparèt in the hot chocolate that Madame lovingly concocted with cinnamon, bay leaves, anise, lime peel, vanilla extract, and a hint of salt. Bòs Cyprien regularly walked forty-five minutes to Tant Céline's house to get Mèt Féfé's favorite konparèt. The only time Bòs Cyprien didn't go to Tant Céline's house for Mèt Féfé's konparèt was when a party or social gathering was happening in the house.

Once Mèt Féfé and the family had their fill of the konparèt, he gave whatever was leftover to Bòs Cyprien. That first Saturday night, Madame decided not to feed Erèz supper because she had taken too long to bring the bread earlier. Bòs Cyprien noticed that Erèz was not going to be fed that night, so he handed the piece of konparèt to her. He didn't say a word to Erèz and headed toward the little house in the backyard where he kept his belongings and slept at night. From where he laid, he observed Erèz through his semi-closed door. After half an hour checking on Erèz on and off, he realized she was frozen where he had left her, still holding on to the piece of konparèt.

Erèz couldn't eat, and she knew Bòs Cyprien was gazing upon her with pity. As a father, his heart hurt to see her like this. He said to himself, "If the girl's parents knew, they would have never sent her here, no matter how bad they have it in their village."

Erèz sat there for a long time, not knowing what to do. The way she was feeling, she couldn't even wash herself. She decided the best course of action was to just go to bed and hope that her body would heal as fast as Sunday morning when she woke up; of course, that was only if the adults and Madame's three children didn't find more reasons or excuses to hit and abuse her.

Back in Guinaudée when she felt sick, her mother gave her two Saridon pills and would boil her some fresh cerasee tea in their rusty tea pot on an open wood fire. From where she was sitting at the bottom of the stairs, Erèz had no one to count on and no one to care that she was hurting. Bòs Cyprien looked concerned, but he was also guarded, not knowing what Madame might say to him if he dared show any type of kindness toward Erèz. The expression on his face from where he was laying on his bed showed care, compassion, and a large dose of anger at the sight of an eight-year-old girl suffering so much agony.

Erèz probably sat at the same spot with her little back bleeding for a good three hours. She wasn't afraid of the thick darkness that surrounded the backyard. In that darkness, she desperately wished there was some magic trick she could perform that would miraculously transport her back to Guinaudée where she could hold Marie-Jeanne's hands forever and feel love and acceptance as every adult's pitit fiy.

As Erèz sat there wishing for endearing miracles and happy things to soothe the pain all over her body, she heard Madame at the top of the stairs holler in Creole, "Are you going to spend the night outside, little zombie?"

Erèz replied in her peasant's voice, "Non, Madame." Madame threw a thin bed sheet toward her that landed on the third step from where Erèz was sitting. Erèz tried to get up, but felt her tiny eighty-five pound body weighing more than the world under so much pain. She limped up the stairs, and it wasn't until she'd reached the top that she realized her little black bag with her belongings, her little dress and shoes, was still under the tamarind tree where she and Andrea cooked the bouyon during the day.

Erèz gathered all the strength she could to go back down the stairs. It was pitch dark, but she was able to remember the exact spot of the black bag. She made it to the bottom of the stairs and realized that it was starting to rain a bit. By the time she located her little black bag, the rain was pouring hard. The drops pummeling her bleeding back caused even greater pain. She tried rushing back up the stairs, but the weight of her painful and sore little body slowed her greatly. By that time, the ants that had crawled into the bag earlier to enjoy scraps of food that fell at the bottom from Bòs Cyprien's plate were now crawling back out and began biting Erèz's arms. Erèz threw the bag to the ground in the dark, but forgot that the rain would get to her only little dress. At that same time, she remembered she couldn't take the bag full of ants inside the house, fearing Madame would beat her again in the morning.

Erèz finally broke down and wept hard. She cried and cried. She cried out of desperation for help that would never come. She felt ill from the overwhelming despair and from the pain that each drop of rain on her back brought her. She pulled the little dress and pair of shoes from inside of the bag and shook them. She left the bag where it was, hoping she would wake up early enough in the morning, at least before everyone, to remove and hide it so that she didn't get in trouble.

As she made up her mind to leave, she heard a voice from inside the bag say in Creole, "La pli, la pli, la pli," and for the first time, she got scared of the superstitious being that might be in the dark. She knew she was the only one in the backyard, and yet someone's voice echoed to pierce the darkness. The voice continued persistently, "La pli, la pli, la pli!" "The rain, the rain, the rain!" She braced herself to look closer in the direction the voice was coming from only to realize it wasn't coming from the bag at all.

In Haiti, all the parrots are called "jako," in Creole, and all the dogs are called "toutous." If anyone calls any Haitian dog by yelling "toutous," it will automatically wag its tail or run toward them, when it is a friendly dog, but an angry dog perceives a stranger trying to befriend them by calling them "toutous" as a trigger to start barking, chasing the person, and protecting themselves.

Under Mademoiselle Carline's window lived a jako in a cage. It paced non-stop, alerting everyone about the rain. For some reason, the parrot only wished to communicate of its own accord when it was raining. When it started raining, Jako always frantically announced to everyone in the house about the rain. If it happened that Madame was in the yard when it started raining, Jako would call her name in a frenzy, hollering non-stop, "Madan Féfé, la pli, la pli, la pli!" "Madam Féfé, rain, rain, rain!" Other than that, in most situations, the parrot kept quiet and rarely let loose its personal thoughts, phrases, or the few words it had learned in Creole or French over the years. Sometimes, the words Jako randomly rambled didn't make sense or were out of context, as if he was upset about something. Everyone ignored him and let him have a go at his mind in his own Jako kingdom. When Jako wasn't interested in a conversation or was being teased to get him to talk like a human, he would remain quiet in hopes that whoever was pestering him with their chatter would come to realize that he wanted to be left in peace.

Upon realizing it was a jako talking, Erèz immediately felt relieved and smiled despite herself. "Bonswa, Jako," she said softly to the green bird. Jako took a moment and turned his head to peer at Erèz. For a few moments, Erèz wondered if she could make Jako her best friend. Could she have a feathered friend with whom to share all her griefs and sorrows while living in this house? In her mind, she pictured Jako quietly listening to her and nodding his head compassionately as she vented to him. Occasionally, Jako would agree or disagree with a little cluck to either encourage or discourage her. Even when Erèz enjoyed the fantasy of befriending Jako, she quickly realized that wasn't a good idea and that the risk was too high that Jako might pick up words or phrases she secretly shared with him and vent them in open air. It would be Erèz's worst nightmare if Madame found out through Jako that she was considered a heartless monster, especially if the whole neighborhood heard.

Even when Erèz couldn't truly befriend the bird in the way she wanted to, she did actively engage with Jako in many imaginary conversations over the years. Whenever her pain and disappointment hit the greatest, she would vent it all to him in her head. When she needed to cry or she missed her family too much, she shared all her nostalgia with Jako in her imagination; thus, she talked to Jako any time she wanted to flee the reality she was living, when she was scrubbing floors, sweeping the yard, or helping Andrea in the kitchen.

Erèz opened the back door. She was soaking wet from the rain and blood on her shredded back. She exchanged the wet clothes she was wearing for the precious dress that her godfather had gifted her two and a half years ago. She took the thin bedsheet that Madame, her cousin, had thrown at her and opened it on the cement floor by the dining room table. That night she struggled to fall asleep because there was too much going through her mind after such a long and tumultuous day. Plus, she had a fever and spent most of the night moaning in pain.

In Guinaudée, Erèz's family wasn't rich financially, but they had an abundance of love that kept them tied together. When anyone had a problem in Guinaudée, everyone joined forces to help the person in need with what little they had. When someone was sick, everyone brought what they had to the family as a sign of support. If they didn't bring fresh food harvested from their farms, then they boiled some tincture or concoction of tea they hoped would bring comfort to the sick. When there was a wedding, everyone pitched in for the reception as best as they could. Knowing and remembering her community back in Guinaudée made Erèz feel even more isolated and miserable as she laid on the cold cement floor. Somehow, Erèz fell asleep in the middle of the night and she slept profoundly. She jumped from her sleep with her feverish body when she felt a splash of cold water hit her head.

Her eyes shot open to see Madame's perfectly pedicured toes pointing through her delicate open-toed white high heels. Erèz looked up from where she was laying on the ground to find Madame's terrifying glance upon her, paralyzing her in place.

Madame said in Creole, "Were you planning on waking up and doing chores, or were you thinking you could sleep all day?"

Erèz gathered what little strength she'd regained overnight to answer rather nonsensically, "Wi, Madame."

Madame rolled her eyes and continued, "Didn't Andrea tell you how to make coffee in the morning?" Erèz shook her head.

"Well, then I suppose Andrea will be in some trouble when she gets here this morning," Madame said darkly as she narrowed her eyes.

Erèz quickly started folding her thin bedsheet under Madame's watchful eye. She felt her bones still burning with a fever and the painful cracking of the dried blood from her wounds that saturated the fabric of her dress in the back.

Madame looked at her and said, "Don't tell me you don't have a toothbrush." Erèz shook her head to let Madame know that she indeed didn't have a toothbrush. Out of nowhere and in reference to nothing, Madame burst out loudly, "Tell me what spirit sent you to this house to kill me!"

"Non, Madame, non!" Erèz mustered in her tiny voice with her head facing down, feeling small and terrified at Madame's tone. As if nothing happened, Madame went to her room to retrieve a toothbrush which had obviously been used to clean more than teeth. She didn't find Erèz worthy of one of the new toothbrushes that she kept upstairs in the little brown cupboard in her boudoir.

Madame kept the new toothbrushes for her rich friends who occasionally traveled from Port-au-Prince to vacation at her home during the year or for the Saint Louis festivities in August. In fact, in just one month, the city of Jérémie would celebrate Saint Louis, the patron saint of the city. People traveled from all over the world to come to the celebration. That year, Madame would be hosting her sister and her brother-in-law who would be coming from Port-au-Prince, and her aunt and her husband who would be flying from Canada to attend the festivities.

The Saint Louis festivities would surely be interesting that year due to the political instability from the American troops leaving the country, as well as the recent constitutional referendum established on June 2, 1935, that extended President Stenio Vincent's term. It left everyone a bit preoccupied regarding which direction the country was headed. A majority of Haitians opposed the presence of the American troops in the country, which symbolized centuries of colonialism and slavery that had ended just over a century ago. Haiti was the first black republic in the world, and the political instability and the usurpation of its freedom brought nothing but terrible resentment.

CHAPTER 18
Mèt Féfé

Mèt Féfé was one of those people who opposed with all his might the nineteen-year-long occupation of Haiti by the United States. In the days and weeks that followed, Erèz would catch bits and pieces of the conversations Mèt Féfé would have with his closest friends. Because they all spoke fluent French, it was difficult for her to understand everything Mèt Féfé and his male friends, who were more like family to him, conversed about.

Occasionally, Mèt Féfé would lose his composure out of frustration, and loudly raise his voice to say, "It is about time these invaders left our country!"

The most frustrating aspect for Mèt Féfé was that he worked in a high level position at Customs Services at the wharf of Jérémie. That meant, he was forced to interact with the foreigners that he called in his conversations, "the usurpers of freedom." It didn't matter if the foreigners were just visiting the country just for the fun of it or if they were soldiers from the American army. He wanted to see them all kicked out.

Aside from his passionate and sometimes heated discussions regarding the American occupation of Haiti and the country's political state, Mèt Féfé was mostly a quiet man. He loved to sit in the living room reading foreign newspapers like the *Wall Street Journal*. After thoroughly reading the newspaper, he remained in his seat pensively. He sat, staring in the emptiness, lost in his thoughts as if he was holding secret meetings with characters in the news articles that he read, all while being careful to keep the premium information private until he was around his friends he felt comfortable with. His readings indicated he was a very informed man, and he spoke English with great eloquence.

Mèt Féfé was not only intelligent, he also was a very grounded man. He held long conversations with Bòs Cyprien about his family in Calas and his crippled son. Sometimes, he would give fifty cents or a couple of gourdes to Bòs Cyprien to send to his mother. Erèz caught Mèt Féfé a few times discreetly slipping the pennies into Bòs Cyprien's hands so that Madame wouldn't catch him. After all, Madame was the manager of the house who knew when to pay Bòs Cyprien and Andrea their salaries each month.

Erèz often wondered if Mèt Féfé was ever able to give his opinion in any of the household decisions. He avoided contradicting Madame in any serious discussion or when it came to simple gossip about people and families around town. There was always the fear that she might fly into a rage and neighbors on either side of the house would hear her yelling at him. Madame was harsh toward Mèt Féfé, and he dealt with Madame's volatility quietly. If the children needed something, they never even bothered to ask Mèt Féfé, knowing that he would simply tell them, "Go ask your mother!" Somehow, it didn't bother Mèt Féfé when the children bypassed his opinion about an issue.

Most Sunday mornings, while Madame and their daughters were at mass, Mèt Féfé's held political discussions with his friends, who tended to drop by unannounced. Topics ranged from local to international politics as they sat across from each other in the antique mahogany chairs. Each chair had large, heavy arms stuffed with high-quality cotton and upholstered with beautiful, expensive fabrics. Erèz always wondered what it would be like to sit in one of them. She didn't even want to imagine what Madame would do if she caught her trying to sit in one of those chairs.

Mèt Féfé and his friends spoke for hours in perfect French, but when they disagreed on something, they mixed street Creole with the French to fully express their disappointments. During their debates and discussions, Andrea served hot fresh coffee in fine white china to Mèt Féfé and whoever his visitor might be that day. When Mèt Féfé wasn't reading or engaging in heated conversations with his friends, he listened to his brand-new radio. He had recently invested in the device so he could enjoy the Spanish music flooding the airwaves through the international radio network CBS (Columbia Broadcasting System). Mèt Féfé's favorite artist was Lydia Mendoza, a new Mexican-Texan who had become extremely popular all over the world. Mèt Féfé seemed to know every single one of Lydia Mendoza's songs and sang along often. Sometimes, the whole house would join him, singing happily when the choruses came up.

He especially loved singing to "La Cucaracha," and "Ayayayay Canta y no Llorés." Erèz had memorized part of the catchy "Ayayayay Canta y no Llorés" as well, but she wouldn't dare sing aloud as Madame would undoubtedly hit her in the head for being a sou moun (disrespectful servant). Her mother had also warned her to not sing around adults in the city, and she intended to stick to that advice. Instead, Erèz sang in her heart when the whole house joined Mèt Fèfè in the chorus of "Ayayayay Canta y no Llorés," and patched in Creole words in places where she couldn't pronounce the Spanish words.

The chorus of that song did something to the spirit of everyone in the house when it came on the radio. They all sang happily with smiles on their faces. The girls would even kiss Madame on the cheeks for no apparent reason as an extension of the happiness the song brought to their hearts. It was fitting as the words mean "Sing and don't cry because by singing, one is happy."

Ay, ay, ay, ay, canta y no llores

Porque cantando se alegran

Cielito lindo, los corazones

CHAPTER 19
Marianne

The first morning, after being woken up with cold water on the cold cement floor on the thin bed sheet, Erèz realized she needed to learn the routines of the household very quickly if she didn't want to enrage Man Féfé in the mornings when she came downstairs from her room. Madame had even told Erèz she would whip her in order to chase away the bad spirits she had brought with her from Guinaudée.

Despite brushing her teeth and rinsing her face, the trace of salt from the tears she shed the Saturday before were still visible to everyone in the morning. Naturally, no one asked her about it. As a restavèk, it was common to be near death from a beating and for no one to care at all. That was something she was going to have to accept, and she would have to count on herself and her good behavior to minimize the beatings and abuses from members of the household.

Madame held out a brand-new tube of Colgate toothpaste. Erèz had been grateful for the old toothbrush in lieu of using her index finger to brush her teeth and scrape her tongue. Plus, she hadn't brought the piece of corn cob that she brushed her teeth with back in Guinaudée. Before deciding if she should take the toothpaste from her hand, Erèz hesitantly looked at Madame very quickly in the eyes just to make sure she was not being teased so that Madame could find another excuse to strike her so early in the morning of a Sunday.

Madame, seeing that Erèz was making her waste her time by taking too long to take the fresh unopened tube said, "It's yours."

Erèz replied softly in her peasant's voice, "Mèsi wi, Madame." She knew she couldn't smile in the presence of Madame, but inside she was smiling. She held that brand new tube of toothpaste like it was precious gold and kept her happiness to herself. In the midst of the little celebration that Erèz was having on the inside of her, she heard Madame say, "Now, get out of my face. You look and smell like you haven't bathed in weeks."

Erèz headed toward the backdoor knowing that if she replied at all she'd likely attract a beating. She didn't say a word and watchfully walked out to the stairs. She limped her way down each step, and then made her way to the backyard. She reached up to one of the clotheslines that Bòs Cyprien had installed for the woman, Man Nini, who came by weekly to do the family's laundry. As she was about to hang her wet bedsheet, she realized it had the strong scent of urine. She couldn't believe it. Had she actually urinated in her sleep during her first night in the city? To erase any doubt, she felt the panties she had been wearing since she had left Guinaudée. They were indeed wet. She was mortified by her nocturnal accident, but counted herself lucky that Madame hadn't realized what had happened. Had she even an inkling that Erèz had urinated in her living room, she would have undoubtedly slammed her head into a wall and made her scrub the floors several times over.

Looking nervously around, Erèz noticed Bòs Cyprien had already swept the backyard with the broom dedicated to that sole purpose. Bòs Cyprien even cleaned the area under the tamarind tree where Andrea cooked the previous day. If it hadn't been for the three rocks that served as pillars for the wood fire and the stain of the ashes in the ground, one would never know a full pot of bouyon had been cooked there just the day before.

Bòs Cyprien also made certain to clean Mèt Féfé's car until it was spotless, just in case he was headed out around town to visit his good friends. Madame came out of the backdoor to shout at Erèz, "Go sweep the porch!"

Erèz replied in that sing-song peasant voice, "Yes, Madame."

She carefully pressed just enough toothpaste on her toothbrush and brushed her teeth quickly. Back in Guinaudée, her mother only brought out toothpaste if they had an overnight guest. Normally, they all used a piece of charcoal or a piece of corn cob to scrub their teeth and tongue in the mornings. The idea that Erèz now had her own toothpaste to brush her teeth in the mornings and evenings brought her great joy.

She grabbed the broom and made her way to the porch where she bumped into Bòs Cyprien who stood quietly observing the still-sleeping town. Besides the few ladies in their well pressed skirts and dresses heading to the six o'clock mass, anba la vil Jérémie looked like a ghost town.

Bòs Cyprien, with genuine concern, asked Erèz, "How is your back feeling, my daughter?"

Erèz lied, "I am not feeling too bad, uncle." She didn't know what else to say to Bòs Cyprien, but they both knew Erèz wasn't feeling well.

Bòs Cyprien left to go about his business as Erèz started sweeping the floor of the porch. The porch of the house was set differently than the rest of the porches on the street; it extended all the way to the road. That made it exceptionally difficult for Erèz to keep it clean. Her main task in the morning as soon as she woke up was to sweep the porch and scrub the bricks with a brush that Madame kept for that purpose only.

She was head down in the middle of scrubbing the porch when she heard a tiny voice her age say in Creole, "Bonjou!"

Erèz lifted her head and locked eyes with Marianne. Marianne said to her, "I didn't know you lived here. Your name is Erèz, right?"

Erèz was happy to be remembered by the other girl, and she replied "Yes, and you're Marianne?" And just like that a beautiful friendship began, one that would last for years.

Marianne smiled at her and gently swung the basket she was holding in front of her. Inside was a pot covered by a white embroidered linen kitchen towel. Erèz could smell the spice coming out from whatever was in the pot, and she thought it smelled just like Marie-Jeanne's mother's spices. Could that mean Marianne had coconut bars in her basket?

Marianne noticed Erèz's interest in what was in the basket and said, "Man Jan sent some plantain porridge and fresh bread for Man Féfé. This time, I better go through the alley because Man Féfé yelled at me when I went through her living room once."

Later on, Erèz would come to know that Mèt Jan was the mayor of Jérémie. Marianne headed to the alley, leaving the smell of the rich cinnamon sticks, lime peel, star anise, vanilla, and butter for Erèz's nose to enjoy and for her mouth to water over.

Around that time, the church's bell rang to announce mass was about to start and not too long after, everyone's little restavèks stepped out on the street to start sweeping and scrubbing the porches. Erèz was almost done scrubbing the floor with that heavy bristled brush when Marianne walked back out empty-handed.

"I will see you later when I come back for the tray," and as she said this, Marianne noticed the blood on Erèz's back. Her eyes widened, but she didn't dare to ask Erèz as she was all too familiar with what had happened in the past to some of the other restavèks who served at Man Féfé's house. Even though the family Marianne was a restavèk to loved her like a daughter, several of her restavèk friends were not nearly as lucky as her. They were constantly being beaten and abused by the adults and children of their households.

CHAPTER 20
Adrien

Adrien was one of Marianne's little restavèk friends. Adrien's dream was always to become a professional soccer player. Sadly, by being given away as a restavèk, his dreams and ambitions were all but nonexistent. Being a ti gason (boy servant) also put Adrien in a social class that didn't allow him the luxury of playing with neighborhood children his age.

In the afternoon, when Adrien was done scrubbing the pots, he would sometimes stand behind the chain-link gate just hoping to catch a glimpse of children his age playing soccer. Most of the time, Adrien cried from sadness, anger, and frustration as he watched the boys run in the street wearing new shoes bought just for wearing while playing so they didn't ruin the good shoes that they wore to church on Sunday mornings, or to school during the week.

One such day, Adrien was especially lost in a fantasy where he was out there on the field with the other boys. He had the ball and the other kids were cheering him on as he set up for a spectacular kick that would surely get past the goalie. Suddenly, out of nowhere, Adrien felt the painful sting of his Madame's matinèt. At that moment, he knew he was never going to be able to watch the kids play soccer ever again as long as he served as a restavèk to his current family. For a split second, that realization made him far more miserable than the painful blow he had just received. As he turned around, one of the matinèt's strands landed painfully on his right eye, which started bleeding immediately and profusely. His Madame didn't care about the blood spurting from his eye and continued beating him.

"It's because you don't have anything better to do that you're wasting time like this. You're good for nothing!" She screamed at him as she continued to beat him.

Adrien bled that entire night and he tried to contain the blood as best as he could with one of his little shirts. In the morning, Adrien woke up with a pounding headache, but he knew if Madame woke up before he did, he would get another round of matinèt beatings. He filled the bucket to scrub the porch with the heavy bristled brush. His head wanted to explode, but he didn't dare express it to Madame. Throughout the day, Adrien's condition worsened, and he developed a fever. His little ten-year-old body couldn't take any more.

Madame noticed Adrien was unwell and trembled a bit on the inside, but didn't actually show concern. Anyway, she didn't care about Adrien's well-being, only about her own reputation. As Adrien laid immobile on the floor on his bamboo leaf braided bed, Madame decided that it was time to address her concerns to her husband, Emmanuel, or Mèt Manno as he was known around the city.

Adrien could hear them both speaking softly about his condition, but didn't even dare to look up toward the direction of the living room where they were trying to hatch a solution. After a brief exchange, Mèt Manno came to where Adrien was lying, visibly shivering from the fever. Mèt Manno looked at Adrien silently and he knew in his heart that his wife had gone too far when punishing the little boy.

"The doctor is on his way," Adrien heard him whisper softly in Creole.

Doctor Emile was every family's doctor in the city of Jérémie. As expected, Doctor Emile, Mèt and Man Manno spoke in French about his condition. However, after living with the family for three years, and despite not having been sent to school, Adrien was able to capture the essence of most sophisticated French conversations.

He heard Man Manno say, "I am hoping the boy isn't blind."

"We'll see," Doctor Emile responded gravely.

Doctor Emile came through the dining room to find Adrien laying down on his face. In broken Creole filled with French words, the doctor attempted to communicate with Adrien, "Boy, how are you feeling?"

Doctor Emile could barely hear Adrien whisper, "I think I have a fever."

Mèt and Man Manno stood there, feeling somewhat ashamed. They wondered what would happen to their reputation if word about Adrien's situation got out. Doctor Emile asked them to leave him alone with Adrien. They obliged, saying, "Let us know if you need anything, Doctor."

"Dear boy, what happened to your eyes?" asked Doctor Emile in his best Creole in a kind, compassionate tone.

Feverishly, Adrien did his best to explain how he got hit in the eye. The doctor turned his body around to assess the damage of Adrien's eye. He concluded that Adrien's optic nerve was damaged, and that the retina would degrade slowly to the point that Adrien would become blind in that eye over the next few years.

Mèt Manno and Man Manno didn't show much emotion or care regarding Adrien when they heard Doctor Emile's diagnosis, but they were definitely relieved they would not be forced to spend more money on paying for a ce n'est rien, or worthless restavèk. Why pay for an insignificant child when you could get rid of him and replace him at any moment for a potentially more promising restavèk? It would have to be another boy, of course. Both Mèt and Man Manno despised the idea of taking on a female restavèk for fear their eight-year-old boy, Jacques, might take too much interest in her.

Doctor Emile cleaned Adrien's eyes to remove the dried blood. He then patched the eye with gauze and taped it securely on the outside to prevent possible infections. The doctor wrote down a prescription for pills and ointments with instructions on how those needed to be administered. Additionally, he said he would be visiting Adrien every three days to clean the eye and advised that Adrien couldn't do any task that would cause him to bend his head, lift anything heavier than two pounds, or stand for longer than thirty minutes. Man Manno was on her best behavior, and agreed to comply with the doctor's instructions. She smiled and nodded in hopes of remaining on the doctor's good side. If she could impress him despite this unfortunate event, perhaps she could secure herself a spot in his circle of friends. She continued to smile and nod as she led the doctor toward the front door. Mèt Manno left right after him to head to the pharmacy. That night, Adrien actually slept a little bit better.

CHAPTER 21
The Williams Family

Just on the other side of the street from Mèt Manno and Man Manno's house was another little boy, Wyatt Williams. He was only two months older than Adrien and also wanted to join the other boys in the street playing soccer. However, instead of peeking through a chain-link gate, he followed the soccer game with great attention from the broad balcony of his parents' house. Often, when Wyatt watched the soccer game from his balcony, his mother, Shirley, would walk outside to check on him. She'd bring him lemonade and ruffle his shiny blonde hair affectionately.

Wyatt was considered a little prince. His father, Warren Williams, was a high-ranking American official. With the privilege of serving the United States on the island of Haiti came a personal maid, a cook, a laundry woman, a chauffeur, and a gason lakou. Wyatt, in turn, had his own private piano teacher, private French tutor, and a professor who monitored Wyatt's academic performance. Wyatt attended Les Frères de l'Instruction Chrétienne primary school, which was five minutes by car and fifteen minutes on foot. The rare times the chauffeur of the house didn't take him to school, the gason lakou, Bòs Pyéro, accompanied Wyatt on the walk, holding his hand. Sometimes on these walks, Wyatt would spy Adrien scrubbing the porch, and Wyatt would cruelly shout to him in French, "Worm!"

Adrien was hurt and angry whenever the ti blan (little white boy) humiliated him by calling him names, but he continued to silently scrub Mèt Manno and Man Manno's porch. If he chose to react, nothing good could come of it, and he'd get an early morning taste of the matinèt.

The Williams family on the other hand, didn't try to integrate themselves in the culture or get to know the people living on the street. Instead, they acted superior to the natives of the city, putting on airs and remaining aloof. The attitude of the Williams enraged Mèt Féfé. With every fiber of his being, he vehemently hated any presence that served as a reminder that the colonial era wasn't quite over. Mèt Féfé didn't want anything to do with the Williams family, and had made his feelings well known. Warren and Shirley knew to avoid him at all costs if possible. Occasionally, Warren and Mèt Féfé would bump into each other on Sunday mornings but never exchanged a word. They didn't even pretend to be cordial toward each other.

The only neighbor who was allowed in the Williams house was the mayor, Majistra Jan, and his wife, Man Jan. Majistra Jan shielded his Haitian family from the many prejudices and misconceptions that the Williams held regarding Haitians. In the eyes of the Williams family, as well as some foreigners, Haitians were generally bribers, manipulators, thieves, or beggars that were always looking for favors or scraps from strangers.

Man Jan employed little Marianne to shower Shirley Williams with all sorts of Haitian treats and desserts. For a penny or two, Marianne delivered treats to the Williams, items like coconut bars made with the freshest coconut and Haitian vanilla, coconut fudge made with rich creamy coconut milk, peanut bars made with freshly roasted whole peanuts, pineapple upside down cake, Haitian liqueur made with fruit syrups, and Haitian Barbancourt rum, the Haitian street rum made from fermented organic sugar cane. Shirley greatly enjoyed these treats. Underneath her prejudice and perceptions about Haitians, she loved Haitian cuisine and spirits in general.

Man Jan was the one friend Shirley had in Haiti, in this culture judged ungovernable by the United States. The presence of Man Jan walking through the little alley on the side of the house to enter Shirley's backyard was always a joy for Shirley. Both Shirley and Man Jan knew enough of each other's language to gossip about other women who lived on the street and laugh together.

CHAPTER 22
Marianne's Good Fortune

Marianne found herself in a wonderful situation as a restavèk. Majistra Jan and Man Jan treated Marianne like the little girl they never had. They had tried to have children for years, but never managed to bring a baby into the world. Both were in their mid-forties, putting Man Jan almost past childbearing age, but she held onto hope that God might bring forth a miracle to make the dream of having their own baby come true.

On Sunday mornings when Majistra Jan and Man Jan made the short seven-minute walk to the Catholic church for mass, Marianne walked closely behind them. With her best Sunday dress, she wore pristine white socks gathered with lace that looked perfect peeking out from her freshly buffed black shoes. In her small hand, she carried a tiny handbag that Man Jan had gifted her to carry to church on Sunday mornings. Colorful ribbons and barrettes adorned and decorated her dark, pretty hair. Marianne sat on the same bench as them at church although she was careful to leave some space between Man Jan and herself out of respect.

Every afternoon, Marianne attended a school dedicated to the restavèks. At twelve years old, Marianne could read French fluently, had mastered her arithmetic principles, and competed with Angelo each quarter for the first-place position in their class. Man Jan and Mèt Jan tried their hardest to give Marianne the best chance to succeed in life. Even at her young age, Marianne was aware of how fortunate she was. She knew the horrifying details of what was happening behind closed doors with some of her other restavèk friends. She was well aware of Adrien's eye damage and of poor Josette who had her forehead split with a pestle. Josette's crime had been to accidentally shortchange her Madame on a bar of soap she was sent to buy at the flea market.

Marianne also understood the unique opportunity that was given to her to study and do well in school. Many restavèks remained uneducated; it was fifteen dollars per year to attend the school, and Man Féfé had already decided that Erèz was not bright enough to invest that kind of money in.

Later, after Marianne graduated from primary school, Majistra Jan and Madan Jan sent her to Ecole Professionelle where Marianne learned sewing, embroidery, crocheting, table etiquette, and culinary arts. By the time Marianne turned eighteen, the beautiful items she produced—table covers, kitchen towels, dresses, and more—were featured among the best handmade articles during the National Labor Day festivities in the city of Jérémie.

CHAPTER 23
Manje

When Andrea arrived to work that Sunday morning, Erèz was facing away from her on the porch. Andrea immediately noticed the dark blood encrusted on the back of her dress and nearly cried at the sight. Overcoming the knot that built in her throat, she exclaimed, "Oh, my daughter! What happened to you last night?

Erèz turned around quickly and said, "Bonjou ma tant."

"I did not expect Madame to be so cruel," Andrea whispered quietly, bringing her hand to her mouth in shock and horror. As they stood on the porch, Madame unexpectedly poked her head through the door.

"What is taking you so long?" She thundered at Erèz. Immediately, Erèz and Andrea proceeded to the backyard through the little alley on the side of the house. Andrea still couldn't believe what had happened to Erèz but decided in her heart she was going to nurse Erèz's back until it healed up. That Sunday afternoon, before Andrea took off for the day, she gently patted Erèz's inflamed back with a cloth saturated in warm water and salt. After patting Erèz's skin dry, Andrea used Haitian castor oil as an ointment to prevent the sores from drying out and creating painful scabs. Andrea adhered to that routine daily for a good two weeks and noticed the steady improvements in Erèz's skin. At the end of her treatment and daily wash, Andrea also gave Erèz two Saridon pills that she believed would bring relief to her pain during the night. After those two weeks, Erèz could finally try to sleep on her back again, and Andrea was quite pleased with her accomplishment and patience in helping heal her little back. Erèz was also confident that her back had healed quickly and safely because of Andrea's discreet and diligent nursing. She was very grateful to have Andrea on her side and knew how lucky she was.

Breakfast for the family on Erèz's first Sunday morning in Jérémie consisted of Haitian omelet with mashed smoked herring, julienned green and red bell peppers, chopped tomatoes fresh from the vine, and green and yellow onions. The delicious breakfast was served with toasted bread purchased the day before from Madan Dikrépen. Andrea knew best how to revive the day-old round bread into a crisp and buttery delicacy. She warmed up a generous portion of butter and allowed the slices of bread to simmer in the sizzling butter for five minutes on each side. Everyone loved eating the bread that way, especially Exavier. Generally a reserved young man, he never hid his eagerness when it came to these toasty buttery bread slices, and he loved dunking each piece in the rich hot chocolate as part of the Sunday morning tradition.

The hot chocolate was in fact quite the treat at the house. Andrea unrolled a few sticks of raw cacao wrapped in green banana leaves to add to the aluminum pot half-filled with water. She then added fresh lime peel, cinnamon sticks, star anise, and a few pinches of salt. It was then strained, and a can of evaporated milk was mixed in. Finally, Andrea sweetened it. Right before emptying the aromatic cocoa into the serving pot, she added a few drops of Haitian vanilla and gave the flavorful concoction a last stir. The scrumptious Sunday morning breakfast was always a hit with everyone at the house.

As soon as the table was set and breakfast served, Andrea, Erèz, and Bòs Cyprien retired to the backyard holding their old aluminum cups filled with whatever was left from the hot chocolate split evenly between them and a meager piece of buttery bread. Andrea's culinary ability was undoubtedly phenomenal. Bòs Cyprien recognized that and always teased her that a woman with such skill and talent should not remain single, but Andrea always rejected Bòs Cyprien's efforts to be her matchmaker. As soon as Andrea felt the dining room had quieted down enough, she and Erèz cleared the table. Between the two of them, they quickly collected everything and took it back downstairs under the tamarind tree to do the dishes. Andrea scrubbed while Erèz rinsed them twice in two different pots and then placed them in the bamboo dish basket to dry.

The menu for the Sunday dinner was even more elaborate than the breakfast. Although she couldn't express her feelings to Andrea, Erèz was rather excited in her little peasant heart; this would be her first time eating such a variety of delicious foods in one sitting. Moreover, she was looking forward to learning how to cook each of the dishes under Andrea's mentorship.

Madame ordered Andrea to cook the goat that Bòs Cyprien brought to the house the day before. Additionally, she wanted Andrea to cook macaroni au gratin (Haitian mac and cheese) along with Haitian Russian beet and potato salad. Madame requested some greenery with the meal, so they prepared a green salad with fresh lettuce, watercress, sliced tomatoes, sliced boiled beets, fried plantains, and pikliz (Haitian spicy slaw). With Erèz's help, Andrea cooked the elaborate Sunday meal quicker than she would on her own.

That first Sunday was a trial for Erèz as she learned the ins and outs of a sophisticated city kitchen, but in only a few weeks she was able to predict Andrea's next steps and take initiative on many of the tasks. As part of her responsibilities around the kitchen while Andrea cooked the meal of the day, Erèz carefully sorted through the tray of di ri péyi (Haitian national rice) to spot and remove tiny rocks and other impurities. The last thing Andrea wanted to happen was for a tiny rock to end up between Madame's teeth. Erèz also set up a fresh pot of water for Andrea to scrub and wash the produce of the day such as green plantains, sweet potatoes, African yams, green bananas, and whatever was available. She also crushed spices and vegetables in the mortar and pestle for the daily épis. Andrea was extremely pleased with Erèz, her sweet little helper. Andrea continued to do everything she could to support her, and to be a kind mother figure to her.

While scrubbing the dishes, Andrea noticed Erèz smelled of urine and asked her if she had washed herself the day before. Erèz confessed she didn't have clean panties and didn't know how to clean herself after Madame had shredded her back with the matinèt. Andrea promised Erèz she would bring her some panties from her oldest daughter that she could rotate through. She then taught Erèz how she could hide behind the outdoor latrine and rinse herself with a water-filled jug while being careful of the painful wounds on her back.

The day before, Andrea marinated and swé the goat meat as she cooked the bouyon. Swé is the process of cooking a meat halfway with the purpose of preserving it. First, the chunks of goat meat were thoroughly scrubbed with fresh sour orange, coarse salt, and lime peel. After rinsing them with copious amounts of room-temperature water and then draining them, the meat was flash-rinsed in boiling salt water and drained a second time before Andrea marinated it in fresh épis.

Usually, when Madame purchased an entire goat, Andrea stir-fried the brain with plenty of lime juice and crushed scotch bonnet pepper to enjoy with cassava bread right away. The liver of the goat was grilled in hot charcoal for the three kids to eat with spicy pimantad, a condiment made with lime juice, salt, a little bit of shredded onions, and freshly crushed scotch bonnet pepper. Other times, when Andrea was not in a rush, she sautéed the liver and prepared a sauce to serve for breakfast on Sunday morning with boiled plantains and fresh, buttery avocado slices.

Erèz helped cook all those dishes on her first Sunday as a restavèk. After all the work she and Andrea put into preparing the dinner, everything tasted unbelievably delicious and Madame acted very pleased. Andrea often asked Erèz to taste this or that as she cooked, insisting on hearing what she thought was missing. Erèz didn't quite know what to say since she always wanted to be respectful to Andrea.

"Does it taste good?" Andrea asked as Erèz sampled the food.

The reply was always the high-pitched intonation of a peasant girl, "Wi, ma tant."

When it came time to set the table, Andrea pulled the good dishes from the dark wooden polished china hutch in the living room. Those special plates were only used for Sunday's dinner. The flowery designs on the long, delicate serving plates, dinner plates, and tall drinking glasses left Erèz in awe. With her help, Andrea was able to set the table in thirty minutes. Every piece of china, silverware, and crystal glass was perfectly placed for a most spectacular table setting. Once the food was brought out, Erèz witnessed for the first time in her life what a truly lavish feast looked like.

CHAPTER 24
Mèt Lemaire and Mèt Eric

Man Féfé and Mèt Féfé regularly had two guests over to the house on Sundays, Mèt Lemaire and Mèt Eric. Mèt Lemaire, a lawyer by profession, had helped the family in various litigations over the years, and Mèt Eric was the godfather to their oldest daughter, Carline. Both men had a great reputation in the city of Jérémie and were well respected. Neither of them had children and both had lost their wives within one year of each other. As long-time friends of Mèt Féfé, and since neither one had kids to provide them with fancy Sunday dinners, there was always a spot reserved for them at the Sunday dinner table. As all well-behaved, respectful Haitian children did, Carline, Sherline, and Exavier always stood up from their chairs to go greet Mèt Lemaire and Mèt Eric when they arrived. The men received kisses on the cheeks from the girls and a firm handshake from Exavier. Carline always preceded her kiss on

Mèt Eric's cheeks with a "Bonsoir, parrain," ("Good afternoon, dear godfather") in perfect French, with a sweet smile on her face.

After the proper greetings, they all returned to their respective spots around the table. Mèt Lemaire and Mèt Eric always sat on opposite sides of each other, close to Mèt Féfé who occupied the head of the table. Man Féfé always sat closest to the back door in case she needed to call Andrea or Bòs Cyprien from the backyard to tend to any dinnertime needs. For some reason, Mèt Eric always wore white. He must have had multiple sets of white suits, white ties, white socks, white shoes, and a variety of white hats to complete his outfits. No one knew why, but every Sunday he was covered in white from head to toe.

When Andrea set the table, she put out wine glasses for Mèt Féfé, Mèt Lemaire, and Mèt Eric, which they would sip on while enjoying their meals. Everyone knew that Mèt Lemaire was a seasoned tafyatè (alcoholic), as were his circle of friends. None of them felt comfortable addressing his addiction. After all, he was a Haitian manly man, and as such he could live his life exactly how he wanted with no questions asked. Often, on Sundays, Mèt Lemaire would drink so much Barbancourt rum and kléren at the house that he would fall asleep right where he was sitting in the living room chair in the middle of lively conversations with Mèt Féfé and Mèt Eric. When he finally awoke, he would act perturbed and ask why they hadn't woken him up to finish their important discussion about whatever political issue was in question that Sunday.

When Mèt Féfé left on Sunday afternoons to visit other friends, he often left the drunk Mèt Lemaire snoring on the living room chair, mouth wide open. One of those Sundays, Sherline cleverly decided to roll a piece of paper in the shape of a cigar to place right in the corner of his mouth, triggering much laughter from the children as he continued slumbering.

CHAPTER 25
A Misstep

As always, Andrea, Erèz, and Bòs Cyprien were never invited to join the upper-class aristocratic family at the table. This distinction of classes under the same roof of a Haitian household was nothing new on Mònn Jibilé or any other street in the city. The upper classes acted no different than the colonizers in the way they treated the slaves they owned or even their servants.

The clear dominance of rich Haitians over poor Haitians became the common way of daily management in a household. The lower-class servants knew they were not allowed the same privileges of their masters and complied with everything that was required of them. That silent submission offered them the chance of a job and a slightly better lives with a few extra dollars to care for their families, potential opportunities to run side businesses with their meager salaries, and the general ability to maintain enough employment to survive on.

Andrea, Bòs Cyprien, and Erèz knew they belonged to that low class of citizens. They ate in the backyard and went about their activities and responsibilities. Bòs Cyprien sat at the front door of his room holding a plate loaded with a sample of everything that was cooked that Sunday, except for the salad. Salads were too fancy for any of the servants to have. As part of his rehearsed custom anytime he got a chance, Bòs Cyprien brought up once more to Andrea that a literate woman who was formally trained in the culinary arts such as herself needed to find a man.

Erèz sat there listening and smiling timidly as Bòs Cyprien teased Andrea's singlehood, but none of the conversations surprised her. It was a common custom among adults in Guinaudée to tease each other about their private relationships and marital status in this way. Parents in Guinaudée often joked among each other about marrying their kids to one another. If a woman had a baby girl or young daughter, she might joke with a man who had a baby boy or young boy by asking him how her son-in-law was doing. Similarly, the man would jokingly ask the woman about his daughter-in-law. In the same spirit, two adult men might joke among themselves about being in love with the same woman just for fun, and they would refer to her as their matlòt (the woman they shared). In the same way, two adult women would joke about their nonm (the man they shared) or being each other's matlòt when they pretended to be in love with the same man. It was all part of the friendly rapport among the citizens of Guinaudée.

Erèz never interrupted the two so as not to be disrespectful, but Bòs Cyprien's jokes toward Andrea always amused her. As Bòs Cyprien carried on with his comments about Andrea's status and laughed at his own wit, they heard the parrot laughing from his cage, mimicking Bòs Cyprien. All three of them laughed heartily with Bòs Cyprien laughing the hardest, stating that even the parrot agreed with him.

Bòs Cyprien always enjoyed the graten diri (the crisp rice from the bottom of the pot). He often commented, "The graten is very oily, just the way I like it."

"If you would learn to cook for yourself, you'd always be able to have rice and graten just the way you like it," laughed Andrea.

Bòs Cyprien, like most Haitians, loved sucking the bone marrow out of the bones on his plate. He would suck on the pieces of bone until he felt he had pulled all the bone marrow and juice out of them. He always placed his request with Andrea for a piece of the goat meat with bones in it for him to suck on.

When Andrea didn't hear much noise coming from the dining room table, she went back up the stairs to clean the table. She knew she needed to be extra careful in bringing so many plates down the stairs so that she didn't break any of them. The one time she had broken one of Madame's glasses, Madame threw a fit for the whole neighborhood to hear and deducted the cost of the glass from her monthly wage. Andrea knew that breaking a glass cost her both reputation and money.

As Andrea piled the plates on top of each other, she noticed that Erèz wasn't helping with the same enthusiasm and asked, "What's wrong my daughter?"

Erèz just shook her head to indicate that everything was fine with her. She didn't want to bring attention to her back, which was itchy and burning due to the long exposure to the sun and heat under the tamarind tree. The pain was so unbearable that it caused her hands and legs to tremble.

Andrea, realizing what the problem was, promised she would give her back a good wash before she headed home that Sunday. As they went down the stairs, Erèz's little legs tripped and one of the porcelain plates flew from her hand to land at the bottom of the stairs.

Madame heard the shattering noise from her room and quickly came out to see what had happened. Instantly enraged, she grabbed the matinèt on her way to the backyard to teach Erèz another lesson on negligence and the cost of displeasing a rich Haitian woman. When Madame made it to the bottom of the stairs, Andrea acted quickly. To protect Erèz, she stood between her and Madame in open defiance, hoping to spare her of another round of beatings. Erèz screamed in agony upon hearing Madame coldly tell Andrea, "You're going to have to choose between your job and that dirty little girl."

As respectfully as she could muster, Andrea evenly said, "Madam, the girl is sick. I don't think her little body can support more of your beatings."

"You better move out of my way immediately if you don't want today to be your last day in my employment."

Andrea knew she couldn't afford to lose this job, and against her own will, she stepped aside to let Madame have a go at little Erèz.

Madame was able to hit Erèz's back immediately right in one of those irritated spots from the previous day's beating. Erèz's body bent and collapsed on the ground from all the pain.

Madame looked at Erèz mercilessly and said, "Get up and let me look at you. I want to see if you are truly a bad spirit sent from Guinaudée to kill me." At that point, Madame stopped hitting Erèz with the matinèt, and called for Bòs Cyprien to get her the ruler. The ruler was not exactly a ruler. It was a piece of flat and heavy wood that Madame kept close for the sole purpose of further punishing little restavèks that disobeyed her orders. Bòs Cyprien returned with the ruler with a heavy sadness in his face. He didn't say a word, knowing Madame would threaten to fire him.

"Extend both your hands out, and you will count each hit up to twenty. Do you understand?" Erèz shook her head yes.

The problem was Erèz didn't know how to count, and on her first Sunday, she paid for being illiterate. She counted to ten and jumped to fifty. Madame continued hitting her while demanding that Erèz start back from number one. With each hard slap of the ruler, Erèz bent her fragile little body from left to right in pain. None of the ruler's many strikes was able to teach her how to count past ten.

After three rounds of hitting and Erèz's palms changing to a deep red, Andrea cried even louder than Erèz, "Madame, please! You wouldn't do this to a little girl over just one plate. Look at how her little body is shivering!"

Perhaps it was Andrea's words or a supernatural voice that only Madame heard, but she suddenly stopped hitting Erèz. With her face completely red, Madame adjusted the front buttons in the pink blouse she was wearing to hide the sparkly white bra underneath and she turned around with her heels clicking angrily to head back up to the dining room.

Andrea was still crying for Erèz after Madame left. Bòs Cyprien silently observed the whole scene from the bed in his room and walked out with eyes red from anger. He tried to offer words of comfort to Erèz, but nothing he said could console her as she cried uncontrollably. Erèz was unable to help Andrea wash the dishes like she did after breakfast that morning. Instead, she sat at the bottom of the stairs with her bloody back and little body shivering, crying her heart out.

CHAPTER 26
St. Peter's Celebration

Erèz wondered how come it felt so long ago that she left Guinaudée when it was only yesterday that her mother had brought her to Jérémie. From where Erèz she was sitting for the past couple of hours at the bottom of the stairs, she could smell the plantain porridge Andrea was preparing for Madame before leaving for the night. The aroma was heavenly as the scent of cinnamon mixed with the star anise, lime peel, bay leaves, and vanilla floated in the air. Erèz had only tasted something like that twice in her life, both on special occasions. Once was at little Patrick's baptism reception and once at the parish celebration that happened every July.

In fact, in just two weeks, the parish of Guinaudée would celebrate their patron saint, St. Peter. The occasion gave the whole community an opportunity to come together to celebrate all day. In the morning, everyone put on their best attire. The men pulled their suits from brown paper bag dust covers under their beds. The women took out their special slips, which they kept in recycled plastic bags for special occasions, to wear under their dresses and skirts. The plastic bags kept bed bugs and other insects from getting to them and messing them up with tiny holes or traces of their fecal matter. Mothers washed their little girls' hair with a bar of laundry soap, greased their scalps, and twisted their hair. They completed the hairdos by adding the loveliest ribbons on each side of their heads and colorful barrettes at the tips of each braid or twist. If one looked closely, some of the white ribbons carried a rosy stain from the ruddy dust from their yards, but what mattered was they wore their best to celebrate Saint Peter.

It was a sight to see everyone in their finest outfits as they attended mass, visited their best friends, and exchanged plates full of the most delicious goodies in Haitian cuisine. In the late afternoon that day, everyone gathered at the park of Guinaudée for the fèt teyatral where children and talented youths performed to entertain the entire community with their dances, singing, and comedy skits. People who could afford to do so slaughtered goats the day before. Families put money together to slaughter cows. Butchers slaughtered cows early in the morning to sell meat for a few gourdes to whoever could afford to buy a few pieces for the special family dinner of the day.

Fèt teyatral means talent show in Haitian Creole. Kids sing, dance, and perform in front of the whole community. These talent shows are held in the middle of summer and for special occasions.

When the day of the big celebration arrived, Erèz and Marie-Jeanne usually ran up the small hill in front of their houses while holding each other's hands and then walked happily to the church. They both waved a quick "bonjou" or "kòman nou yé la a" when meeting children they used to be friends with as they lowered their heads in embarrassment of how their outfits looked compared to theirs.

Because their parents couldn't afford to send them to school and they didn't know how to read and write, that automatically put them in a lower social rank among their childhood friends. Saint Peter's Day was also the only day that Tant Lucienne went to church. Even the pain in her feet that took over most of her body and sometimes paralyzed her couldn't keep her away. Marianne's mother carried little Patrick on one hip and with her other hand, she held Tant Lucienne's hand to keep her from falling as they both tiptoed on small rocks and pebbles. When they got to the church, everyone was jovial and in celebratory spirits. Erèz and Marianne always sat together in the same area in the back with all the other kids whose parents couldn't afford to send them to school.

Many children who graduated from the primary school of Guinaudée and went to high school in the City of Jérémie came back for summer vacation by that time. They were fully involved in planning and executing most of the festivities and community activities surrounding St. Peter's Day at the parish alongside their parents. Some of them served as altar boys at the church, assisting the priests during mass by lighting the church's candles and aiding with the Holy Eucharist.

Ti Roro, Erèz's godmother's son, always served as an altar boy at the church. He was often barely recognizable wearing the white cassock, cotta, soutane, and clerical collar while he assisted the monastics during the church services. As a young child, Ti Roro aspired to be a priest. His parents scrimped and saved to send him to school so that he could have a chance at achieving whatever he dreamed to be and do. Due to the fact that most of the family's spare money went toward Ti Roro's school tuition, he was eventually unable to continue attending church on Sundays because they couldn't afford buying the clergy's required outfits.

Ilèyis, on the other hand, never allowed what he was materially lacking to prevent him from attending the celebration of St. Peter and praising God and the saints. He wore one pair of tennis shoes that a friend brought him from Port-au-Prince three years prior. The shoes hardly fit and barely held together and the white laces were stained with red dirt from the yard and neighbors' gardens, but he proudly wore them regardless. He closed his eyes and ears to anyone trying to stop him from attending mass for St. Peter's anniversary. Yaya always managed to borrow some clothes and shoes from her friends to sing in the church's choir. She usually sang her heart out happily. It was as if the joy boiling in her heart transcended her soul and entire being, causing her face to shine brightly. Erèz's mother joked that Yaya was allowed to sing in the choir as long as she behaved herself, but there was never a risk of Yaya acting poorly and shaming her family in any way as she respected the community and cared for her reputation as a virgin and young girl.

The bishop usually traveled from Jérémie to attend mass on St. Peter's Day. If he couldn't make the trip, he sent one of the priests serving in the Catholic Church of Jérémie to represent him and join the monastics with a special sermon. Erèz, Marianne, and their friends were always extremely curious, much like everyone else, to catch a peek of the special envoy from the Roman Catholic Church of the diocese of Jérémie. Perhaps if they got really lucky, they might have the chance to shake his hand along with the hands of all the nuns and brothers, or anybody else who counted as part of the cortege. The children who took catechism classes dressed in all-white uniforms for their first communion. Often families of those children traveled from Port-au-Prince to celebrate that memorable event in their lives and accompany them in this new stage of commitment to their Christian faith.

Erèz's mind was flooded with all those memories as she sat at the bottom of the stairs. She relived the beautiful memories as the smell of Andrea's plantain porridge continued to fill her nostrils. Erèz knew she was going to miss the celebration of the parish that year, and her heart broke. She knew there was nothing she could do about it besides fantasizing about the many "what ifs" of still living in Guinaudée peacefully with her parents, hanging out with Marianne and little Patrick, and fleeing from the angry chicken chasing her.

She cringed at the nostalgia of being so far away from her community and the pain of being separated from what she loved most. The idea of pleasing her parents and the whole community of people she admired and loved the most seemed an impossible request. They would never know how cruelly Madame, her own cousin, behaved toward her. She wondered if anyone would believe her if she would tell them the details of her miserable transition to city life.

In the meantime, Andrea finished making the plantain porridge for supper and came down the stairs still upset from witnessing Madame beating Erèz. She didn't say a word, but proceeded to clean under the tamarind tree where she had cooked dinner earlier.

She broke her silence by saying, "My little daughter, tomorrow, I will give you a bush bath, but today, I am just going to pat your body with lukewarm water and salt." Erèz nodded yes, thankful to have at least one person who cared for her well-being.

Bòs Cyprien also cared, but Erèz didn't think he would get involved as much as to pat her back with lukewarm water and tend to the slashes on her back. As any Haitian man would do, Bòs Cyprien dealt quietly and privately with his feelings regarding Madame's abuse of the poor children that had the misfortune of landing in her household.

Around four-thirty, Andrea couldn't hear Madame's voice or hear her wandering around the house. She was probably taking a nap or sitting at her sewing machine in her boudoir, fixing hems on the girls' dresses or on Mèt Féfé and Exavier's pants. Madame was, in fact, a very skilled seamstress. Over the years that followed, Erèz was able to learn some basic sewing skills simply from watching Madame from a distance and studying the steps she took to fix different styles of garments. Erèz's careful observations of Madame at the sewing machine while cleaning and scrubbing the boudoir's floor were enough to help her craft her own dresses later on.

Andrea took the opportunity of that moment of peace and quiet around the house to warm up the water and a handful of coarse salt. Hopefully, patting Erèz's back with the lukewarm water would help her muscles to relax and allow her to get some restful sleep. For the treatment, Andrea emptied the pot of hot water into one of the old tin pots the laundry lady used to wash and rinse old rags on Wednesdays.

"Come, my little daughter," said Andrea as she signaled with her hands for Erèz to come close. Behind the small latrine across from the tamarind tree, Andrea used a piece of towel to rub Erèz's body gently. Erèz's little body trembled as Andrea applied pressure to her body with the towel soaked in the lukewarm salty water. She sobbed, but recalled exactly what her mother would tell her, "This is for your own good." She tried as much as possible to hold back the tears, but couldn't stop them from rolling down her cheeks, let alone control the contortions of her body from so much pain. Her little back was burning, but Erèz knew that the lukewarm salt water would work healing wonders.

"Wash yourself my daughter because the 'thing' smelled like pee today." Andrea said to her gently. That brought a smile to Erèz's face, and after saying the usual "wi, ma tant," she bent as low as she could so that the water could hit her bottom and clean away unpleasant smells. Andrea, seeing her struggle a little, helped her rinse her bottom. Unfortunately, despite being clean now, Erèz still had to wear the same blood-stained dress from the beatings with the matinèt. Andrea gave two Saridon pills to Erèz and told her to be strong.

At six o'clock, it was time for Andrea to go home to take care of her own children. She packed up her little khaki bag with the sandals she wore around the house during the day and exchanged them for a good pair of shoes she wore to get to and from Madame's house. Andrea left that evening with a blessing to Erèz, "May God watch over you my daughter." That would be Andrea's nightly blessing until she left Madame's house some years later for a better paying job as a bònn at a Haitian army officer's house. Every time Andrea left in the evenings, her absence weighed heavily on Erèz as she felt she was left alone at the mercy of Madame's fury.

After Andrea left, Erèz sat for a long while at the bottom of the stairs listening to the neighbor's children as they happily laughed, played hide-and-seek, and chased each other around their backyard. In her heart, she wished and hoped she could join them, but she was a restavèk, after all, and had no business playing with regular children. She could dream all she wanted about having fun with other children, but the notion of having fun wasn't unfortunately part of her social rank.

CHAPTER 27
Sherline

Later that Sunday, Erèz was taking a short moment to herself on Bòs Cyprien's bed when her little heart leaped in her chest. She jumped to a standing position as she heard Madame bellow, "Where is that little werewolf?"

As Madame approached, she noticed that Erèz had showered but was still wearing the same dirty clothes. Madame looked at her scornfully and clicked her heels right back into the house to see if her second daughter, Sherline, had clothes she no longer wore to give to Erèz. One thing that Madame, her cousin, took very seriously was her reputation. She didn't want people in the neighborhood to misjudge her based on the clothes her little restavèks wore; therefore, even though Madame couldn't care less about Erèz's appearance behind closed doors, she made sure Erèz looked her best before she headed out to Madan Dikrépen's house to purchase fresh bread for supper that Sunday. Sherline was four years older than Erèz so the dress Erèz wore to go buy the bread fitted rather loose and baggy, but at least it was clean and smelled good.

On Sundays, Madan Dikrépen didn't bake as her workers had the day off, but she sold from her leftover stash.

"Bonswa ma tant," said Erèz in her high-pitched peasant voice as she arrived at Madan Dikrépen's house. Erèz indicated how much bread she needed and handed her the small handmade bamboo basket with the white hand-embroidered linen folded neatly at the bottom. Moments later, Madan Dikrépen handed the basket, now full of bread, back to Erèz who paid her the money she had been entrusted with.

As Erèz walked out to the street, she caught Dodo riding his bicycle down the hill. Once again, he looked as though he was in heaven from catching a glimpse of Carline through her window upstairs. She made sure to be there around the time she knew Dodo would be passing by on weekend afternoons. On her way back to the house, Erèz felt Carline scrutinizing her, but she didn't dare look up and continued to walk through the little alley to the back of the house with the basket full of bread.

That evening, Madame asked Erèz to set the table for supper. Being a quick learner, Erèz remembered all the details Andrea taught her during the earlier food service. Although Madame didn't say a word, she seemed to approve of the way Erèz set the table. Madame started warming up the pot of fresh plantain porridge and stirred it. She then filled each cup with plantain porridge and added just enough in two old cups for Erèz and Bòs Cyprien. She directed Erèz to take each brimming cup to the table. Erèz carefully tiptoed holding each cup as she walked toward the table, knowing all too well that if one of those cups broke, Madame would beat her for a fourth time in just two days.

As Erèz carefully carried the last cup to the table, Sherline walked down the stairs and looked at Erèz as if she was the most disgusting thing she'd ever seen. That was the first time that Erèz truly had a good look at any of the children in Madame's household. She paused, slack-jawed, and stared at Sherline longer than she intended because she was literally the most beautiful girl she'd ever seen in her entire life. Instantly, Sherline became furious. Even though she thoroughly understood that Erèz could barely communicate in a Creole that made sense to people in the city, Sherline asked Erèz in French, "Is this the first time you've seen a human, little zombie?" Erèz didn't understand a word that was being spoken, and she continued to stare at Sherline who walked right up to her and punched her in her right eye.

That blow to the eye was painful enough that Erèz fell two steps back. However, despite the pain, Erèz's biggest concern was making sure that the cup didn't fall to the cement floor to attract Madame's rage. Fortunately, Erèz managed to keep the cup from falling, but she couldn't prevent some of the porridge from splashing on the plate holding the cup.

Erèz could not fully escape Madame's wrath over this infraction. An entire slew of abusive words and nearly nonsensical thoughts came flying forth from her mouth, "You, little werewolf! Look at your face, you stupid little zombie! They sent you to kill me!" The slurs continued on and Madame tossed the little bit of porridge set aside for Erèz back into the pot as her punishment for the night. As if that punishment wasn't enough, Madame put the slice of bread previously set aside for Erèz back in the basket.

Madame then shouted at Erèz to get out of her sight. Erèz walked away as quickly as she could with her head down as the humiliation weighed heavy on her heart.

That night, Bòs Cyprien walked down holding his peanut butter-covered kabich (bread roll) in one hand and the cup of plantain porridge in the other. He asked Erèz if she had eaten her supper already, and she explained the whole horrible story about Madame punishing her after she had been punched in the eye by Sherline. That was when Bòs Cyprien noticed that Erèz's right eye was swollen and bright red from the blow.

Bòs Cyprien didn't say a word, but he handed his food to Erèz. Erèz couldn't help herself as her mouth watered from the smell of the peanut butter alone. Erèz devoured the bread and savored every sip of the plantain porridge from the battered cup.

Erèz slept with a headache, a sore body, and a painfully swollen eye that Sunday night of her second day in the city of Jérémie, but at least her tiny belly wasn't completely empty, thanks to Bòs Cyprien.

CHAPTER 28
A Moment with Marianne

Come Monday morning, Erèz wasted no time getting herself up immediately upon the rooster's first crow. She had no desire for Madame to find her on the cement floor, or to be woken up again by having cold water thrown on her.

As she got herself up, Erèz realized she hadn't sleep well at all. The trauma of the previous day plagued her dreams, and her right eye had only become more swollen during the night.

Despite the pain in her eye and the general soreness of her entire body, she rapidly folded the bedsheet she had slept on and headed to the back door with the used toothbrush and fresh tube of toothpaste that Madame had given her. She made sure to keep the toothbrush and toothpaste with her at night because she didn't like the idea of keeping them in a hole in the back wall of the latrine.

Once she took care of her hygiene, she filled the bucket from the yard with water and grabbed the brush with the heavy bristles in order to scrub the floor of the front porch. As she was preparing to unleash a vigorous scrubbing on the bricks of the front porch floor, she heard a small voice behind her speaking Creole.

"How are you doing?"

Erèz turned around to see none other than her new friend Marianne holding a tray with a coffee pot and what appeared to be bread rolls. Erèz would later discover that Man Jan made fantastic coffee that Madame simply loved. Occasionally, Man Jan would send Man Féfé some coffee, especially in the morning around festivities.

"Your dress is way too big on you!" Marianne exclaimed, not unkindly, but as a matter of fact.

"I don't have any other dress." Erèz answered simply. Marianne remained quiet for a moment, wondering if maybe she had made her new friend feel self-conscious.

"What are you doing today?" ventured Erèz.

"I'm going to Bonbon with Man Jan to visit her mother," Marianne said with a smile on her sweet face.

Erèz considered that for a moment and realized nothing like that would ever happen with her and Madame.

"I don't think Madame will ever take me anywhere. She says I'm a ghost. And a zombie. She thinks I'm a spirit sent from the countryside to kill her before she's old."

Marianne laughed at all the mean nicknames, thinking it was silly of Man Féfé to say such mean things.

"I really didn't think Madame knew all of these kréyòl rèk words!" Marianne said between giggles. *Kréyòl rèk is a term meaning "raw Creole words."*

She then continued in a more serious tone, "But Erèz, I hope you know that you are beautiful. You are not a ghost. You are not a bad spirit. And you are definitely not a zombie! You are Erèz, and you are beautiful, yes?"

Erèz could hardly respond to the kind words, and she was rather in awe that Marianne could spend all that time chatting without fear of getting into severe trouble with Man Jan. Erèz, on the other hand, made sure to continue scrubbing that porch as she chatted with Marianne. Their chat was interrupted as Andrea arrived to work and made her way to them down the pathway leading to the house. Andrea immediately noticed Erèz's swollen eye.

"What happened?" were the first words out of Andrea's mouth.

"Nothing, auntie," Erèz said quickly out of respect, but also because she didn't wish to go into the horrific details of what had happened to her in front of Marianne.

Andrea didn't need to ask further as it was quite obvious that Erèz had suffered more abuse after she had left for the evening the day before. She walked past the girls to the narrow alley that led to the back of the house. It not only broke her heart, but it also infuriated Andrea to know Erèz was suffering such violence. Sadly, there was next to nothing she could do about it.

CHAPTER 29
Monday

Of Madame's children, Erèz had only met the horrible Sherline so far. She had yet to meet or really see Carline, Madame's oldest daughter. She had caught a glimpse of Carline in her window upstairs, but that was the extent of it. Exavier, who would finish high school the following year, also remained a mystery to her. Erèz's curiosity to meet the other two children of the household was severely dampened after Sherline had delivered to her the painful welcoming gift directly to her right eye. The last thing she wanted or needed was to meet more people who might be eager to abuse her physically.

That first Monday miraculously went without any unfortunate incidents. Madame asked that Andrea take Erèz with her to the flea market so she could learn her way around and begin negotiating with vendors to make purchases around the market.

Andrea gave Erèz a straw hat to wear to hide and protect her swollen eye. Andrea wasn't entirely sure as to what she could do for Erèz's poor eye except to allow time to pass, but she did tell Erèz not to irritate it by scratching or scrubbing it.

Erèz adored her bonding time with Andrea at the market. The flea market of Jérémie was far more sprawling and elaborate than the one Erèz was used to attending with her mother on Wednesdays. She admired the elegant ladies who shopped in high-heeled shoes and forced themselves to speak Creole with the peasants who had come in from the various countryside villages surrounding the city.

How did they come to be so elegant and refined? Why didn't they hire a bònn or a restavèk to do their shopping? How did they know Creole? Erèz wondered, but out of respect, didn't dare ask Andrea. Instead, she carried their shopping basket silently and paid attention as best she could to the way Andrea bartered with the vendors.

Andrea noticed Erèz was physically uncomfortable and picked up some Haitian castor oil for a few pennies to use on Erèz's back later. It was a slightly risky move considering that when she returned from the market, Madame would meticulously scrutinize the items she brought back in the shopping basket to make sure that Andrea didn't steal from her.

When they got back to the house, Andrea cut both ends of the okra she had purchased and allowed it to sit in a bowl of water on the kitchen counter for a few hours. She wanted to use the mixture of the okra's natural juices and the water as eye drops for Erèz's injured eye.

Being careful not to get caught by Madame, Andrea removed the okra from the water. Pulling Erèz's head backward, she dropped a couple of okra droplets into Erèz's eye using the thin tapered tip of the okra. She secretly continued this procedure every hour or so and by the end of the day, the eye did in fact look less inflamed and irritated.

Madame requested that Andrea make légim with blue crab, pork, and shrimp, along with mashed assorted veggies such as eggplants, carrots, cabbage, spinach, and watercress, which will be served with black bean sauce and cornmeal on the side the next day. Erèz's mother used to make mayi moulen all the time with smoked herring sauce or with black bean sauce but sautéed mashed chayote squash with smoked herring was the closest she ever got to making légim. The dish, in its classic form, was far too expensive, and her mother couldn't afford to make it.

The légim was creamy and decadent. Andrea loved coconut milk in her légim and so did Madame. Andrea made sure to make the mayi moulen piping hot because it hardened when cold and nobody wanted a cool plate of hard mayi moulen.

Bòs Cyprien, Andrea, and Erèz sat outside eating their delicious meals from old dented bowls, drinking fresh watermelon with lime juice from beaten tin cups like always, but it didn't matter what the food was served in, everyone enjoyed the delectable meal. As usual, Bòs Cyprien asked Andrea for a piece of bone to suck on to enjoy the bone marrow.

When they were done eating, Andrea and Erèz went back inside the house to clear the family's table and carry the dirty dishes out to the backyard under the tamarind tree to wash and scrub them. Andrea also cleaned the upstairs kitchen and swept the backyard including the area around the three rocks that was used for the open wood fire to cook the beans. Once that was done, she went back upstairs to prepare lemongrass and cinnamon tea for Mèt Féfé and hot chocolate for the rest of the family.

Madame was in a happy mood that day as she occasionally was. Happy moods meant that she kept rude comments and judgments to herself, and most importantly, Erèz was safe and not physically harmed. That night, Madame fed Erèz a piece of bread and hot chocolate that Andrea had prepared before she left for the day. It was warm and delightful.

Erèz was very pleased as she enjoyed all the spices dancing and swimming in that chocolate. She could taste the flavor of broken cinnamon pieces, star anise, lime peel, and the vanilla that Madame added right before she poured the chocolate in each cup. She was glad Madame saw it fit to add the vanilla to her cup as she did for the rest of her family.

As Bòs Cyprien sipped on his chocolate, he didn't say much. He was exhausted from the two-hour round trip by foot he had made to the countryside locality of Calas that afternoon to visit his mother and paralyzed son. He came back looking preoccupied but kept his thoughts to himself and retired early.

As Erèz sat at the bottom of the stairs later that night, she recalled how good Andrea had been to her in the past few days. She loved hearing the blessing, "May God watch over you, my daughter," each afternoon on Andrea's way out to her house. Through those words, Andrea strengthened Erèz's faith in her God and the goodness of Saint Peter. Andrea's words made Erèz believe in divine protection despite how homesick she was and how deeply she missed everyone from her former life.

CHAPTER 30
Madame's Children

The following morning, Erèz once again made sure to wake up at the first rooster crow. The pills Andrea had given her had helped her sleep through the night without a headache. Unfortunately, her eye was still itchy and swollen, and her back was still too sore to lay on. She quickly ran through the same routine of tidying her bed and folding the clothes she used as a pillow before heading to the backyard to brush her teeth and wash her face.

Now it was time to work. She filled the bucket halfway and grabbed the brush with the heavy bristles to scrub the bricks that comprised the floor of the front porch.

She was hard at work scrubbing when Andrea's voice interrupted her, "How are you doing this morning, my daughter?"

Erèz stopped long enough to smile inwardly and say, "Good morning auntie. I am well." Andrea knew she wasn't well, but she was satisfied enough with the answer and proceeded toward the little alley at the side of the house.

That morning, Madame sent Andrea to the flea market very early to buy some akasan (corn porridge) to serve for breakfast with bread. Andrea came back and prepared the akasan with milk and a touch of vanilla essence. Surprisingly, Madame didn't object to feeding Erèz, and Erèz enjoyed dipping each piece of her roll in the akasan in her cup.

After the family finished eating, Andrea and Erèz cleared the table. Madame glanced around as she stood up from the table and decided that the entire floor of the living and dining rooms—along with the floors of the four bedrooms upstairs—needed to be scrubbed.

It didn't matter that Erèz's body was sore or that the marks from the matinèt hits were still raw. Madame didn't care how she felt as what she truly wanted was for Erèz to know who was in charge. She needed Erèz to understand clearly that all of her commands must be blindly obeyed, and also to know what could happen to her if she displayed any sign of disobedience. Madame's rules also include situations that arose outside of Erèz's control; bread not being ready at Madan Dikrépen's house when she went to buy some, for instance.

That morning, out of the blue, Erèz was ordered to scrub the entire floor of the house on her poor, sore little knees. Madame gave her a new heavy bristled brush that was reserved to clean the inside of the house. Erèz had never cleaned any house in this manner in her life, much less a large house like Madame's and didn't know what to expect.

She didn't help Andrea do the dishes that morning, but instead spent almost the entire day scrubbing all the house floors. Andrea checked on her often to make sure she didn't damage the floor with the brand-new brush or break any of Madame's bibelots. Andrea knew that Erèz's fragile frame couldn't handle another round of Madame's matinèt on her frail back or legs. Erèz was grateful to have Andrea in her life, and Madame didn't object to Andrea's constant guidance of Erèz.

Madame knew Andrea cared for the house better than she ever could, and she truly appreciated everything Andrea did; however, due to her extensive hubris and pride, she would never spit words of appreciation aloud to her.

This day of scrubbing led to Erèz uncovering every room in the house. It was also the first time she set eyes on Mademoiselle Carline and Monsieur Exavier. Madame had instructed Erèz to use "Monsieur" in front of Mèt Féfé and Exavier's names. When addressing Carline or Sherline, she was to address them as "Mademoiselle."

Erèz found her mother's advice to not look people in the eye to be sound. Perhaps, she would not have received that brutal punch from the horrible Sherline had she kept her eyes down. The lump that developed in Erèz's eye after that blow never went away. Despite Andrea's best efforts at treatment, the lump remained in her eye forever to remind her of her painful ten years as a restavèk, zombie, werewolf, and evil spirit.

Once Erèz finished scrubbing the living and dining rooms, Andrea took her upstairs to show her what needed to be done. With her head down, she entered Exavier's room after Andrea. He was laying down in his bed trying to nap after the hearty breakfast. His room was quite bare other than a few shoes on the floor and a dark wooden dresser filled with pants, suits, and dress shirts. The floor upstairs was made of slats of wood in all of the four rooms, but the floor in Exavier's room seemed to be recently redone. Andrea instructed her to sweep first and then scrub using less water for this room.

As Erèz scrubbed the floor, she bumped the little wooden table that supported a tall chamber kerosene lamp. The chimney of the lamp fell and a small piece of the tip broke. Instantly, Erèz was terrified that she was going to receive another round of the matinèt and another taste of Madame's rage.

Exavier, who was resting facing the wall under his brown bedsheet, rolled over to see what had broken. He looked Erèz up and down from head to toe with some amusement and said in Creole, "Why are your legs so skinny?"

"I don't know, Monsieur Exavier," she replied while keeping her gaze to the floor.

Exavier burst into a friendly laughter that eased much of the tension in Erèz's body. She even looked up for a quick moment and managed a genuine smile.

Exavier locked eyes with Erèz, and said in Creole, "I will tell my mother that I was the one who broke the tip of the lamp."

Erèz wasn't sure what to say other than to let another wide smile spread across her face. Exavier wrapped himself back in the bedsheet and rolled over to his previous position where he remained while Erèz continued scrubbing the floor. Once she was done scrubbing, she started drying the floor with a piece of burlap.

Over the ten years that Erèz served the house as a peasant restavèk, Exavier was very supportive of her and treated her with respect. When Exavier was in front of Madame, he behaved disdainfully toward Erèz, but anytime he was alone with her, he treated her well. One of the reasons why Exavier was appreciative of Erèz was because she was the mediator and special envoy between him and his girlfriend, Jasmine. Exavier would leave love notes under his plates before he headed back upstairs to his room. Erèz would inconspicuously take them and give them to Jasmine who could often be found out on the porch of her one-story house around the same time in the afternoon that Erèz usually went to Man Dikrépen's house to buy bread.

Sometimes, Jasmine would have a love note ready to give to Erèz to take back to Exavier. Erèz was thus the carrier of good news for both of them. Later on, Erèz would do the same for Dodo, Carline's boyfriend. Both Exavier and Carline waited anxiously for the love notes that Erèz delivered by placing them under their plates at supper. Because Erèz didn't know how to read and write, Jasmine always marked Exavier's note with a blue X so that Erèz didn't confuse who the note was for.

Erèz especially enjoyed her interactions with Dodo. She usually found him at the bottom of the hill on his bike, waiting for her. Dodo was a gentleman, and most of the time he brought Erèz candies, which she looked forward to with great anticipation.

Madame somehow never suspected all of these love affairs happening under her nose and roof. If she'd found out, that would have brought a great deal more grief to Erèz's life. Madame's goal was for her children to finish high school and graduate from the university with a firm career in place before they could date and start a love relationship. Thus, she raised her kids in such a fashion that they spent much of their time confined to their rooms reading, writing, painting, sewing, crocheting, knitting, sewing, and hand-embroidering. That way of life, in Madame's perspective, kept them out of trouble and away from other youths who might distract them from their education.

The next room Erèz entered was Sherline's. Her room was one of the messiest in the house. As per Andrea's instructions, she entered the room with the broom and took to sweeping the floor. Sherline, who had been lying on her bed until this moment, suddenly sat up on the bed with a straight back. She eyed Erèz sweeping timidly in a corner of the room and angrily tossed her sheets aside.

Erèz glanced up to see Sherline moving toward her rapidly and aggressively. She immediately put her head back down in hopes of avoiding whatever was to come next; however, she couldn't avoid Sherline's wrath. Erèz tried to shrink away as Sherline grabbed a fistful of her hair and started slamming her head against the wall.

"You never walk into my room without knocking!" Sherline screamed, as she continued to bash Erèz's head against the wall. After the third slam, Erèz started crying. When Sherline grew tired of knocking poor Erèz's head into the wall, she shoved her to the ground by the hair she still had clenched in her fist. Erèz sobbed as she cowered on the floor, trying to shield herself with one arm in case Sherline planned on further abuse.

Forcing herself to speak in Creole, Sherline hatefully said, "If you ever come into my room without knocking again, you'll wish all I did was knock your stupid head into the wall." She was about to turn, but thought better of it and decided to spit on Erèz on the floor. Feeling proud of herself, Sherline calmly returned to her bed to continue her nap.

Erèz slowly crawled away from the corner once Sherline was back in bed. She softly cried the entire time she scrubbed Sherline's floor. She didn't want to cry at all for fear of renewing Sherline's attention, but she couldn't contain the physical and emotional pain she felt.

After Erèz finished in Sherline's room, she went straight to Madame and Mèt Féfé's room, as Madame was still downstairs. She was amazed at how spacious the room was and at how meticulously clean Madame kept it. The room didn't contain much. There were fresh white linens on the bed. Long flowing drapes adorned either side of the tall wooden windows, and in the right-hand corner of the bedroom was Madame's sewing machine. There was essentially nothing to break or anything that might lead to finding trouble with Madame.

She swept the floor and started scrubbing right away. Once she had dried the floor very well, she dropped the heavy bristled brush in the bucket, and proceeded heading downstairs to get clean water.

Walking down the stairs was more difficult than she expected as her head wanted to explode from Sherline smashing it repeatedly against the wall. She went downstairs as carefully as she could so as not to fall, but some water ended up splashing on one of the steps. Madame, standing at the bottom of the stairs, witnessed the small spill and began shaking her head at Erèz.

Madame waited for Erèz to make her way to the bottom and proceeded to yank her by her right ear, pulling Erèz toward her while pinching as hard as she could.

With her other hand she slapped her on the side of the head and said, referring to the spirits Erèz might be possessed with, "Did they send you to kill me?".

Erèz knew she couldn't cry aloud as Madame would triple her beatings. Tears flowed involuntarily to release the pain in her head. Madame freed her with a shove, and Erèz continued on her way to empty and fill the bucket. To her surprise, when she came back to the stairs with the bucket full of water, Madame still stood in the same place studying her from head to toe with a look of great disdain and disgust.

Madame whispered under her breath as Erèz stepped on the first stair, "What is wrong with that little zombie's face?" The constant zombie references extremely dehumanized Erèz as they reduced her to feeling like she was the vilest creature that could possibly occupy space in Madame's house.

Erèz reached the top of the stairs, faltering at Carline's room. She expected anything to happen, as that was the very first time Erèz was going to meet Carline. She took a moment to gather the will and strength to knock, but she didn't hear a voice giving her permission to walk in.

Erèz's little body trembled, and she once again gathered enough strength to knock a second time. That time she heard a sleepy voice say in French, "Come in."

Erèz pushed the door slowly to step into a room covered with chaotic piles of paper scattered all over the floor. Carline noticed the look on Erèz's face and said in a tone indicating she was forcing herself to lower her standards by communicating in Creole so that the little peasant standing before her could understand her, "Is that you? The girl with skinny legs? Just put the papers on the table."

Carline went back to sleep as she didn't seem to care much that Erèz was there picking up the papers scattered around the room and that brought great relief to Erèz. She picked up each piece of paper and placed the pile on the table with care.

Erèz didn't know how to read and write, but she noticed the beautiful drawings over most of the papers that indicated to her that Carline was quite an artist. Other pieces of paper had groups of parallel lines all over, and it took her a while before she realized they must be music sheets. She swept and scrubbed the floor as she did in the other three rooms, and she finished by drying the floor with burlap. By the time she was done, Carline was faintly snoring away, and Erèz tiptoed out of the room to head downstairs.

Erèz went through the back door without incident. Under Andrea's direction, she rinsed the bucket and handwashed the piece of burlap to hang it dry on the clothesline.

Behind her, Erèz heard Madame say, "You didn't scrub the stairs?"

Andrea came to Erèz's rescue to say, "I didn't tell her to, Madame. I scrubbed all the stairs just a few days ago on Saturday." Madame didn't like when Andrea showed any sign of disagreement in front of other people. Choosing to listen more to her ego than Andrea, she replied with authority, "The little zombie spilled filthy water all over them so now she must scrub them."

The beautiful hand carved wooden stairs were the envy of all the wives who came in to gossip with Madame in the living room. Erèz's eyes, those stairs symbolized more of a nightmare. She needed to clean in between the heavy round balusters with a towel. She then swept them from top to bottom, and scrubbed each stair on her knees.

With her tired and frail body, she went back to the house carrying the bucket filled halfway with clean water, the heavy bristled brush, and the piece of wet burlap to tackle the stairs. Erèz was hurt all over, but didn't have the option of not completing the task.

She slipped and nearly had several big falls from the top of the stairs during her second round of wiping the excess water and squeezing the piece of burlap. When she arrived at the last stair, Madame was at the dining room table crocheting. Fortunately, she didn't look in Erèz's direction. Instead, Madame kept her eyes on her crochet needle, making sure she was following her pattern to the T. Erèz quietly snuck out the back door to clean and hang the piece of burlap to dry.

Andrea asked, "How are you feeling, my daughter?"

"I am fine, auntie." Andrea knew that Erèz was lying, but left it at that.

That afternoon, Andrea prepared a bush bath for Erèz with fresh leaves she had collected in her neighborhood that were known to help soothe muscle pain. Andrea filled a pot with water and added soursop, papaya, lemon grass, sour orange, and several other leaves that her neighbors recommended and brought them to boil. Right before she emptied the concoction into the old aluminum tin laundry tub for the bath, she sliced a sour orange and placed the two pieces in the hot ashes. She left the slices there until the juice started bubbling and the fresh green peel sparkled and darkened in the fire as it became almost carbonized. Andrea tried to be as inconspicuous as possible in her preparation, as she didn't want Madame to start questioning her and interrupting the regimen of natural treatment she was working on for Erèz's back and now her eyes.

As Andrea rubbed Erèz's back with a cloth, she realized that Erèz had a fever. She scooped some liquid from the tincture for the hot bath and asked her to drink it straight from her hands just like Erèz's mother used to do when she had a fever.

"It's good for you," Andrea said kindly as Erèz drank it. To help with Erèz's splitting headache, Andrea gently rubbed her head with the boiled leaves from the brew. Unfortunately, even those soft touches caused Erèz to feel as if her head was about to explode. Neither of them knew that Erèz was suffering from a concussion caused by Sherline's earlier abuse. Sadly, Sherline banging Erèz's head became a regular punishment. For the next ten years, Madame and Sherline would often knock her head against the wall as a quick and painful punishment whenever she didn't deliver on a task required of her. In fact, Erèz went on to suffer heavy migraines and headaches all her life.

CHAPTER 31
Long Days

On Tuesday afternoon, dinner was quite hearty and substantial. It was a feast of African yams cooked in bean sauce with cured salted pork belly and pig feet, steamed white rice, and Creole red fish sauce served with icy passionfruit juice. Madame also asked Andrea to prepare her much-loved Haitian chocolate. It was made with Haitian cacao bars wrapped in green banana leaves which helped to contain the fresh cacao grease that floated to top of the milky chocolate. Andrea made sure to teach Erèz how to make the Haitian hot chocolate just in case Madame designated her to make it one day for supper while Andrea was not around.

Andrea and Erèz sat under the tamarind tree eating while Bòs Cyprien sat at the front door of his small room sucking endlessly on the piece of bone in his plate. Their laughter as they ate dinner that day was extra boisterous. Madame overheard the three of them laughing and shook her head in disgust. She found herself very irritated that her three servants dared to have a bit of fun for an hour or so out of their day instead of dealing with her berating and constant tantrums and mood swings. She tried to ignore the annoyance as she continued conversing with her children over dinner. Madame shared her plans for how she was going to get the house ready to receive her extended family traveling from France and Canada to Jérémie for the Saint Louis celebrations in a few weeks.

Mèt Féfé always ate alone in the afternoons when he got home from work around four o'clock. Madame usually sat on the other end of the table recounting all the mishaps that had happened around the house while he was at work.

Mèt Féfé listened patiently as always, and he had long since learned to comment just enough so as not to enrage his wife. If during these conversations Madame felt that he wasn't showing enough appreciation for her hard work around the house, she would launch into an angry tirade accusing him of only caring about his work at the Customs Office in downtown. Mèt Féfé knew it was best to humor Madame on most matters and thus maintain the peace.

These routines didn't change that Tuesday as Andrea left for the evening with the blessing, "May God watch over you, my daughter." As she had done the past few days, Erèz went to Madan Dikrépen's house to purchase bread in the afternoon. Madame had also asked her to pick up some butter in a little bowl from Madan Octave who owned a shop down the street. This would save Erèz a trip to the flea market. Of course, this second errand to purchase the butter made Erèz extremely nervous. She knew there would be trouble if it took her too long buying both the bread and the butter in two different locations.

Fortunately, she found that with each of these little getaways in the afternoons, she became more and more familiar with the names of the neighbors who lived on the street, and with the streets' names and shortcuts.

That particular afternoon, she ran into Marianne at Madan Dikrépen's house. She was wearing her brand-new pair of red flip-flops. Erèz marveled at the shine and color.

"Your sandals are so pretty," she remarked.

"Thank you," replied Marianne. "Today I went with Man Jan to pick out fabrics so she can make me new dresses for the summer," Marianne explained excitedly. Erèz was happy that Marianne had such a good life with her family, but it didn't stop her from wishing that she too could be as lucky as Marianne who was clearly loved by her family despite being a restavèk.

"Hey, what happened to your eye?" Marianne asked, suddenly noticing the swollen eye looking back at her.

Despite the newness of their friendship, Erèz trusted Marianne enough to let her know exactly what had happened with Sherline as she cleaned her room.

"But, please promise not to tell anyone. If Madame finds out I told anyone, she will make things even worse for me. She doesn't want anyone to know how she really acts when nobody's looking."

"I won't tell…" Marianne replied quietly while looking at the ground and feeling extremely sad for her new friend.

That night, Erèz and Bòs Cyprien were not given butter for their pieces of bread. Madame judged the butter too expensive to share with the lowly servants who had more than enough in their lives to be thankful for. After all they had a roof over their heads, electricity, clean running water, and were fed three free meals a day. However, much to Erèz's joy, she and Bòs Cyprien were allowed to enjoy the flavorful hot chocolate she had helped Andrea prepare earlier that afternoon.

That night, the family stayed up around the table longer than usual as they discussed plans for the Saint Louis festivities. Erèz was unable to remain awake until they were done with their meal, and she fell asleep right at the bottom of the stairs where she usually sat to eat her supper.

It was obvious to Bòs Cyprien that Erèz was completely exhausted and drained. While he did want to offer her the comfort of his room, he knew he couldn't because the risk of flaring Madame's anger was too high. When he noticed the talking and laughter around the table had come to a complete stop, he got off from his small bed to wake Erèz up where she sat profoundly asleep. She cleaned the table in a daze. Afterward, she groggily headed to the little room filled with the bags of charcoal and charcoal dust to get her toothbrush, toothpaste, and pick up her bedsheet.

The night was restless as Erèz had fever-induced nightmares and babbled in her sleep all night. At one point, Erèz screamed so loudly in one of her nightmares that she woke up everyone in the house. Madame, outraged that she had been woken up in her sleep in the middle of the night, immediately made her way downstairs and filled a cup with icy cold water to mightily splash on Erèz. She stared unsympathetically at the tiny sleeping shivering figure on the floor and uttered to herself, "Look at this pathetic worthless zombie!"

It didn't take Erèz long to realize that one nightmare was over and another one was about to begin. She was unsure if she was still deep asleep in a nightmare or if she was awake and covered in icy cold water as she pinched herself back to life, staring astonished at Madame's immaculately polished toes. Erèz looked up to meet Madame's cold, pitiless eyes. They glared at her with disdain underneath hair rolled in large and puffy pink sponge curlers. Even in her half-asleep state, Erèz knew she didn't want to trigger any beating in the middle of the night. As soggy her body and hair were, she quickly proceeded to grab her flip-flops, fold the wet bedsheet, and feverishly rush her way toward the back door while Madame's glare continued to pierce her silhouette.

Madame yelled after her sarcastically as Erèz carefully closed the door after herself, "Count yourself lucky this time! I dare you to wake me up again in the middle of the night in my own house."

CHAPTER 32
Julianne

It was still pitch dark out at four in the morning when Erèz stepped outside. Aside from the crickets chirping and the occasional clip-clap of people's shoes heading to the early mass, Erèz stood in the middle of the backyard all alone. She was perplexed, unaware of what had triggered Madame to come downstairs at this hour and toss cold water on her on the cement floor. She hung her wet bed sheet on one of the clotheslines in the backyard and set herself down on the ground hoping she could catch a few more minutes of sleep before heading out to the front porch to scrub it.

Eventually, Bòs Cyprien woke up and started his daily routines. Erèz half-heard him, but was too tired to move in one direction or another and fully wake herself up. Somehow, she managed to fall back asleep for an hour or so and remained on the ground in a fetal position holding her knees close to her chest for support.

Fortunately, the sound of the first rooster's crow woke her up. Erèz knew it was time for her to start moving, fighting the desperate desire to sleep a couple of more hours. Her head was still throbbing and her entire body was sore, but she didn't want to run into more trouble with Madame by procrastinating on her daily tasks.

She brushed her teeth hurriedly and collected the bucket and scrubbing brush to begin scouring the front porch. Nothing unusual occurred as Erèz went about her work on the porch. The occasional rooster could be heard crowing, and several women passed by heading to mass, chatting along the way.

Andrea arrived that morning almost out of breath because she was running thirty minutes late. With a kind, but quick, "How are you doing, my daughter?" She headed to the backyard to get started on washing the dishes, preparing the coffee for Madame, and cooking breakfast for the family.

Luckily, Madame woke up later than usual that Wednesday morning, and Andrea accidentally escaped a reprimand for her tardiness. Madame instructed Andrea to prepare omelet with smoked herring and slices of creamy avocados. Additionally, she requested freshly pressed orange juice and Andrea's much loved buttery toasted bread.

After the family was served breakfast, and after Andrea, Bòs Cyprien, and Erèz had retired to the backyard to eat their breakfast, Madame stuck her head out the back door hollering:

"Andrea, tell that little zombie to keep an eye out for those peasants heading downtown with ripe bananas because I would like some for breakfast tomorrow."

Andrea walked with Erèz up to the front of the house.

"When you see the vendors selling bananas, ask them to wait, then come get me and I'll take it from there. Don't scream for me as

Madame doesn't like the neighbors to know what she is buying or anything else that happens within the four walls of this house for that matter! Do you understand?" Erèz nodded her head yes.

As Andrea was wrapping up her explanation to Erèz, she stopped in the middle of her sentence and her jaw dropped. Erèz followed her stare and saw a young woman walking up toward them from the bottom of the hill. As she walked, she rummaged through a glittery purse covered with numerous colorful and sparkly beads. She seemed to be searching for something that was irretrievably lost, but she was still determined to find it at any cost.

Andrea muttered, "Gadé, gadé, gadé," ("look, look, look") in disbelief and chagrin. She knew Madame wouldn't be pleased with what was about to happen, "And just when I have to head out to the market! Ah, Julianne..." Andrea wondered if she would be able to extricate herself from the situation that was about to unfold.

Erèz, on the other hand, couldn't believe a young lady could be so beautiful and fashionably put together so early in the morning on a Wednesday. Julianne wore a long flowing buttoned skirt that flared at the bottom. The pattern was colorful and vibrant. When she walked, it moved and swished all around her. On top, she wore a button up periwinkle blouse with large-squared shoulders. A rather tiny hat with a large silk bow adorned her head and revealed perfect undulating curls. Erèz stood there enthralled, staring at her. As Julianne continued searching through her colorful beaded purse, another woman approached Andrea and Erèz.

Man Nini, the laundry servant, greeted the two brightly in a peasant tone, "How are you doing?" Andrea turned around simultaneously, startled to see Man Nini there, realizing that she hadn't gathered the dirty laundry from everyone's room for her to wash and iron for the week. Andrea darted in the house to collect the laundry.

Julianne stopped walking and rummaged frantically through her purse. Finally, a vendor passed by with loads of ripe bananas, mangos of all sizes and colors, and freshly harvested quenepa in her bamboo-braided basket. Erèz asked the vendor to stop and went to get Andrea who accompanied her back to the front porch with a heaping pile of laundry.

Andrea helped the vendor unload so she could view and pick the best bananas. After bargaining her way through for the bananas, Andrea asked the vendor if she could try a quenepa before purchasing one of the bulging packets tied with thin pieces of banana leaves. Indeed, they were sweet, and Andrea obtained a pack for five cents. Erèz tried the quenepa and loved how the flavorful acidic sweetness filled her mouth.

Glancing in Julianne's direction, Andrea saw her recollect herself and start walking toward the house again. She decided it was time to let Madame know that Julianne was on her way to the house.

Madame scratched her scalp and sighed in irritation and disbelief, "Why did they let her out on a Wednesday?" Before she could say anything else, Julianne had already walked through the living room and into the dining room.

"Now why wasn't the front door open to let in some fresh air?" Julianne inquired casually in perfect French to no one in particular.

Madame sighed and responded in French, "How are you, Julianne?"

"Yes, Aunt Féfé, Sonsonn and I were out for a walk yesterday, and he said he loves me. I think he's going to ask me to marry him soon." Julianne smiled broadly, unaware or uncaring that she had completely ignored Madame's question. Madame tried to conceal her frustration as this was not unusual when communicating with Julianne.

Nurse Godson, who went by Sonsonn, was a nurse at the center where many of the people of Jérémie with mental disabilities were housed. Julianne was obsessed with Sonsonn. The other nurses who worked at the center found Julianne's delusions about marrying Sonsonn amusing, and they teased him often about it. Sometimes, Sonsonn laughed along with them, and other times he found no humor in the matter.

Julianne often stalked him around the building to catch him off guard and try to kiss him. Sonsonn didn't appreciate her advances on a personal or professional level. Sometimes, he tried to reason with Julianne and explain why they couldn't be in a relationship, but those conversations always resulted in Julianne becoming very upset and creating massive scenes where she would throw a tantrum. She would roll on the floor while clutching her neck as if someone was choking the life out of her. This was disruptive to other patients, as she never cared who was around when Sonsonn tried to let her down gently. Sonsonn, against his better judgment, ultimately agreed to play along with Julianne to maintain peace in the ward.

Erèz stood amused by the doorway, looking at Julianne and wondering what might be wrong with her. That was when Julianne noticed her and asked in perfect French, "Es-tu la nouvelle servante?"

Erèz did understand the word "servante," which sounded like the Creole pronunciation "sèvant," but didn't have a clue how to answer back. It was then that Madame realized Erèz was being distracted by Julianne. Madame moved like lightning toward Erèz and slapped her as hard as she possibly could, channeling all her frustration that had built up due to Julianne's presence.

Erèz was shocked back to reality as her lip split open and blood spilled down her chin. Julianne, equally startled by what just happened, screamed as if it was her who had just received a mighty blow from Madame. Julianne started crying and sobbing uncontrollably. Neighbors on either side could easily hear Julianne sobbing, and Madame didn't like that at all.

Julianne unleashing her frustration in such a manner to alert the nosy neighbors was exactly the kind of scenario that Madame feared would happen when she showed up. None of the kids emerged from their rooms to check what was going on because they knew their presence would have only escalated Julianne's mood and further irritated their mother to a whole new level.

Andrea was coming down the stairs with her hands full of dirty clothes when she noticed Erèz rushing through the back door with her lips split, blood gushing down her chin and tears streaming down her cheeks. Just when Andrea thought nothing worse could happen to poor Erèz, Madame split open her lips.

CHAPTER 33
Man Nini

After some of the commotion around the house had died down, Madame ordered that Erèz stay home to learn how to do laundry with Man Nini instead of heading to the flea market with Andrea.

Erèz was in no physical condition to do much due to the recent beatings. Man Nini was not unaware of Madame's ways. She knew Madame couldn't keep a restavèk for long, and so Man Nini didn't ask much of Erèz.

She patiently explained the steps to Erèz on how to handwash the white clothes, undergarments, bras, underwear, socks, and towels. First, you scrub the white clothes in plain water to remove the dust. Second, you hand wash them with soap. Third, you rinse them once. Fourth, you wash them again with soap in diluted chlorinated water.

Fifth, you rinse them again a few times, and at the end, you rinse them in light blue water by shaking a little blue chalky ball tied in a piece of cotton fabric. Fifth, you prepare lanmidon (cassava flour) for all the white garments made of cotton fabric to give a good crisp to the creases when ironing the clothes. Sixth, you shake and dry all the clothes.

To each explanation of the step, Erèz replied in her little high-pitched peasant tone, "Yes, auntie."

Internally, Erèz wondered if she would ever be able to remember all the steps when it came her turn to do the laundry for the house. The process of doing laundry in the city was all so complicated compared to the simplicity of how it was done in Guinaudée by the river. Back home, everyone went by the river to do their laundry on Saturdays. The steps to wash white clothing in the countryside were as simple as hand-scrub each piece with a bit of laundry soap, let the clothes sit under the sun on some gravel on the river shore, turn the pieces of white clothing on each side under the sun, wait for the stains to fade and disappear, dampen them in the river to rinse the soap out, and finally throw the garments and clothes on the gravel to let them dry. Doing laundry in various tubs and using different laundry ingredients in the steps seemed too complicated to follow, but out of respect, Erèz kept replying, "Yes, auntie," and continued to assist with the few things Man Nini asked her to do.

When Andrea returned from the maché, she was able to care for Erèz's wounds peacefully without fear of Madame intruding. Julianne's presence always wore Madame out to the point that she cared less about what was happening in the backyard with her three servants. Andrea tended to Erèz's eyes with fresh okra water every hour or so, and Man Nini suggested tying the okra in a piece of fabric around her head to help soothe Erèz's headaches. While it seemed a great idea,

Andrea feared angering Madame if she came to discover that she'd been caring for Erèz.

Man Nini didn't leave until nine o'clock that day, and Erèz enjoyed her company and patience in teaching her very much. Man Nini took one break during the day from hand washing the laundry to eat the scrumptious meal Andrea handed to her in the old aluminum bowl: shrimp in Creole sauce with boiled plantain and Haitian dark mushroom rice with tiny dry crawfish.

Erèz enjoyed the one lone shrimp on top of her black mushroom rice and savored the little bit of sweet watermelon and lime juice at the bottom of the old plastic red cup. Bòs Cyprien wasn't there to enjoy the meal with them because Madame had sent him to negotiate with Bòs Antoine about laying cement in the backyard in preparation for her family's upcoming visit from France. Madame wanted a quote to redo and replace the brown dirt and tiny rocks in the backyard before her family's arrival.

Bòs Cyprien came back late that day tired from walking, gathering prices from the few hardware stores, and seeking out individuals who could load sand and rocks. He ate his dinner cold and didn't joke much. After dinner, he climbed the mango tree and hopped on the wall that enclosed the yard, straddling it with one of his legs hanging inside the yard and the other on the street. He watched people passing by, either heading south toward the road inside the cemetery or north toward the Cathedral Saint Louis. Occasionally, someone would greet him with a "Bonswa Bòs Cyprien," and he would reply back politely, but he was not his usual cheerful self that day.

That night, Erèz sat at the bottom of the stairs in her usual spot observing Man Nini's patience in ironing every split in the family's various dresses, cotton slips, skirts, and pants. She hung each piece delicately on beautifully polished wooden hangers. Watching Man Nini warm the little brass cast iron in the open charcoal fire and then wipe it each time on a piece of towel before actually ironing the garment looked very tedious.

Man Nini carried all the clothes upstairs to place each hanger one after another on a large nail on the dining room wall strategically placed there for that purpose.

That Wednesday night, everyone went to bed early. Julianne's tantrums throughout the entirety of dinner had taken its toll on them. She spent dinner seamlessly pivoting from laughing to crying to sobbing to screaming within minutes, then the cycle repeated itself. Julianne was Madame's niece, the daughter of Madame's sister, Man Mona, who was a rich former slaveowner. They opted for a gilded Parisian lifestyle, and they decided Julianne with her mental illness would be too great a distraction from their extravagant life in Paris. Julianne's parents made Man Féfé Julianne's legal guardian and enrolled her at the Saint Joseph Health Center of Jérémie, which specialized in treating and rehabilitating mentally disabled individuals in the city.

Madame couldn't wait for Mona to visit from France during the Saint Louis festivities so she might take a much-needed mental break from Julianne and her wild and unexpected mood swings. Additionally, Man Mona always brought her the latest and most fashionable clothes, hats, and shoes from renowned French designers and seamstresses. Anytime Julianne stepped out from the confines of Saint Joseph Medical Health Center, people looked at her like she was from another world with her splendid, fashionable attire.

Julianne left right before Mèt Féfé showed up in the afternoon, and Madame headed upstairs, exhausted, to lay down. Mèt Féfé sat quietly at his usual spot by himself, pensively lost in thought as he ate every bite of his meal. Undoubtedly, he was grateful that his nagging wife was nowhere to be seen that afternoon, which offered him some much peace and space.

Before leaving, Man Nini emptied the pieces of hot burning charcoal under the tamarind tree and threw a bucket of cold water over them. When she came back the morning of the following day, she cleaned up the ashes and laid the pieces of charcoal on a piece of old tin to dry under the hot sun. Usually, Andrea mixed those old pieces of charcoal with fresh ones to cook, or she would leave them for Man Nini for the following Wednesday when she came to do laundry. Madame was incredibly pleased with Man Nini's work but was too prideful to say it or even say a simple "merci" for a job well done.

CHAPTER 34
A Terrifying Night

Erèz's first Friday in Jérémie was a melancholic one as she imagined all she was missing out on during Fèt Sen Pyè (Saint Peter's Celebration) in Guinaudée. She woke up especially missing her mother; Marie-Jeanne; little Patrick; Tant Lucienne; Mèt Robèto; Ilèyis; her father; Ti Roro; her godfather; and even the angry chicken that traumatized her so often.

She couldn't wait to see her mother in October. She cried quietly from missing her mother's touch and love while she performed her daily tasks. In fact, she cried even harder during the night and didn't sleep much. Erèz was extremely homesick. Missing everyone and all that she enjoyed most about Fèt Sen Pyè weighed on her. She dragged herself through the monotonous day with a heavy heart. At least the day went without some incident that might incur the wrath of Madame or Sherline. In the evening, she was glad to finally lay down at the bottom of the stairs and get the whole miserable day over with.

It took her a while to fall asleep, but when she finally did, something happened that would forever change Erèz's perspective about sleeping, or even sitting, at the bottom of the stairs. As if through a dense fog, she heard the voice of an old woman reprimanding someone. The sound of the voice became louder, and Erèz realized the old woman wasn't only angrily chastising a young girl, but she was also beating her mercilessly with a tree branch. Erèz wanted to run away, despite feeling horribly for the girl. No matter which way she went, she bumped onto the woman beating the girl. Sometimes, the beatings seemed to be happening behind the backdoor. Other times, the little girl was being beaten in the middle of the cemetery. Erèz couldn't escape it no matter how hard she tried to navigate through the dense mist of this dreamscape.

At times, she felt as if she was the girl being struck while simultaneously watching herself from afar. She could feel the tense anticipation before every hit just as much as she could feel the stinging of the branch against her skin. Though she couldn't see a single soul during any of this, Erèz heard footsteps of people who carelessly ignored the abuse as they walked by. It was as if they had seen this a thousand times before, and they couldn't be bothered to acknowledge or care about the recurring event consisting of a horrible woman of advanced years mercilessly beating a small child.

As Erèz watched and lived the scenario in that eerie world, a faceless old woman walked toward her and gripped her arm painfully tight. She thought the woman's long dirty nails were going to pull a piece of flesh from her arm. She opened her mouth to scream, but no sound came. Something had swallowed her entire voice and the more she tried to scream, the more that vile faceless woman pressed her nails through her flesh in her arm. The pain was excruciating, but couldn't defend herself. The pinching in Erèz's right arm eventually stopped after what seemed an eternity, and she managed to wake up. For a second, she wasn't sure if she had woken up to real life, or another dream. She wondered if her dream was real. Had she been transported to some world inhabited solely by unkind and bafflingly strong little old ladies?

It all felt too real and too terrifying to ignore the nightmare and Erèz just couldn't just shake the horrible feeling from what she just lived. The dream lingered upon her. She looked at her arm where she had been pinched and clawed at in the dream. It appeared to be normal and in good condition, but she rubbed it gently anyway. Despite wanting to sit up to process the dream some more, she got up quickly because worse than that nightmare she'd had was being struck on the head by Madame for getting up too late.

Bòs Cyprien still wasn't his cheery self that morning. He hadn't gotten back to being himself since the day he returned from visiting his mother. He asked Erèz as soon as she reached the bottom of the stairs, "Did you sleep well last night?"

Erèz lied, replying with a "Wi, tonton,"

As if Bòs Cyprien knew Erèz wasn't telling the truth, he persisted gently, "Are you sure?"

"Wi, tonton," repeated Erèz, less sure of herself.

Bòs Cyprien said quietly as he shook his head, "These werewolves didn't let anybody sleep last night."

Erèz didn't say a word to that, but she knew how much she'd struggled in her sleep with the powerful devilish forces and dream characters that plagued her the entire night. With that last simple comment from Bòs Cyprien, she never viewed the backyard the same. She became extremely fearful about the idea of living so close to the cemetery, and her skin developed goosebumps at the slightest noise when she sat at the bottom of the stairs waiting for everyone to go to bed. She couldn't explain what had happened during the night to anyone, not even Andrea.

Interestingly enough, that same morning, Andrea brought Erèz a protection prayer chain. The necklace portion was made of a piece of kitchen twine. The square flexible pendant was covered on the outside with a piece of blue chambray fabric, and the inside contained a prayer to the saints. The entire pendant was wrapped in a piece of clear waterproof vinyl to protect the prayer from the rain or any type of liquid. Obviously, Andrea had carefully handsewn the prayer with the white thread and meticulously hand-stitched all around the piece of blue. She placed it over Erèz's head and said, "Always hold on to this prayer! May Mary, the Mother of Jesus along with all the saints protect you!"

Later that morning, Madame noticed the necklace, but as a fervent Catholic woman, she chose not to comment on a pendant that contained the Lord's Prayer. Erèz never parted with that necklace as she saw it as a great source of comfort and protection. Whenever she found herself in the backyard in the darkness, she pulled the pendant from inside her dress and kissed it as she whispered, "May Mary, the Mother of Jesus, and all the saints protect me!" She never knew the words to the prayer that Andrea wrote in the little piece of paper inside the piece of vinyl, but repeating the words Andrea blessed her with when she placed the necklace around her neck made her feel safe. At one point, she started blessing her mother, godmother, Yaya, Ilèyis, Marie-Jeanne, and Tant Lucienne with the same words and she made that her official prayer throughout her life.

CHAPTER 35
Preparations

By Sunday, the pain and itchiness of the wounds on Erèz's back weren't quite as uncomfortable as they had been at the beginning of the week. The soreness in her palms no longer prevented her helping Andrea. Andrea managed to give her the okra water drops a couple of times that day, and to her delight, noticed that the inflammation had diminished significantly. Sadly, the tissue growth in the cornea of Erèz's right eye had become more pronounced.

Madame never said a word although she knew quite well the substantial amount of physical damage she'd done to Erèz in just one week. She still looked at her and treated her like an insignificant freeloader when, at only eight years old, Erèz had already done more than all of her three children combined.

The Sunday dinner turned out to be another elaborate one. Upon seeing Andrea set the table, Erèz realized how much she had already forgotten about properly setting the table for the special Sunday dinners. The menu for that Sunday was rice and black beans, chicken in Creole sauce, macaroni au gratin with ground beef filling, fresh lettuce, watercress, tomato salad, and sweet potato pudding served with freshly pressed pomelo juice on the side. As always, Erèz and Andrea disappeared into the backyard to eat their food. Miraculously, Bòs Cyprien's happy spirit had returned to his being, and he couldn't stop praising Andrea's talents in the kitchen while enjoying sucking on the piece of bone in his mouth. He spent several minutes removing meat from each vertebrate of the chicken neck with a smile on his face.

Mèt Lemaire and Mèt Eric joined the Sunday dinner table as was their custom. Before they even finished their dinner, they had managed to drink an entire bottle of Barbancourt rum between the two of them. Of course, none of that was new to Mèt Féfé, Man Féfé, or the kids, but it always seemed strange to Sherline that her own godfather couldn't distinguish her from her sister Carline when he got drunk. After all, Mèt Féfé always managed to keep his lucidity when he was drinking rum.

That afternoon, as both of his friends sat on the large vaulted wooden chairs in the living room snoring with their mouths wide open, Mèt Féfé canceled his regular Sunday afternoon visit to his other friends downtown before the new week started. Instead, he turned on his vacuum tube wooden cabinet radio to listen to love songs like "Tell Me About Love," by Lucienne Boyer, "I Have Two Loves," by Joséphine Baker, and "If You Were Not Here," by Fréhel.

Mèt Féfé sang and sang as his two friends snored the afternoon away. At one point, he got up to stand on the porch and watch the people and cars going up and down the street. It just happened to be around the time when Dodo was riding by to wave at Carline in her window. Mèt Féfé looked at him suspiciously, wondering why a young man about Carline's age looked so giddy riding in front of his house, but he didn't say a word. Dodo caught himself just in time and swallowed the smile meant for Carline. He figured he just saved both Carline and himself a great deal of trouble. Regardless, Mèt Féfé narrowed his eyes and glared at Dodo riding his bicycle down the street until he disappeared at the corner of the street that led to the front of the Saint Louis Cathedral. He wanted to protect his girls from the distraction that was "boys without a future," as he called them.

Andrea left that afternoon with the regular blessing, "May God keep you, my daughter!" She left the little kitchen adjacent to the dining room spotless, and trusted Erèz to sweep, scrub, wash, and clean the dining room and kitchen floor. Erèz did such a great job that, upon seeing it the next day, Andrea exclaimed, "Bravo, little madame!"

Erèz smiled from ear to ear and replied proudly, "Thank you, auntie."

The weeks that succeeded were a blur of countless tasks and chores to get the house ready to receive Man Mona from France and other family members traveling from Port-au-Prince.

When Man Mona traveled to Jérémie, Man Féfé filled out a formal request at the hospital to release Julianne for the time her parents would be in town. Madame didn't really care to have Julianne around due to the non-stop turmoil she created around the festivities, but in order to prove to her sister that Julianne was in good hands, she made sure to have her around the house during those two weeks.

The work in the backyard had also started, and that was the most disruptive aspect of Madame's to-do list as Andrea couldn't cook under the tamarind tree until the bricks had been carefully laid and the cement between the layers had dried. All the food was cooked inside in the tiny kitchen using fresh charcoal. Madame complained to Mèt Féfé about how much charcoal was being wasted from cooking the beans in the kitchen instead of an open wood fire in the backyard. Mèt Fefé wisely refrained himself from commenting, knowing there was nothing he could do about it, as Man Féfé herself spearheaded all those changes to show her wealth off to her side of the family.

The workers were loud and some of them ended up intoxicated from drinking too much kléren under the hot sun. Madame complained to Mèt Fefe about that part also, but Mèt Féfé just replied noncommittally in Creole, "Really? Is that so?" Madame looked very irritated with that answer, but she also knew that Mèt Féfé wasn't an easy one to bait and draw into an argument.

During this time of construction, Erèz located a strategic corner where she could observe the two neighboring girls who lived on the left side of the house. They couldn't see her unless they were specifically staring at the house, so Erèz was able to secretly watch them play all sorts of games.

One afternoon, Madame opened the door to look for her and couldn't spy her anywhere. She hollered loudly, "Bòs Cyprien, have you seen the little zombie?"

Bòs Cyprien glanced in Erèz's direction, their eyes meeting for a quick moment, and then he turned toward Madame and said, "She is cleaning behind the door."

It was a deliberate effort to lie and protect Erèz while also alerting her to the impending danger, but it was already too late. Madame swung open the door assuming rightfully that she would catch Erèz watching the neighbors' children at play. Madame grabbed her as hard as she could by her right ear and slapped her in the back of the head saying in Creole, "If they've sent you to kill me, you are not going to find me!"

Erèz cried loudly, and the kids stopped to look straight toward where Madame was cuffing her non-stop in the head. Madame became extremely embarrassed as she realized the neighbors' two young girls were witnessing her mistreat and abuse Erèz. Madame roughly pulled Erèz inside the living room by her right ear where she removed one of her heavy-heeled sandals to start pounding Erèz indiscriminately all over her body. Her head, back, face, and forehead took the worst of it. Blood covered her face and hair, but Madame was relentless.

That afternoon, Erèz headed out with the basket to purchase the bread from Madan Dikrépen, dried blood covering her forehead and encrusted in her hair. The line was long and the crowd was especially boisterous that day, but Erèz didn't join in the laughter and gossip. She tried to remain as quiet and unseen as possible while waiting for her turn to purchase bread.

When it was her turn to finally get bread, Madan Dikrépen was busy directing her workers. She caught sight of Erèz and did a double take.

"That woman is killing you. Don't you have any family?" She asked Erèz in Creole.

Erèz couldn't let one word escape her mouth as she was still dazed and mentally numb from the pain that overwhelmed her entire body. She felt weak and dizzy, and her thin and skinny legs barely held the weight of her body under all the pain.

She met Dodo on her way back, but was unable to return his smiles and enthusiasm. She took the carefully folded pink piece of paper from his hand and the lollipop and walked straight back to the house. Erèz had mastered the drill of hiding Dodo's love notes under

Carline's plates and picking up Carline's love notes for Dodo after the mid-day dinner. Andrea knew about the exchange of love notes and how Erèz got caught in the middle. She was always terrified that Madame would find out and blame Erèz for introducing eighteen-year-old Carline to boys and a life of promiscuity.

Andrea could hardly keep up with the massive abuse suffered by Erèz's body, but she continued caring for her with the bush-bath treatments as often as possible. During the baths and just as she laid herself to sleep, Erèz held tightly to the prayer chain that Andrea had given to her and whispered the same prayer she always said before she closed her eyes to sleep, "May Mary the Mother of Jesus protect me."

Because of all the work being done in the backyard, Andrea couldn't comb, wash, and grease Erèz's hair with Haitian castor oil for over a month. Andrea knew that Erèz's puffy hair needed help, but didn't know how to care for her hair under Madame's watchful eye. Now that the backyard had been cemented, Madame would open the backdoor constantly just to admire the new remodeling she'd just invested in. Fortunately, a week before the Saint Louis festivities, during one of those moments when Madame found herself admiring the results of the money she had spent to redo and cement the back-yard, she said loudly, for both Andrea and Erèz to hear, "Does that little zombie know how to untangle that bird's nest on her head? Can you comb her hair, Andrea?"

"Yes, Madame," Andrea responded without betraying the relief she felt that she could now wash and comb Erèz's hair without risk of punishment.

As Andrea gently started upon her hair, Erèz remembered Marie-Jeanne's mother back in Guinaudée who lovingly untangled and combed her hair on Saturday evenings, then greased her scalp and each strand of her hair. Andrea noticed that the reddish part around Erèz's hair that was so prevalent when she first arrived was gone. This obvious indication of her malnourishment had disappeared in just the past month. Andrea didn't make any comment, but was pleased that there was at least some benefit in Erèz's favor.

It took a long time to untangle Erèz's hair. Between simple neglect and the fact that some of the medical treatments for her headaches ended up tangling her hair further, it took Andrea at least two hours to do Erèz's hair. Erèz was incredibly happy with her beautiful new hairdo, although the tight braids made her scalp more tender and elevated her headaches. Erèz noticed that her hair was done in the same way Marie-Jeanne's mother used to do it back in Guinaudée. The only difference was that Marie-Jeanne's mother used black threads to weave each braid into each other. Andrea looked at her work, exhilarated. She decided that the hairstyle could last in Erèz's hair for a month or so before she would undo the braids and moisturize Erèz's scalp and come up with another braid style.

Madame had Bòs Cyprien revive the front porch with a touch of paint, clean the tall ceilings in each room of the house, and repaint the two rooms reserved for visitors. Man Féfé couldn't care less about elaborate dinners during the week preceding Saint Louis. Instead, she had Andrea focus on washing all the plates, glasses, and silverware in the tall china cabinet in the dining room. She also directed Andrea to scrub the pots to the point that she could see her face reflected back at her in each of them.

The day preceding Madame's family's arrival, she had Erèz scrub the floor of the porch and every floor in the house. Madame acted very stressed, but oddly was still in a good mood. Within herself, Erèz fed on that positive energy even though she and Madame rarely exchanged a word, and Madame still refused to address her by her name and kept calling her and referring to her as "the little zombie," "skinny-legged," or "werewolf."

Andrea and Erèz washed all the plates, glasses, and silverware under the tamarind tree. Because the backyard was now cemented with bright multicolored bricks that needed to be kept clean, they used a large piece of clear vinyl as a waterproof cover. They placed each plate face down on the vinyl after rinsing them.

At the end of all the preparations, the house looked almost brand-new, with the linen drapes that Man Nini rinsed and pressed and the fresh touches of paint on the ceilings and walls. Madame went from room to room unhooking the handmade brass latches from the shutters to let fresh air and sun enter the house. With everyone's focus on Madame's demands, the house was pristine and immaculate. Finally, after days of intense cleaning, scrubbing, sweeping, painting, drape washing, and remodeling, Madame felt relieved and ready to receive her family for the Saint Louis celebration.

Madame planned on an especially extravagant dinner for the day preceding Saint Louis Day, inviting all of her friends from the neighborhood. She arranged for Bòs Cyprien to purchase half of a pig, one goat, three turkeys, and five chickens to have enough provisions during the two weeks that Man Mona and her husband would be around. The goat, turkeys, and chickens were all kept in a coop in the back right corner of the backyard to prevent them from wandering off or from defecating all over Madame's newly remodeled yard.

Madame's cousin, Bòs Wilner, came from the countryside of Abriko bringing fresh plantains, oranges, freshly picked soursops, pomelos, pieces of sugar cane, sweet potatoes, and African yams. Madame noticed Bòs Wilner standing on the porch with his feet full of dust from the two-hour walk from Abriko and pretended not to see him for a while. She did so to humiliate him. She held on to her deep desire to see him turn around to head back to where he came from, but she eventually yelled in Creole, "Andrea, go see who is on the front porch for me!"

Bòs Wilner knew the drill to go around the house to the little alley to get to the backyard. Even though Bòs Wilner and Madame were first cousins, Bòs Wilner behaved like a peasant, just like Erèz's mother, and he was treated as such under Man Féfé's roof. Like all peasants from the surrounding countryside, Bòs Wilner was never invited inside to eat or to sit on any of the polished wooden chairs that Mèt Lemaire and Mèt Eric sat on each Sunday.

When Bòs Wilner got to the backyard, he took the twisted bamboo basket from his head and sat on one of the little benches reserved for low-class visitors. Erèz stepped out from her chores through the backdoor and said, "Bonswa tonton."

Bòs Wilner smiled and replied, "Good afternoon, my daughter."

Madame had Andrea place all the things that Bòs Wilner had brought into the kitchen adjacent to the dining room. She then asked her to prepare fresh coffee and a buttery bread roll to serve to Bòs Wilner. Andrea advised Madame there was no more bread, and Erèz was sent to Madan Dikrépen's bakery.

With the money in one hand, and the basket with the hand-embroidered white linen in the other hand, Erèz headed down the hill. On her way back, Marianne waved to Erèz from her front porch. Erèz waved back to Marianne, and she signaled Erèz to come toward her.

They talked and complimented each other on their hairstyles. Erèz asked, "Did Man Jan press your hair?"

"Oh, no. Man Jan and I went to Madame Margaret. Do you know Madame Margaret?" Marianne went on to explain that Madame

Margaret saw to all the beauty needs of the aristocrats' wives in town. Erèz looked at Marianne, wistfully wishing she could have a Madame who cared for her at least a little.

Unbeknownst to her, Madame was on the porch observing her chatting and laughing with Marianne. When Erèz returned to the house and opened the backdoor, Madame hit her with the matinèt. The blow landed right on her little chest. She hit her viciously several times more before Bòs Wilner decided to come to Erèz's rescue. He stood on top of the first set of stairs, pleading with Madame with his two arms open in sign of supplication, "Have pity Fé! Have pity! She is so little." Bòs Wilner nicknamed her "Fé" as a kind diminutive of Man Féfé. Surprisingly, Madame stopped hitting her, but she remained out of breath from the hits she'd delivered with the matinèt.

"Andrea, bring me the grater." Madame said resolutely.

"Madame, please!" Andrea, whispered.

"Do not make me repeat myself." Madame said ominously.

When Andrea returned with the wide, flat grater, Madame instructed Erèz to kneel on it.

"You think you have come here to beat me?" Madame said scornfully as Erèz lowered herself to kneel on the grater. The pain of the sharp grater removing the outer surface of skin of both her knees was excruciating, and though Erèz wanted to cry her heart out, she knew that would bring another round of matinèt beating. That was the last thing she wanted. She suffered as silently as she could as the sharp little grater blades slowly but surely cut into her knees' flesh.

Her soft little moans and whimpers would have broken most hearts, but not Madame's. She calmly went about her business as Erèz remained in agony. Andrea could not bear it and pleaded with Madame to release Erèz from the cruel punishment. Madame intended the punishment to last for four hours, but with Andrea begging Madame to release her, Erèz was allowed to stand after three. When Erèz lifted herself from the grater, her raw little knees were bleeding heavily. She trembled as she found herself barely able to walk to the yard. Warm blood dripped down her shins, and tears continued to roll down her face from the massive amount of pain she had just endured.

Watching Erèz hobble to the yard was too much for Andrea to take and she decided in her heart then to actively start looking for another family to work for. She had witnessed too much suffering of the little restavèks who served at Man Féfé's house during her ten years working there as a servant. There had been numerous little Erèzes who had arrived and then left. As a longtime spectator to the physical and emotional abuse, Andrea could no longer stomach it.

CHAPTER 36
Man Mona and Misyé Pyè

Andrea knew she was in for extra long hours of work for the following two weeks. Sadly, her pay would remain the same. Soon, she would be attending to Madame's guests and also dealing with Madame's exaggerated demands and displays; Madame loved impressing her guests by demonstrating how she exercised full authority over the affairs of her house, including her servants. Her antics would be more unbearable than usual during this time and Andrea made sure to be mentally ready for all of it.

Julianne moved in the day prior to her parents' arrival. As always, Julianne's presence created more chaos than Madame's patience and short temper could handle. Julianne became immediately fascinated with Erèz after witnessing Madame's brutal slap. She fantasized about spending time in the backyard to sympathize with the little restavèk who could barely express herself in French and spoke Creole with this interesting peasant-like sing-song voice. Even Julianne knew that was going to be out of the question. Madame would never tolerate it.

Unless Erèz was setting up the table and helping Andrea, she was not allowed to be in the house or near the dining room table. Still, Julianne did what she could to satisfy her curiosity about Erèz. Peeking around corners and looking out the right windows, she was able to spot Erèz going about her day from time to time. Julianne especially loved seeing Erèz's little head poking over at the neighbors' yard to interact with the two girls jumping, laughing, and playing. Julianne smiled to herself as she watched Erèz have a little bit of secret fun. Despite her mental illness, Julianne understood the best she could do to protect Erèz from any more abuse from Madame over the next few days was to take no visible notice of Erèz and to simply keep her mouth shut about her.

Man Mona and her husband traveled by boat on *La Belle Jérémienne* from Port-au-Prince and arrived in Jérémie in the middle of the night. Mèt Féfé waited for them all night at the wharf to pick them up. To keep her out of sight, Madame made Erèz sleep in the little room that contained the sacks of charcoal. The cockroaches and rats that resided around the property traveled easily back and forth between the latrine and this little room, giving them free rein to bite Erèz throughout the night. Erèz had many sleepless nights during those weeks when Madame's family was in town. Between her recent nightmares, the proximity of the cemetery, the werewolves Bòs Cyprien talked about so often, and now the cockroaches and rats running over her at night, she was unable to get any decent rest.

Erèz was already awake when Man Mona and her husband, Misyé Pyè, walked in after four in the morning. Their presence had caused quite the stir. Man Mona was especially boisterous and laughed with Madame loudly enough for the whole street to hear. Misyé Pyè, on the other hand, seemed to be a quiet man. As with Mèt Féfé, his quiet and passive nature helped provide some balance in the relationship with his wife, who was far less restrained.

At the sound of the first rooster crowing, Erèz jumped from where she was lying to go pick up the bucket and brush to start scrubbing the front porch. Andrea arrived shortly after. She had made sure to come to work earlier than usual as she had no interest in finding herself on Madame's bad side during her family's stay.

"Why is your face so dark?" Andrea asked, noticing the smudges on her little face.

"I slept in the little room, auntie."

Andrea shook her head, muttered to herself, and proceeded to the alley. She started cooking immediately and made sure to refill the tea pot for Man Mona. Mona, who came from the French aristocratic life, was a great lover of the beverage and drank her expensive tea all day long.

Breakfast was an elaborate display, and per Madame's request, Andrea wore a pristine white bandana and a freshly pressed white apron with gatherings and lace at the bottom. This was to be her uniform for the next two weeks.

Man Mona enjoyed Andrea's cooking and before her return to Paris, she always made sure to discreetly fold a few dollars in Andrea's hand whispering, "To buy cola for the kids."

Andrea always welcomed the extra money with much gratitude. She used it to buy clothes, barrettes, ribbons, and sandals that her monthly income could never cover.

Madame called Andrea to bring more hot tea. As she poured the tea, Man Mona took great interest in asking her about her kids, and how she was handling raising them alone. Andrea responded using as few words as possible to avoid saying the wrong thing in front of Madame, but as she walked away she heard Man Mona say with great confidence, "Fé, don't ever let her go! You found a good one—no, a great one."

When Erèz finished scrubbing the front porch, she hurried herself up the stairs to help Andrea in the kitchen. Upon seeing her covered in soot from her night in the charcoal room and her morning cleaning the porch, Andrea advised her that she was going to have to take a shower.

"Quickly, my daughter, before Madame catches you dirty like this," Andrea said.

Erèz rushed right back down to the yard, filled the bucket and carried it behind the latrine where she vigorously scrubbed herself and rinsed the charcoal and soot from her body. She then wore her oversized denim hand-me-down dress and flip-flops. When she came back, Andrea glanced at Erèz from head to toe very satisfied with the way she looked.

Back in the kitchen, Erèz helped Andrea with whatever she needed: mashing the spices in the mortar and pestle, sorting through the rice for impurities, scrubbing and rinsing the rice, mashing the beans with the pestle in one of the pots, and washing dishes and utensils. As Madame mostly wanted to keep Erèz out of sight, she followed Andrea around to the dining room only when she thought it was safe for her to do so. Erèz picked up on the hints very quickly, and Andrea was incredibly pleased.

When the kids came downstairs along with Julianne, the dining room turned into quite the joyous scene. Man Mona and her husband's luggage had still not been taken up to their rooms upstairs, causing the kids great excitement in anticipation of the gifts they contained. They kissed Man Mona and Misyé Pyè on both cheeks several times, and palpable and infectious joy filled the air.

Breakfast was served and Man Mona enjoyed her eggs; they were perfectly cooked over-easy, just the way she loved them. The chatter around the table that morning had everyone in a collective good mood, and Julianne decided this was the perfect time to announce that she was engaged to Nurse Sonsonn. Man Mona couldn't help but laugh, and Misyé Pyè shook his head. Quickly realizing this might hurt her feelings, they pretended to believe her and asked why they were only just now learning of the engagement.

Julianne responded in perfect French "Well, with such news, I just had to share it face to face." Misyé Pyè gave his daughter a strained smile knowing her fantasy would never come to reality. At ten o'clock Man Mona decided she was tired and they needed to bathe and rest a little after their long journey. Mèt Féfé, Man Féfé, Misyé Pyè, all the kids, and Andrea helped haul the heavy luggage upstairs. Man Mona calmed the anxious kids and Julianne about going through the luggage for their gifts by assuring they would do so together after dinner. That was quite a disappointment, but after four hours of catching up with Man Féfé, the only thing she had energy for was putting herself to bed.

Misyé Pyè and Man Mona slept for about five hours until Madame knocked on their door to wake them up for dinner. Once they reached the dining room table, their eyes lit up upon seeing the goat in Creole sauce, a dish they'd not eaten for a year now. Man Mona sucked on all the bones on her plate and all five fingers that held them, which of course was out of the question for any kind of Parisian table etiquette. It didn't matter though, as she appreciated the freedom to eat as she wished with trusted family members within Man Féfé's four walls instead of worrying about proper table etiquette during high-class dinners. She ate her broiled plantains with creamy yellow avocado pieces soaked in the sauce but skipped the rice, saying that she wanted to leave for Paris with her waist the same size.

Man Mona and Misyé Pyè continued to share stories of their lives and adventures in Paris over the past year. The kids burst out laughing at some of the tales, especially the one where Man Mona fell right on her face on their way out of Folies Bergère, the very exclusive and sophisticated cabaret in Paris. She'd had a little too much alcohol in her blood, and her heels kept getting stuck in the hem of her long opera dress. As the fun continued around the table, Bòs Cyprien, Andrea, and Erèz sat under the tamarind tree making their own jokes about Man Mona's strong perfumes and heavy jewelry. The clanging bracelets and bangles made so much noise that they were convinced she could wake up a few of the dead people resting in the cemetery. Bòs Cyprien jokingly mourned the podyab (poor souls) who couldn't even sleep peacefully in the afterlife from the noise of Man Mona's jewelry. All three laughed heartily.

Bòs Cyprien also joked about Misyé Pyè, who looked more like Man Mona's restavèk than her husband as she ordered and pushed him around like a human zombie. This comment, of course, resulted in more laughter. As Bòs Cyprien reached the last bite of his meal, he said in a more serious tone, "I am laughing and I kid, but Misyé Pyè is a kind soul. Misyé Pyè always sends money to my mother. He is a good man."

Bòs Cyprien also shared an interesting story with Andrea and Erèz about Misyé Pyè's. During one of Misyè Pyè's visits to town, he committed adultery with Man Magalie, the wife of his best friend, Misyé Jean Claude. Man Magalie became pregnant and gave birth to little Judith. Misyé Jean Claude had no idea about the tryst and cared for baby Judith as his own; at least until after a few years, when Judith started looking more like a little replica of Misyè Pyè! Misyé Jean Claude confronted Misyé Pyè who admitted to the extramarital affair with Man Magalie, which put an end to their friendship. Misyé Jean Claude continued to love Man Magalie and Judith, and he ultimately swallowed his pride to care for baby Judith as if she was his own.

Amusingly, Man Mona knew both Magalie and Judith very well, but she considered them too poor and beneath her to be included in her circle. Misyé Pyè, on the other hand, always held Magalie close to his heart and also Judith, who was only two years younger than Julianne. Thus, when Misyé Pyè came home to vacation, he always arranged to give money to Bòs Cyprien to take to Man Magalie for Judith.

Man Féfé and Mèt Féfé knew about the scandal as well, but never dared to bring up the subject during family get-togethers. It seemed Man Mona was the only one who was kept in the dark about her husband's illegitimate baby.

CHAPTER 37
Saint Louis Day Eve

After breakfast, Erèz went through the same routine of assisting Andrea in clearing up the dining room tables and bringing the dishes under the tamarind tree to wash. Andrea washed and scrubbed, and Erèz rinsed them twice in two different pots of water.

When they got to the cooking pots, Andrea told Erèz that it was time for her to start learning how to scrub the aluminum ones. Together, they grabbed pieces of corn husks, dampened them in water, and then, with a handful of fresh ashes started scrubbing the pots. After rinsing the aluminum cooking pots, they scrubbed them a second time, then washed them with soap so that, like Andrea always said, they could see the reflection of their smiles shining back at them. From then on, Erèz always scrubbed the pots alongside Andrea so that she could perfect doing the dishes from A to Z.

As they continued scrubbing and cleaning, they both heard the fun the kids and adults were having upstairs unwrapping gifts. New dresses, shoes, and jewelry were just the beginning. Erèz could hear Carline's voice clearly thanking Man Mona for her brand-new set of paint brushes. Although the conversations happened in fluent French, Erèz understood the word "pinceau," which is pronounced the same both in singular and in the plural (pinceaux), but spelled differently in Haitian Creole: "pinso." At one point, Sherline became extremely excited about a gift as they could both hear her running back and forth on the wooden floor above them screaming wild thank yous to Man Mona. It was a good ten minutes before Sherline seemed to finally settle down.

Madan Dikrépen didn't bake the day before Saint Louis as she too was focusing on receiving family members from the countryside and Port-au-Prince at her house for the festivities. Madame asked that Andrea prepare some banana beignets that she would serve with milk for supper. Andrea prepared them right before she left that evening as they couldn't be served cold. Man Mona and Misyé Pyè enjoyed their supper very much. Man Mona enjoyed it so much that she opted to clean her fingers by licking all ten of them, once again taking advantage of eating in her home country.

The plan was to go to bed early that night as they were looking forward to a busy schedule for Saint Louis Day. The Haitian virtuoso pianist, Ludovic Lamothe, was holding a concert for the Saint Louis festivities at Hotel Lamarre in Bordes. Man Féfé, Mèt Féfé, Man Mona, and Misyé Pyè were eager to attend to catch up and mingle with the elite members of town. They planned on taking Julianne, Carline, and Exavier, but excluded Sherline, who was still too young to attend concerts and dances.

Erèz sat outside at the bottom of the stairs like usual, exhausted after a long day of work. As the talking and laughter echoed through the wee hours of the night, Erèz concluded she would be better off getting herself situated in the little charcoal-dusted room she shared with the crickets and cockroaches. She had a restless night. She couldn't sleep and felt very unhappy, but there was no one she could talk to in the thick darkness. Occasionally, a cricket chirped, and a couple pieces of charcoal moved around from a rat shuffling about in the little room. Erèz knew to brush her teeth very well and rinse herself from any grease smells that might cling to her in order to prevent any mice or rats from nibbling around her lips, fingers, and toes. A good cleaning didn't ensure a quiet night of sleep, but it helped.

That night of Saint Louis's Eve, Erèz dreamed that she was walking on a long road paved with fresh dirt. On both sides of the road, there were vibrant blooming roses in a variety of vivid colors. She found herself alone on that beautiful road, but she was happy and felt peaceful. At the end of the road, she noticed a woman waiting for her with her arms wide open, but the bright ethereal light that surrounded her form didn't allow Erèz to study the features of her face. In Erèz's little mind, she couldn't wait to get to where the lady was, but the more she got closer to that being, the farther away the lady seemed to be. She was tired from walking in the dream, but the scent of the beautiful flowers alongside the road kept her energized and made the long walk bearable. In the dream, she wished to remain there forever instead of going back to the harsh reality of that cold cement floor she was sleeping on. She jumped awake from her dream, wondering where exactly she had been and concluded in her heart that the illuminated woman who awaited at the end of the road with her loving arms wide open definitely was Manman Mari or Mary, the Mother of Jesus.

"Manman Mari is watching over me," Erèz thought, feeling safe and secure, at least for a few moments.

She woke up not from a rooster singing, but from the neighbors' dogs barking non-stop. They barked for a long time that night, and Erèz was unable to fall back asleep. She wondered what werewolves or spirits were roaming through the streets that caused the dogs to bark so zealously. Her body almost froze with fear on the floor, and she wished the sun would hurry up and rise so that she could feel more at ease.

The following day during dinner under the tamarind tree, Bòs Cyprien mentioned that there were likely powerful voodoo ceremonies being conducted in the cemetery the night before. They must have been raising the dead from their resting places in the ground to serve new masters in the form of zombies. Erèz gulped and was too terrified to comment about her experience during the night.

When she arrived at the front porch for the usual morning scrub on Saint Louis Day, the street of Mònn Jibilé felt somber and was void of any traveler. It was so quiet, Erèz could only hear the distant crashing of the cerulean waves of the ocean as they hit the coast in downtown Jérémie and rolled back. She noticed the breeze from the ocean that morning made the air a little bit chillier than usual.

As she brushed the bricks, she thought she felt someone watching her. When she couldn't ignore the feeling any longer, she turned around to find Marianne dressed for the occasion in a crisp new fitted dress. Her pressed hair was in pink sponge rollers, indicating she was half-ready to go to mass with Mèt Jan and Man Jan. She waved at Erèz brushing the multicolored bricks of the porch, and Erèz sadly waved back a bit mesmerized at how pretty she looked.

That morning Andrea came to work early again to prepare the extravagant breakfast before everyone left for mass at eleven o'clock. Erèz remained vigilant alongside her, helping with anything she needed.

Andrea made omelet with smoked herring, as that was one of Madame's preferred dishes. Madame also requested lime juice and coffee with milk that only Andrea knew how to make in just the right way to please her. Andrea also made Madame's favorite buttery bread to serve with the eggs. For Mèt Féfé and Misyé Pyè, she prepared salted cod fish sauce with crispy semi-cooked slices of yellow onions and freshly boiled green plantains that she served with a green lettuce salad topped with round slices of juicy tomatoes and green watercress. Andrea also sliced two meaty avocados and set the lightly salted slices on a separate plate for them to enjoy as they pleased with their hot pieces of boiled plantains. That morning, everyone raved over Andrea's incredible culinary skills and talents.

Everyone was in the most upbeat and jovial of moods, and the loud sounds of laughter and talking rang through the entire house and out into the backyard. Exavier and Carline were especially excited that day, anticipating not only the concert, but also being able to see their secret lovers who would also be in attendance. Man Mona, of course, was extra ostentatious. Julianne appeared to be having a good day as no tantrums occurred to derail anyone's enjoyment of breakfast. Like everyone else at the table that morning, she was in the Saint Louis celebration spirit.

Man Mona's musky perfume traveled from the dining room table to the kitchen. Erèz never met her or Misyé Pyè face to face, so she only really knew Man Mona by the smell of her heavy perfume, loud bouts of laughter, and her unique style of communication, which was mixing French with Creole as she saw fit. Though she was able to get her meaning across to her family when she spoke, her accent and strange way of speaking clearly screamed to everyone else, "I am from France and not from around here!"

After everyone finished eating, and the ladies went back upstairs to brush their teeth and freshen their faces. Misyé Pyè stepped outside through the back door searching for an opportunity to slip some money to Bòs Cyprien for Judith without Man Mona knowing. It weighed heavily on Misyé Pyè's heart that he couldn't go visit his daughter, but the situation was so complicated on both ends that the best he could do was to stay away and not disturb the house that sheltered his daughter and her family.

Upon receiving the money, Bòs Cyprien managed to very swiftly take it to Judith's house before she and her household headed to Saint Louis mass. When Bòs Cyprien knocked at Misyé Jean-Claude and Man Magalie's door that morning, Misyé Jean-Claude poked his head through the wooden door. He looked at Bòs Cyprien suspiciously from head to toe and asked him why he was at his door so early on this Saint Louis Day.

With a demeanor that simultaneously expressed his rush and his reverence, making sure he didn't look Misyé Jean-Claude straight in the eyes, Bòs Cyprien said, "Misyé Pyè is in town for the Saint Louis Day festivities, and he sent me here to give this to Mademoiselle Judith," as he handed the tightly folded U.S. dollar bills to Misyé Jean-Claude. Misyé Jean-Claude snatched the money from Bòs Cyprien's hands, mumbling unhappily without an intelligible word crossing his lips, and Bòs Cyprien turned around as fast as he could, and left without looking back.

CHAPTER 38
Saint Louis Day

Everyone headed to church, and the house became silent. Andrea and Erèz got to work right away emptying the table, doing the dishes, and prepping for the scrumptious midday dinner. The day prior, Andrea had slaughtered, marinated, and cooked a turkey halfway to preserve the meat overnight for the extravagant Saint Louis dinner. For the menu of the day, as requested by Madame, Andrea cooked macaroni au gratin with ground beef filling, steamed white rice, gungo pea soup, fried turkey in Creole sauce, and Haitian Russian potato and beet salad. The rest of the turkey such as the head, neck, liver, and gizzard swam in the sauce for Mèt Féfé and Misyé Pyè to enjoy with slices of half-cooked yellow onions on top.

Right when Andrea was about to start making the sauce, she noticed she was out of fresh thyme and sent Erèz to the flea market to fetch some. Of course, being Saint Louis Day, there were hardly any vendors at the flea market, even though it was on a Monday that year. Vendors from the countryside didn't travel to the city, and that made it harder for Erèz to acquire the fresh thyme Andrea needed. She wandered around the flea market wishing one of the few vendors would have some thyme, but she had no luck finding it.

After an hour and a half of diligent but fruitless searching, Erèz decided to return to the house. On her way back to the house, she heard the bells of the Saint Louis Cathedral ringing loudly, indicating mass was over. Everyone who had attended mass would now be lining up in front of the church, getting ready for the church's procession around the city. As she dragged her feet in Sherline's old flip-flops, she spotted Madame and her family across the street in their best Saint Louis Day attire.

She didn't dare glance in their direction for longer than a moment, but she was extremely curious to catch a good glimpse of Man Mona. She couldn't stop herself from peering at them. As she did, Madame's eyes locked right on hers. Startled and terrified, she quickly turned around knowing what might be reserved for her later on as a punishment. Adrenaline pumped through her body, and she sped back to the house as swiftly as her feet could carry her in those oversized flip-flops. No one said a word as they noticed her jump and shuffle off back toward Mònn Jibilé. She knew she was in a world of trouble, but hoped that perhaps on this special day Madame's heart would soften. After all, she had just attended mass to pray to the patron saint of the city of Jérémie.

On her desperate rush back, she also noticed Marianne, who was all dressed-up with her fresh curls showing from underneath the brim of her little white hat. A shiny blue ribbon decorated with delicate little flowers wrapped around the crown of the hat to meet in a giant bow. Marianne was holding her regular little church purse and wore a pair of gleaming black shoes that must have been bought just for today. Marianne walked closely behind Misyé and Man Jan, indicating she still held the restavèk rank instead of that of a legitimate child. In other situations, this would likely have been a painful emotional reminder for any little restavèk that they were unequal and unloved; however, Marianne was grateful for all her good fortune with her loving family and walking a few paces behind was a small price to pay.

As she continued her walk, Erèz thought about how Man Jan loved fixing Marianne's hair. Sometimes she braided it. Other times, she twisted her hair right after washing it with imported pouches full of fragrant shampoo. Erèz always admired how beautiful and healthy Marianne's hair looked, always well-oiled and perfectly parted. Erèz wished someone cared enough to buy her pomades and oils for her bushy and long wavy hair.

Erèz and Marianne made eye contact, and secretly greeted each other without saying a word. Erèz turned her head right back toward the house fearing that staring too long in Marianne's direction would raise suspicion about her close friendship with Marianne. Unfortunately, Madame took notice as she was following her closely with her eyes. When Erèz got to the front porch, she rushed straight through the hall to the back door. Andrea greeted her with surprise. "I thought you were lost. What happened?"

Erèz responded by telling her there wasn't much happening at the flea market and that the few vendors who showed up were not selling thyme. Andrea was disappointed that she would be unable to cook the bean and Creole turkey sauces without the fresh herby flavor she was looking to create, but knowing way too well that it was not Erèz's fault, Andrea only responded with, "I hope Madame didn't see you." Erèz remained quiet, knowing that Madame had in fact seen her and that she was likely in for an unpleasant scolding on Saint Louis Day.

The group announced their arrival before Andrea or Erèz even laid eyes on them. Man Mona was laughing almost hysterically while trying to explain something in her mixture of French and Creole, and her perfume once again filled the house as if she'd never left.

Andrea had prepared a pot filled with clean water, a bar of hand soap, and a clean white towel in a corner of the living room for everyone to wash and dry their hands with when they got back from mass. One by one they poured water over each other's hands above the white enamel bucket. They had chosen to skip the church's procession around the city under the hot August sun. They were determined that attending mass and participating in the Eucharist were good enough Christian deeds on this Saint Louis Day. After Madame had washed her hands, she excused herself to Man Mona and Misyé Pyè and headed to the kitchen. She spied Erèz crushing boiled beans in a small pot for Andrea's bean stew.

From behind, Madame yanked Erèz by her left ear, whipped her around harshly, and said in Creole, "Did the spirits of Guinaudée send you for me?" Erèz stared at Madame in shock with her mouth wide open as her ear was pinched even tighter to inflict as much pain as Madame's strength allowed. As if that wasn't enough, Madame dragged her away and slammed her head several times against the kitchen wall.

Erèz knew Madame expected her to stifle her tears or cries, but Erèz was unable to do so under the prolonged beating. Madame became further infuriated as Erèz's crying was loud enough for the entire neighborhood to hear. Erèz's sobbing embarrassed her as it didn't fit with the image she liked to portray as a refined aristocratic woman. Moreover, Madame had no desire for Man Mona and Misyé Pyè to think differently of her. She clamped her hand over Erèz's mouth to quiet her, but Erèz was sobbing too uncontrollably from the pain and fear to be silenced. There was nothing Madame could do to hide those screams from anyone in the house or in the neighborhood.

Man Mona, overhearing what was happening, cringed a bit and awkwardly mentioned to Mèt Féfé that she didn't know that Man Féfé had a little girl servant. Mèt Féfé nodded in the affirmative, but didn't elaborate about Erèz out of the sheer embarrassment and shame that his wife brought upon all of them by beating the girl on such a holy day. Mèt Féfé stewed silently, knowing he would never be able to convince his wife to stop raging on the child and to instead enjoy the day with family in peace.

Marianne, who was outside playing when the screaming started, ran. Marianne had heard Erèz shriek and cry a few times before from her house, but that time in the middle of the day after mass seemed to be much worse than what she was used to hearing. Almost instinctively, she ran to see what was happening to the little girl she called her best friend, rushing through the hall on the side of the house. Madame clutched Erèz by the hair and covered her mouth with her hand as Erèz's entire body shook. Marianne stood there, peeking through the small window of the kitchen, shocked. Marianne knew that even though she was just a restavèk, she couldn't stand idle and that even though Madame was terrifying, Marianne couldn't stand to witness what was happening. Her eyes filled with tears against herself at the sight, and she mustered up all her courage she could and took it upon herself to shout in the most defiant tone she could manage, "Man Féfé, today is Saint Louis Day! Stop it! Stop it!"

Those simple but blunt words seemed to take hold of Man Féfé so much so that she let go of Erèz's hair. She glared at Marianne, but didn't say a word to her for fear her guests would step out to also reprimand her for her behavior on this Saint Louis Day. Man Féfé headed right back to the living room, leaving Marianne to console

Erèz on the ground. Erèz continued to cry as the bump on her head from the numerous times Madame had bashed her grew bigger and bigger in minutes.

Man Mona asked about the little girl servant in Creole, but that question from Man Mona only made Madame angrier and further fueled her wrath. Man Mona, not wanting to contribute to any more violence or commotion on a holy day excused herself saying, "I am going to take a nap. I need to stretch out my legs after being on these high-heels all morning." Man Féfé nodded absentmindedly in agreement as she sat at the table lost in thoughts of how she'd made a fool out of herself on Saint Louis Day.

In Madame's fantasy world where she saw herself as an aristocrat of the highest order, everything revolved around her and the image she wished to maintain. As long as she could portray and project the image of being part of the elite in town and living a high-class lifestyle, nothing else mattered to her. As a very light-skinned mulatto, she had a tacit badge of acceptance among the city's elite, and she would fight at all costs to keep that approval.

Outside, Andrea kept repeating in hushed tones, "Oh my God! Oh my God! Oh my God!" She was in a fair amount of shock from seeing Erèz so savagely beaten. And for what? For running an errand where Madame could catch sight of her? Andrea didn't say a word, but frantically continued cooking so she could serve dinner on time. She wanted no part in enraging Madame further.

CHAPTER 39
Concert

The tone at the dinner table was rather dejected after Madame's fiasco earlier. Misyé Pyè tried to get Mèt Féfé to engage in a conversation about the American family down the road, but Féfé looked preoccupied on a day when he should be happy. Mèt Féfé always expressed his feelings about how he couldn't wait to see them disappear from the city and go back to the United States where they belonged. Misyé Pyè knew well that Mèt Féfé saw them as the constant sour reminder of French colonialism still present on the street and in the city, but even the mention of the Williams family couldn't elicit a response from Mèt Féfé. He clearly remained troubled over his wife's violent outburst on the little servant Erèz.

"Mother," interrupted Julianne, "did you tell everyone that I am going to marry nurse Sonsonn?"

Man Mona played along, "Oh, no, I forgot my darling. You only just told us, and it slipped my mind among the festivities."

At that Julianne shot up from her chair, angrily tossed her napkin onto her plate and shouted, "How could you forget something like that, Mother?"

At that point, everyone at the table was trying not to laugh while keeping their eyes lowered to their plates in an attempt to avoid attention from Julianne. They knew if they interfered, they would be targets all night as well. In order to maintain peace for themselves, they allowed Man Mona to take the brunt of Julianne's anger and indignation all by herself.

In the backyard, Andrea, Bòs Cyprien, and Erèz ate their dinner silently, unable to lighten the mood due to the fact that Erèz remained in excruciating pain. Andrea warmed up water with salt to set on Erèz's swollen forehead. That seemed to have helped as the swelling had decreased, and the area appeared to be less inflamed. Andrea had grown so tired of the way Madame treated her little restavèks and especially Erèz. She knew she had to stay in order to feed her family, but she also knew she needed to find a better employment situation soon.

The afternoon continued free of disturbance as everyone retired to their respective rooms to rest and freshen up for the evening concert. Andrea and Erèz silently did the dishes, and Bòs Cyprien climbed the mango tree in the back to watch people as they went to and from the cathedral wearing their best attire for Saint Louis Day.

After Andrea left for the night, the house grew even quieter. Bòs Cyprien's occasional passing conversations with people on the road were the only sounds that interrupted the silence. Erèz remained in the backyard, but didn't bother to shower. She didn't have the strength or energy to care about being clean as the weight of all the injustice and humiliation pressed heavily on her young soul.

Eventually, the two little girls to the right side of the house started jumping rope. Unknown to them, their voices, laughs, and their simple presence brought so much joy to Erèz's defeated heart and soul and battered body. The girls knew Erèz couldn't join them for their games because she belonged to the restavèk rank of social class, but they were kind to her and would sometimes secretly wave or smile at her. They knew they couldn't interact with Erèz in an obvious manner for fear their parents would not even allow them to play in the backyard anymore.

The house woke up as everyone started getting ready for the concert happening in just a few hours. Before they even made it downstairs, Man Mona's floral-scented perfume traveled all the way to the backyard as usual, and that amused Erèz even in her current miserable state. They headed out toward Hotel Lamarre in Bordes for the concert, leaving Erèz in the same spot she'd sat for hours now. At one point, Erèz leaned her back against the wall and just stared into the dusk, listening to the sounds of chirping crickets and various songbirds serenading the evening away. Her first Saint Louis celebration in Jérémie left a very sour taste in her entire being. She went to bed feeling very depressed, without eating supper that night or even saying good night to Bòs Cyprien.

When Man Mona, Man Féfé, Misyé Pyè, and Mèt Féfé arrived at the hotel for the concert with their children, they were all greeted by the most esteemed members of the aristocratic class of Jérémie. The women and girls wore skin-toned tights underneath their long dresses as all respectable ladies did. Man Féfé and Man Mona also wore elaborately styled wigs. Their elegant shawls were decked with delicately hand-placed pearls all around the edges. It was quite the elegant flair.

Man Mona had brought the shawls from France and gifted one to Man Féfé. They engaged in conversations with other reputable ladies in town as Exavier and the girls grouped with their friends.

Mèt Féfé and Misyé Pyè immediately acquired stiff drinks and took a spot next to the main entrance scanning the general audience. Other concert goers and friends stopped by to greet them, and they conversed casually about de tout et de rien (random subjects and anything).

When Nurse Sonsonn walked in with his fiancé, Magdala, Misyé Pyè feared it wasn't going to be the best of nights for his daughter. Nurse Sonsonn introduced his fiancé to Misyé Pyè, and Misyé Pyè thanked him for taking such good care of his daughter. He light-heartedly teased Nurse Sonsonn's fiancé about how Julianne was also getting ready to marry her fiancé. She laughed heartily, but was otherwise very reserved as all well-behaved single ladies were. Magdala had obtained her PhD in psychology in Bordeaux, France. The pair had met at the clinic where they both worked, and the courtship started almost immediately. Because they worked at opposite ends of the building and in different departments, it never caught anyone's attention that they were in a serious relationship, let alone newly engaged. The night went fairly smoothly for the family. The presence of some of the town's political representatives annoyed Mèt Féfé, and he decided he was not going to mingle much.

When Ludovic Lamothe finally appeared on the stage, the room stopped to applaud him in awe. He took several deep bows and located his place at the piano. As expected, he played pieces by Frederic Chopin, but then the real performance began when he played his own pieces such as *Nibo, La Dangereuse,* and *Lisette.* Man Féfé and Man Mona made their way through the crowd to find Mèt Féfé and Misyé Pyè for their first dance. They danced for as long as the music lasted, and the men immediately returned to their former location. None of them gave much thought to their children dancing with the opposite sex, thinking they were just happy to be out with classmates they hadn't seen since school let out in June. That was the most freedom the kids had enjoyed with their paramours in their parents' presence. They remained careful not to be too brazen or to raise any suspicion that would negatively affect their ability to interact with each other in the future.

Despite Nurse Sonsonn's best efforts, he was unable to avoid running into Julianne. He introduced his fiancé Magdala as his cousin to avoid any sort of outburst on Julianne's part. Julianne attempted to hold his hand upon seeing him, but Sonsonn told her they needed to maintain their love relationship a low profile for now.

"Sonsonn, you must tell my mother of our engagement. She has to hear it from you before she goes back to France," Julianne said as she proceeded to grab Nurse Sonsonn's hands and drag him through the crowd looking for Man Mona.

Man Mona smiled wistfully as her daughter beamed and blushed from sheer excitement as she introduced Nurse Sonsonn, not as the medical professional who cared for her, but as her soon-to-be husband. Man Mona gave Sonsonn a knowing look, and played along, and Nurse Sonsonn let loose half a smile and wondered about what he could possibly do to put a stop to that farce.

As the night wore on, people stepped outside to breathe some fresh air and continue their conversations in a cooler environment. The heat generated from their moving bodies dancing had made the place unbearably warm in that mid-August heat. Exavier and Carline cleverly took advantage of that moment away from the adults. They remained inside, finding corners to sneak kisses with their lovers, vowing their love to each other, and whatever else young lovers their age did.

When Mèt Féfé and Misyé Pyè stepped back inside, they were surprised to see Man Féfé at the piano performing *J'ai Deux Amours* with Ludovic Lamothe. She sang loudly, projecting her surprisingly beautiful voice across the room hitting all the notes perfectly. That performance alongside the renowned Ludovic Lamothe earned her a new wave of respect and admiration from all the high-ranking citizens present that night.

CHAPTER 40
Mother

The days passed quickly and rather uneventfully for the rest of Man Mona and Misyé Pyè's stay. As was their custom for every visit, they made sure to slip tightly folded money to both Andrea and Bòs Cyprien before their departure.

Andrea wanted to give some of that money to Erèz, but she needed to get Madame's approval first. If Madame were to ever find the money given to Erèz, she would no doubt think Erèz had stolen it from her. Andrea didn't even want to think about the kind of beating that would result from that. To Andrea's surprise, Madame gave her the permission she sought. Andrea then gave Erèz one gourde all to herself. Erèz was overcome with joy and promised herself she was going to save that money to give to her mother when she visited in October.

Before Erèz knew it, it was the first Saturday of October and her mother finally traveled from Guinaudée for a visit. Erèz's mother appeared to be quite unhappy despite the smile she wore upon seeing her daughter. The weight of poverty in the village of Guinaudée left its marks on her face in a very visible way. Erèz couldn't help but notice how pale and sickly her mother had become in just a few months. Out of respect, Erèz didn't ask her mother any questions, although she worried for her.

Madame didn't bother to step out in the backyard to greet Erèz's mother until a good two hours after her arrival. Of course, she acted that way intentionally to show how little she thought of her as a peasant.

"How are you, sister?" said Madame nonchalantly in Creole. She made sure to use "sò" instead of "sè," the proper Creole translation of the word "sister," in order to mimic peasants' sisterhood greetings. Madame quickly went on to explain how Erèz had disrespected her multiple times and how she was strongly considering sending her back to Guinaudée.

Madame didn't have much else to say and didn't even bother to ask about life in Guinaudée or the rest of her family. In fact, all she could focus on was how much she wished Erèz's mother would administer a satisfying thrashing to Erèz for having been so disrespectful to her. Erèz's mother didn't respond to the accusations. She knew how Madame her cousin exaggerated facts whenever it suited her and her inflated ego. Sadly, Erèz's mother also knew that she couldn't take Erèz's side either. She feared Madame her cousin would ask her to take Erèz back to Guinaudée with her, right then and there. Knowing she couldn't afford caring for her baby girl, Erèz's mother remained silent, pondering on how she was going to encourage Erèz to be a better girl for Madame so that she could finally be sent to school to learn how to read and write like she had always wanted.

Erèz feared she was in trouble with her mother, but as soon as Madame turned on her heels leaving wordlessly, Erèz saw the look in her mother's eyes and knew that she wasn't in trouble at all. Erèz's mother rubbed her hand gently over Erèz's head as she playfully pulled on her thick braids, and at one point, she said, "Guinaudée doesn't offer us much and you know that way too well. Try to do better, fanm mwen!"

That was the first time Man Renise referred to Erèz as "my woman." Erèz nodded silently in agreement that she would try to be better, all the while knowing there was truly nothing she could do to stop Madame or Sherline or anyone else in the house from abusing her violently for the slightest mishap.

With a smile, her mother said, "Meat is growing on your bones, fanm mwen!"

Erèz asked her mother to wait for her as she'd saved her a gift. She quickly went to the dark little room where she slept amongst the sacks of charcoal and the crickets that roamed at night. She'd been waiting for that moment for a long time, and Erèz eagerly pulled the one gourde that Andrea had given her two months ago from where she'd hidden it among the soot. She came back with her hand tightly gripped around the gourde. Erèz smiled proudly as she handed it to her mother. Her mother smiled from ear to ear looking at the gourde and was hugely grateful that Erèz thought of her and saved her the money instead of spending it on herself.

"Thank you, my daughter," she said proudly. Hearing the love and pride in her mother's voice was all the gratification Erèz needed and had been looking for the past two months since she'd received the money.

Erèz asked about everyone in the neighborhood in Guinaudée including her best friend Marie-Jeanne and little Patrick. She released the widest smile when she inquired about the angry chicken that chased her up and down the yard and traumatized her so many times.

Erèz's mother updated Erèz on all that was happening back home. One of the most exciting tidings was that Benjamin's parents came to the house to officially ask for Yaya's betrothal to him. As Benjamin was a good and respectable young man in the village with a bright future, neither she nor Erèz's father objected to the relationship. Yes, Yaya would definitely have a good future with Benjamin. Man Renise continued to tell Erèz that the clergy of Saint Peter's church also approved of Yaya and Benjamin's relationship and that arrangements for their wedding were underway. The happy event was to take place in July around the Saint Peter Day celebration. This was exciting news as Saint Peter's celebration in Guinaudée was as festive as Saint Louis Day.

Erèz remembered Benjamin as a very quiet young man, always pensive as if he was studying thoughts and ideas in his mind that he wanted no one to know about but himself. He always wore a suit to mass on Sundays, alternating between the only two he owned, the brown one this Sunday and the black one the following Sunday. He wore the same pair of shoes, tie, and shirt underneath both suit colors, but he earned much of his regard by the way he treated everyone around him with dignity and respect. His tireless and successful work as a bush doctor, helping parents of small children suffering with worms, malaria, and typhoid also ensured that the townspeople greatly revered Benjamin.

When Benjamin graduated middle school, his parents couldn't afford to send him to the city of Jérémie to pursue higher education and attend high school. Regardless, the blessing of his natural intelligence along with the ability to read allowed him to pursue natural healing in a community where medical care was scarce and almost nonexistent. In very little time, he'd become highly sought after for his herbalism skills and knowledge of natural medicine. During the American occupation, impromptu clinics popped up in the yard of the Saint Peter Church to treat people around Guinaudée and the surrounding little villages. Benjamin was a fixture at these pop-ups where he not only helped heal, but also acquired more knowledge to aid his village.

Erèz chuckled to herself thinking how different Yaya and Benjamin were in so many ways. Yaya was outgoing and outspoken, faithfully led worship at mass, sang in the choir, and led youth ministry. Benjamin, on the other hand, clammed up when he was around too many people, retreated into his shell, and remained quiet. Really, Yaya was the yin to Benjamin's yang, with his calm demeanor and stern composure.

Erèz's shiny brown eyes lit up at the news of the impending nuptials and asked her mother to ask Madame's permission to attend the wedding. As much as her mother wished to have her in attendance, she was too fearful that Madame would respond by saying that if she traveled back to Guinaudée with Erèz, she might as well go ahead and keep her there forever. Erèz was heartbroken when her mother denied the request, but as was generally the case in her current life, there was nothing she could do.

As Erèz and her mother continued to talk, Andrea came down the stairs and handed a cup of hot coffee and a leftover breakfast roll to Man Renise, who was incredibly grateful. She ate the bread roll and enjoyed every sip of the freshly made coffee. She remained only a little while after eating, knowing she couldn't keep Erèz from her tasks all day. She left quietly without formally excusing herself with Madame. Man Renise stood up and affectionately said, "I am leaving, fanm mwen," reiterating to Erèz that she was her big girl now. Tears rolled down both of Erèz's cheeks and she wiped them right away as best as she could, but she knew her mother wanted her to be strong and didn't appreciate her displaying so much sadness. In truth, Erèz buried a lot of emotions and experiences that she would never recount to her mother. Man Renise couldn't help but notice the tears, and she tried reassuring Erèz by saying, "Don't cry, fanm mwen! I'll come back for the festivities!" She was of course referring to Christmas and New Year, but that all seemed so far away to Erèz.

CHAPTER 41
Time

The Monday after her mother left was back-to-school day for the city of Jérémie. Not for Erèz. Instead, she was sent to purchase fresh bread from Madan Dikrépen for Madame's kids' breakfast before they headed to school wearing their brand new uniforms, socks, and shoes. On her way to get bread, she saw happy parents were already going down the hill holding their smiling children's hands. She stared at the freshly pleated skirts, shorts, knee-high socks, and hats. Most every family attended the early mass at the Cathedral of Saint Louis to pray for God's and the Saints' blessings over their children and the new school year.

Erèz was mesmerized with all the well-behaved children her age holding their mothers' hands or skipping gleefully in front of their parents. She still longed for the day when she'd be sent to school. One day, she imagined, she could be just like those children. In another life, perhaps. It definitely didn't seem to be in this life where she was relegated to spending all her time scrubbing pots and floors while wearing oversized hand-me-downs.

Going to Madan Dikrépen's house to buy bread for breakfast became her favorite thing to do. When school reopened in January after the Christmas break, the well-dressed schoolchildren walked down the hill to school alone, and some of them behaved in a friendly manner toward Erèz. Although both Erèz and the students knew they couldn't interact much due to her restavèk status, they still had some tacit exchanges that helped carry Erèz through her day. The kind-hearted kids would shyly smile at Erèz before looking away. Sometimes they would offer her a sneaky small wave. Of course, others brandished closed fists at her to let her know that one of those mornings she would get a pounding if she insisted on staring at them. Erèz knew to turn her eyes away immediately from the group of mean-spirited students who made sure she exactly understood how they felt about her.

On one of those days in January when Erèz was on her way back from buying bread, a sweet little girl named Josiane met Erèz. She smiled at her and handed her a fabric baby doll. Josiane was with her mother, and Erèz understood her mother must have approved of the gift, but she also knew by accepting the gift that there would be problems with Madame. She knew Madame would beat her within an inch of her life if she was caught playing with a baby doll of unknown origin.

Erèz looked down sadly and shook her head no. Josiane and her mother respected Erèz's decision, and they continued to always act kindly toward her every morning. One day not long after, Josiane asked her in Creole, "What's your name?"

"Erèz" She responded.

"Well, then my baby doll will be named Erèz," said Josiane brightly. This caused Erèz to smile from ear to ear and she felt joyful for the rest of that day.

In December of that year, Erèz's mother didn't make it to the city to visit Erèz. Her father came in her place, bringing fresh loads of farm vegetables, avocados, sugar cane chunks, oranges, and African yams. He also brought the unfortunate news that Erèz's mother wasn't feeling very well.

The news of Man Renise being sick of course saddened Erèz, but she was very happy to see her father for the first time in six months. Madame didn't come out to greet Erèz's father, but that didn't bother him. He was well aware of exactly how she acted toward family members from the countryside. A cup of hot coffee from Andrea and a warm bread roll always helped erase the painful sting of humiliation that people faced when around that house. As Erèz spoke with her father, she held on to just a glimmer of hope that she could head back to Guinaudée with him, but she knew deep down that wasn't an option. She knew that any pleading or begging on her part to her father to go see her mother would be shut down. She could almost hear him telling her that she had it good in the city and to appreciate how much better off she was here than in the village of Guinaudée.

Andrea carried the fresh provisions little by little upstairs to the kitchen, and not too long after that Erèz's father left for home. He promised that her mother planned on coming down to the city for Easter. Though she was sad to see him go, she didn't feel the same ache in her gut as she did when her mother left after her visit the last time.

Erèz's mother didn't come for a visit for Easter as expected. Then, neither of her parents came to visit or bring freshly harvested fruits and vegetables for the Saint Louis Day celebration that August. Erèz felt lost and abandoned in a world that seemed to hate her. Man Mona and Misyé Pyè returned from France for the Saint Louis Day festivities and the same chaotic energy filled the house as it did on their last visit. Not one incident surprised Erèz.

Time passed and yet another school year started that October. Erèz felt alone, but small things helped her make it through. Josiane still acted kindly toward her every morning and waved each time she had the opportunity to do so without attracting the attention of any-one who might frown upon her interacting with a low-class restavèk, including her classmates.

Erèz also still saw Marianne frequently enough. Marianne had started at the school for the restavèks, which was held for two hours in the afternoon. Sometimes on her way from buying ingredients for dinner, she met Marianne on their way back to the hill and conversed about what Marianne had learned that day. Marianne always wore her uniform while Erèz still stumbled around in Sherline's old yellow flip-flops, which now had holes at the bottom and didn't protect the soles of Erèz's feet.

Often, when Erèz was sent out later in the afternoon to buy ingredients, she'd greet Marianne by asking, "How are you doing?" Marianne seemed preoccupied some of the time and would reply that she was stressed from her studies and homework deadlines. Erèz let her be and wandered on her way in her half-broken sandals softly saying, "Okay, see you tomorrow."

CHAPTER 42
News

One day, two years later, Andrea and Erèz were out shopping for their usual ingredients at the flea market. At first, they thought it was their imagination when they heard someone calling Erèz's name.

"Is that Erèz? Is that Erèz?" Realizing it was not her imagination playing tricks on her, Erèz recognized her godmother's voice and turned around right away. Her godmother rushed toward her with tears rolling down her cheeks.

"How are you, pitit mwen?" Her godmother said, grabbing her close and holding tightly onto her. She then took a step back and noticed that Erèz had gotten taller since she had left Guinaudée. Her heavy curly hair was now shiny and had regained its dark color from proper nourishment in the city.

"Oh my goodness, pitit mwen, has no one given you the news?" Erèz's little heart raced. She knew the protocol of sharing bad news in the village of Guinaudée. Phrases such as that were generally to prepare the person for receiving heartbreaking information. It was to give them just a moment or two to brace their heart for the heavy blow that was to come.

"Your mother passed away six months ago, but we didn't know how to let you know because your father is also sick." Andrea stood there by Erèz's side, shocked to hear the news, and dismayed knowing there was now no chance she would ever go back to her family.

Meanwhile, Erèz felt the world darken and spin around her. The news had hit her entire being like a brick. Everything suddenly felt cold in her mind and soul. Her heart sank to the pit of her stomach and she could barely stand. Her godmother held her, crying as if she was reliving the funeral all over again. Her godmother cried especially loudly and even wanted to scream as was common in Haitian funerals to prove sadness and grief over the loss of a soul.

Erèz faced the ground stunned, and her godmother folded one gourde into her palm.

"Thank you, godmother," she muttered almost involuntarily. After a few more words, her godmother blessed her with a "May God be with you, my daughter." They parted ways, and Erèz silently followed Andrea with her head down. For once, she truly felt like the soulless zombie Madam always accused her of being. Erèz was inconsolable, and Andrea knew there was nothing to say to bring peace to her heartbroken little soul. Usually, Erèz would hold the straw bag for Andrea to add ingredients as they purchased them, but after such horrific news, Andrea carried the bag on her own, feeling that was the least she could do on such a terrible day in Erèz's life.

Tears rolled down Erèz's cheeks nonstop on the entire way home. As soon as Andrea got to the house, she looked for Madame, who was taking her mid-morning nap. When Andrea knocked at the door she heard her move, but she didn't want to open the door without Madame inviting her in. Andrea heard the shuffling of her bed sheets and then complete silence. She waited for a few minutes and hesitated before knocking again.

Madame's voice erupted loudly startling Andrea, "What do you need? Come in!" On that order, Andrea pushed the door and unhooked the latch from the outside to enter. Madame's eyes were red and her hair was a wild mess framing her face. For the past eight years that Andrea had been a servant at Madame's house, she'd never seen Madame in such a state.

"Are you okay, Madame?"

Madame brushed off her question asking, "What's going on? What do you want?"

Andrea proceeded to tell her that Erèz's mother had passed away six months ago.

"We found out at the flea market just now. Erèz is inconsolable and I wanted to let you know," Andrea said gravely. Madame looked at Andrea with great disdain before saying, "Is this the reason you chose to disturb me?" Madame noticed the shock that came over Andrea's face at this response and continued, "She has food, a place to shower, and a place to sleep. She'll get over it."

Andrea couldn't believe her ears. She thought even Madame couldn't be so heartless in light of such tragic news. Andrea turned around without saying a word.

A month later, Madame was still spending much time in her room. She had been feeling lethargic, suffering from headaches, and she was urinating often. She didn't come downstairs nearly as often as she used to. Sometimes, she still came down to eat with everyone, but other days Andrea brought her food upstairs and a plate that she barely touched.

Madame was losing weight quickly, and Mèt Féfé gathered every ounce of courage to talk to his stubborn wife about bringing Doctor Emile into the house for a consultation before her health deteriorated completely. Much to his surprise, Madame agreed.

Doctor Emile examined Madame and studied her symptoms and he came to the conclusion that she was diabetic. She was ordered to cut out the intake of coffee, refined grains, bread, and processed sugars.

During the three-month roller coaster with Madame's health, Erèz had time to grieve the passing of her mother in relative peace. For many nights, it was difficult to fall asleep. She kept waking up thinking she heard her mother's voice calling her or talking to her. At one point, she thought she felt her mother's body lying next to her on the thin bed sheet she slept on. Erèz was convinced that she could feel the warmth of her body and smell her familiar scent. The sensations in the middle of the night were all so vivid and too real to be fake. When the rooster crowed, she was often relieved to finally wake up. Seeing her mother in her dreams and feeling her presence did not comfort her, but rather filled her being with a sense of dread, loss, despair, and anguish. Those nightmares persisted for at least a year after learning of her mother's passing, and she did her best to process the sense of abandonment that plagued her in her dreams and waking life. It didn't help that her father, perhaps due to his own ailments, never came to visit. Fortunately, Erèz often bumped into her godmother at the flea market, and she always greeted her with the widest and most sincere smile on her face and a "How are you, pitit mwen?"

Her godmother lovingly touched her long thick hair which was often tangled because she rarely combed and washed her hair, let alone greased her scalp with lwil maskréti, Haitian castor oil. She couldn't help but notice that day that Erèz's beautiful curly black hair was in need of a wash, detangling, and rebraiding, and that her scalp needed to be moisturized.

On a similar occasion, her godmother said to her, "I saw you have breasts?" Erèz was unable to respond, but simply smiled out of embarrassment knowing Andrea stood right there as well as other vendors who could hear everything her godmother was telling her.

Erèz's godmother closed her right hand over one gourde and spoke the usual blessing over her, "May God be with you, pitit mwen!"

Every Saturday, Erèz wished and hoped to bump into her godmother at the spot she usually occupied to sell her goods. Her godmother was the only one she saw regularly from the people back home who meant the most to her. Sometimes, Erèz's godmother brought Ti Roro down with her, but Erèz and he didn't interact much outside of casual hellos, waves, and smiles.

CHAPTER 43
Alone

When Erèz turned twelve, four years after she arrived at Madame's house, Andrea quit working for Madame. It was the last day of August, just four days after the Saint Louis celebration.

During dinner on the Sunday prior to her quitting, she shared the secret with Bòs Cyprien and Erèz that the following week would be her last. Bòs Cyprien and Erèz were both shocked. Erèz, who saw Andrea as a mother figure, was devastated by that news. Tears streamed down her cheeks, and Andrea tried to comfort her by saying they would still see each other around the city or at the flea market. Andrea went on to share that she had found a job at the house of a Haitian lieutenant that paid double her current salary. Bòs Cyprien was happy for her and tried to lighten the bittersweet mood by joking that she was leaving before he found her a boyfriend. As usual, he was able to make Andrea and Erèz laugh.

Madame had no clue that Andrea had found new employment and would soon be gone, but she continued treating her the same as always by bossing her around, threatening to fire her at any occasion, and complaining about anything that bothered her around the house. In turn, Andrea also behaved as she always did with Madame.

"Wi, Madam," was always her response, but each time, she privately celebrated her victory of having found herself in a much better situation at the lieutenant's house.

Madame was completely blindsided when, upon receiving her twenty-dollar monthly salary, Andrea said to her with her head facing the floor, not knowing how best to deliver the news to her, "Today is my last day, Madame."

Madame was dumbfounded for a moment and couldn't hide the shock from her face as she said, "It's just now that you're letting me know?"

Man Mona and Misyé Pyè had not yet left for Paris, and when Madame told them the news. Man Mona rushed to the kitchen to convince Andrea not to quit. Of course, it was useless as Andrea had been desperately trying to get away from Madame for years. She humbly replied, "Non, Man Mona." Man Mona and Misyé Pyè gave her the biggest tip they ever had, knowing how much they'd enjoyed her cuisine and the respectful way that Andrea had attended to them whenever they visited. Andrea gave five gourdes to Erèz, who nearly jumped for joy despite her heartbreak on Andrea's last day.

To Bòs Cyprien and Erèz's surprise, Madame decided that Erèz could replace Andrea instead of hiring a grown woman to run the house. Perhaps it shouldn't have been a huge shock, as Madame was saving herself twenty dollars a month by not hiring an adult who knew her way around the kitchen. Erèz tried the best that she could, but the six months that followed Andrea's departure were a complete nightmare for her.

She had never made any of the family's meals on her own while Andrea was still working for Madame and had only helped Andrea with parts of the cooking process. The food that Erèz cooked during those first few months was always found lacking in flavor in some way: too salty, tasteless, dry, stringy, and so on, and because she cooked three meals a day, she was beaten multiple times a day each time Madame was unhappy. Madame asked Mèt Féfé's friends, Mèt Lemaire and Mèt Eric, to stop coming on Sundays because the food quality had become so poor and flavorless. Madame told Erèz she had better figure herself out, or she could pack up and go back to Guinaudée. Erèz was losing sleep over the threats and wondering how she could possibly improve her cooking to please Madame. Did Madame not understand that Andrea had formal culinary training and that she was a twelve-year-old who barely had enough kitchen experience to put together a simple meal? Madame's expectations were unreasonable, and Erèz was hoping and praying that all the saints she prayed to at Saint Peter's church in Guinaudée would miraculously teach her what she needed to know to please Madame and survive in this house.

By Easter the following year, Erèz's cooking had begun to improve. Her Easter dinner was a mashed palm heart, salted cod fish sauce, boiled beets, a green salad with lettuce and watercress, steamed white rice, white bean sauce, and chicken in Creole sauce. Everyone enjoyed that dinner greatly, but Madame was too proud and unkind to congratulate Erèz for a job well done. That was the first day since Andrea left that Erèz felt a heavy weight lift from her being. She breathed deeply relieved that at least tonight Madame wouldn't come to the kitchen and smash her head against the wall or strike her with her heel.

That night, like most nights, she fell asleep as soon as she sat at the bottom of the stairs at seven o'clock, right after serving dinner and prepping for the following day's breakfast. On the weekends, her non-stop schedule of prepping and cooking the Sunday dinner left her completely exhausted. It was all on her to prepare the bouyon, cook any other food, set the table, clear and wash the dishes, scrub the pots, and take all the dishes and pots back to the kitchen adjacent to the living room upstairs. Once she showered and had braided her hair, she would pass out the second her head laid on the roll of clothes she used as a pillow.

Doctor Emile continued coming to the house intermittently to monitor Man Féfé's blood sugar. The worst that could happen was for her to fall into a diabetic coma due to her blood sugar being too low or too high. From time to time, she felt lethargic and that was a sign that her blood sugar spiked. When that happened, Bòs Cyprien would be sent immediately to get Doctor Emile. With each of Doctor Emile's visits came a new bill, but Mèt Féfé could afford paying for each. Although there wasn't much love between him and his wife, and even though Man Féfé irritated him most of the time, he didn't like the idea of losing her. He didn't want to have to finish raising Sherline by himself, and their two other children were still somewhat dependent on both of them despite being young adults studying abroad after high school.

CHAPTER 44
Changes

Erèz continued to see her godmother at the maché over the years. Her already light interactions with Ti Roro began to change after she turned sixteen. In a subtle, but clear move, Ti Roro said to Erèz, "How are you doing, sister?"

The word "sister" was used politely to indicate that there was still a connection between them through his mother, her godmother. Yet there was also the understanding in that statement that he was now in a new class of educated citizens that she would never be part of due to her status as an illiterate restavèk. Erèz understood what Ti Roro meant and decided in her heart that due to her complexes of inferiority, she was going to distance herself from being too friendly to him the next time she bumped into him in the streets of Jérémie. Despite having lived in the city for the past eight years, there was still something very peasant-like about her demeanor that made her status very obvious.

Her godmother kept her up to date on Yaya's new family. She now had a son with Benjamin that they had named Roberto. Erèz wanted nothing more than to visit her sister to meet her nephew and spend some time holding and playing with him. She knew if she asked for Madame's permission to take a few days to see her family, she would be told to stay there forever and never come back. In reality, Madame feared that Erèz would not return if she left for a visit, but she didn't dare to be vulnerable in front of Erèz by showing her emotions. Madame would no longer have access to free labor and someone to abuse at will; therefore, she used manipulative tactics to keep Erèz from ever visiting Guinaudée.

Erèz and Marianne remained best friends. Marianne had grown into a beautiful teenager and had many boy restavèks from school chasing after her. Marianne paid them no mind and behaved wisely, listening to Man Jan and Mèt Jan's advice to focus on completing her schooling before entering into any kind of romantic relationship with boys. Marianne eventually graduated from school and went on to pursue culinary training and home economics so she could run her masters' house in their old age.

Julianne still visited regularly and spent the day with "ma tante Féfé" as she called Madame. Her fantasies about Nurse Sonsonn continued, and she often cried to Madame about their imaginary lovers' quarrels. One day, Julianne arrived at the house sobbing, with tears streaming down her pretty face. She was completely inconsolable, telling Madame that Nurse Sonsonn had broken up with her. Man Féfé didn't know quite what to say. In truth, she was the one who had initiated a conversation with him a couple days prior, suggesting that the faux relationship caused more psychological damage to the girl than helped her. Nurse Sonsonn was in agreement and decided to finally put an end to the charade once and for all.

Bòs Cyprien's mother died and that took a heavy toll on him. After her passing, he went to Calas and stayed for an entire week. He was never quite the same after he came back. He definitely didn't act as jovial as he used to be, which was understandable. The dinners in the backyard had quieted. Boss Cyprien ceased telling jokes, and Andrea was no longer there for him to flirt with or tease. He was often lost in his thoughts throughout the day. It pained him that he had wanted to do so much for his mother before she passed, but never was able to save enough money to make her happy in her last years of life.

Moreover, his paralyzed son no longer had a caretaker. Bòs Cyprien hired a woman he once courted in his youth named Rosemarie to care for him. He would send her money through the merchants heading to Calas after a long day at the flea market under the hot sun.

Erèz soon found herself fending off constant sexual advances from the sixty-five year old Bòs Cyprien. Erèz, at sixteen, had only ever seen him as a father figure. Now, he often made inappropriate implicit sexual comments about how beautiful she was and how much he admired her perky little breasts. Unknown to Erèz, the lecherous man even discovered a way to position himself through the entrance door of his room to stare at Erèz's naked body as she scrubbed herself behind the wooden latrine. Unfortunately, it was extremely common in the neighborhood for the gason who were responsible for the house upkeep to develop relationships, consensual or otherwise, with servants. The fact that many of them had spouses at home didn't matter.

Even at her young age, Erèz knew that Bòs Cyprien's attempts to coerce her was part of the quiet but acceptable way that society allowed men to sexually assault women. Erèz usually brushed off his unwanted sexual comments and lewd advances by mumbling curse words at him and removing herself from his vicinity when possible. Bòs Cyprien always laughed when he saw how uncomfortable Erèz became each time he made advances she had no interest in. Unfortunately, Bòs Cyprien was not the only man Erèz was forced to deal with in this manner at Madame's house.

CHAPTER 45
Misyé Noël

O n Friday nights, Mèt Féfé invited over his closest friends from around town. The group varied from seven to ten people in size, but two consistent regulars were Bòs Latou and Misyé Noël.

Bòs Latou was a mulatto mechanic with enough good looks and charm to seduce almost any woman he wanted. He proudly joked that he had lost count of how many children he had; that he was simply trying to fulfill God's command to go forth and multiply; and that he was well on his way to populating the Earth single-handedly.

Despite being a married man, he went about town having reckless sex, getting women pregnant, and then abandoning the majority of children he co-created. Mèt Féfé knew that when it came to the way he treated women Bòs Latou was a despicable man, but he had a child with Roseleine, one of Mèt Féfé's sisters. Roseleine's baby was one of the rare and lucky children that he actually assumed responsibility for by regularly providing Roseleine with money, food, and clothes for baby Isabelle. Roseleine was counted among the women he remained with long-term over the years. Sometimes, he slept at Roseleine's house and helped her with the baby. Other times, he stayed away for months at a time running around town exploring new sexual escapades. Roseleine still felt committed in her relationship with Bòs Latou despite knowing how much of a womanizer he was. Some of the women he was involved with somehow felt it was a badge of honor to be in the privileged group that he bounced around among to satisfy his sexual appetite.

Though most men knew to stay away from Bòs Latou's women, sometimes Bòs Latou found himself being the one cheated on by one of his many mistresses. If one of his women eventually engaged in love affairs with other men, he felt betrayed and his fragile ego was deflated. In such cases, he would go about publicly shaming and badmouthing the women, often by calling them whores and prostitutes. Still, Mèt Féfé embraced him as part of the family and Bòs Latou admired and respected Mèt Féfé. He always spoke highly of Mèt Féfé saying that he was an intriguing man with an enigmatic mind.

Misyé Noël was also a married man who was known to have extramarital affairs with several women in town, but he had a different energy and demeanor from Bòs Latou. He was a quiet man most of the time and more often than not looked pensive and lost in his own thoughts. He listened more than he talked. When conversations around the table became loud and heated and needed to be settled, the men always looked to Misyé Noël for his say. He would then offer his thoughts and considerations, and miraculously bring everybody into agreement. Misyé Noël's calculated interjections in conversations always contained well thought-out arguments, relevant facts, and a great deal of confidence that suggested he had done his research on the subject. He definitely commanded the respect of that semi-drunk Friday night circle.

On the other hand , the group debated Bòs Latou's interjections every time. It was very possible Bòs Latou had valuable inputs and opinions to share, but his bad-boy reputation stained whatever he had to say, and he was never taken very seriously by the group.

As the men entertained themselves over glasses of Barbancourt rum, Erèz mostly kept herself busy in the kitchen making malanga frites; frying hushpuppies, plantains, gryo (deep-fried pork) and making the men's all-time favorite, pikliz. The men usually harassed the seventeen-year-old Erèz right in front of Mèt Féfé. The more graphic and viler the sexual comments were, the louder everyone laughed. Erèz wished she could escape this demeaning environment full of filthy married men who constantly undressed her with their eyes and never kept their lascivious thoughts about her to themselves.

Erèz always kept her composure in spite of the revulsion and grief she felt over being objectified and degraded every Friday night. It didn't help that she'd become quite skilled at styling her hair in all sorts of attractive ways, and Madame always asked her to be extremely presentable and look her best for the men.

One Friday afternoon, the gathering took a turn for the unexpected worse when Madame addressed her for the first time in French. "Go wash yourself. Misyé Noël will be coming over this evening, and he will want you to massage his feet. I will cook for the men tonight."

What?? the bewildered Erèz exclaimed to herself. She had never seen Madame set foot in the kitchen since that Saturday years ago when she'd first come to Jérémie. Distressed, Erèz continued to wonder what exactly was going on. She knew she couldn't object because even at her age, Erèz still got her head slammed into the wall from time to time at Madame's whim.

Her heart started racing as she thought about it more. Why was Madame going to cook when she never cooked? Did she even know how to cook? Why wouldn't Misyé Noël have his wife massage his feet? Why was it so imperative that she wash herself in order to massage his feet? These questions rushed through her mind, and she knew none of the answers she fabricated worked in her favor. She washed herself like Madame requested, and Madame handed her a bright flowery dress that she had seen Carline wear before. This was absolutely not a dress Madame would ever offer to Erèz just for the heck of it.

Madame spoke French on and off with Erèz while also behaving in an extremely friendly manner around her. After living under her roof for close to ten years, Erèz understood most of what Madame implied in French, although she couldn't formulate French sentences to reply to what she was saying. Madame treated her that Friday like a daughter heading to her first dance with a boy. This terrified Erèz even more as she got the sense she was being prepared for something sinister.

The men showed up well-dressed as always that Friday night. Some arrived in their office work clothes, cotton sleeves rolled up for the casual gathering. Bòs Latou always brought a couple of bottles of Barbancourt rum with him, and tonight was no different. What was different was that they all had an odd ceremonious air about them unfamiliar to Erèz. Were they celebrating something? Clearly, they were all in on some secret that Erèz was not privy to.

With a curt "Messieurs," upon his arrival, Misyé Noël headed straight upstairs to the spare room where Man Mona and Misyé Pyè stayed when they vacationed. Some of the men smiled darkly and knowingly at each other, quietly acknowledging among themselves what they knew was about to happen between their man and the attractive young girl they all very openly lusted after. Unsurprisingly, Madame made a mess of the food that night, but Erèz couldn't comment on mistakes being made in front of her. Madame knew best after all. She signaled to Erèz that it was time to head upstairs to massage Misyé Noël's feet.

She said in an uncomfortably overly friendly tone while snapping her fingers, "Turn around," and Erèz did just that. Madame pulled an old necklace from her pocket and placed it carefully around Erèz's neck. She then whispered in Erèz's ear, "Go make Misyé Noël happy!"

Any doubt that existed in her mind about what was going on tonight evaporated. What was going to happen to her innocence suddenly seemed all too real and she couldn't defend herself. She was to be given to this man so that he could sexually abuse her as he'd always wanted.

Madame had been maliciously planning and arranging this crime with the silent approval of Mét Féfé for several months. Madame had even tracked Erèz's cycle to ensure she would not be bleeding the night of the act.

Erèz timidly headed upstairs, barely able to move one foot in front of the other as each foot suddenly weighed heavier than lead. She knocked at the door and heard the familiar voice of Misyé Noël. She detected undertones of violence and danger in his voice snarling from behind the door.

She walked in the room to find Misyé Noël lying on the bed topless with his pants still on. Erèz stood there paralyzed as she wished she didn't hear him. He said, "Come on, my daughter. Massage your father's feet."

Erèz closed her eyes and braced herself. After months of hearing the men's disgusting comments to her while attending to them and serving them food on Friday nights, she knew exactly what this loathsome man had in mind.

The music being played from the box radio downstairs drowned out any sound from upstairs that might have been heard by the men below. Eventually, the music faded through the night as the men started to depart one after another.

Madame counted that Erèz and Misyé Noël were in the room for a total of three hours. After, Erèz clutched the banister to stabilize herself as she slowly and painfully made her way down the stairs, Madame was sitting across the dining room table facing her direction, waiting for her. She noticed how Erèz's skinny legs trembled with every weak step she took. Blood dripped down from between Erèz's legs, staining and saturating the hand-me-down dress. Erèz clutched the folds of fabric to herself in an attempt to soothe the searing pain. When she managed to make it past the table, Madame pulled her around by her shoulders to face her, and Erèz diverted her eyes to stare past her as she whispered, "Bònn nwit, Good night."

Mèt Féfé sat in the living room listening to his favorite music in an effort to calm the sense of indignation he started feeling from having allowed this orchestrated rape to occur under his roof. The house went completely quiet afterward, and the only noise that interrupted the eerie silence was Misyé Noël's shoes clicking and echoing on the wooden stairs on his way to his room. He passed the dining room table as if he didn't notice seventeen-year-old Erèz's quivering, sobbing form laying on the thin sheet on the cold cement.

Erèz cried uncontrollably that night and slept with a fever, but the following day was bouyon day and there was no time to lament or process last night's events. Madame acted as though nothing heinous or unusual had happened between the walls of her house the night prior. At most, perhaps she and Erèz had shared a fleeting bad dream.

CHAPTER 46
A Visit

From the suffering of the night before that transformed Erèz's body into that of a woman, the morning started against her will with the smell of Misyé Noël's heavy perfume haunting her. She went about her business with the usual chores around the house and brushed off the idea of interacting with Madame during the day.

Every Saturday since the death of poor Man Nini, Erèz hand-washed everyone's clothes in the afternoon and ironed them using the charcoal-filled iron. Between doing the laundry and cooking the bouyon, she barely had time to breathe. She was jumping back and forth between stirring the pot, scrubbing the clothes, rinsing them, and so on. She carefully managed her time and efforts so that everything ran smoothly, but it was no easy task.

She was just in the middle of stirring the bouyon pot, when she heard someone knocking at the front door. The knock sounded peculiar. She wondered who could possibly be knocking at the door on a Saturday at eleven o'clock in the morning when the person should be busy straightening their own house. The knock persisted, and she reluctantly interrupted her work flow to go answer the door. As always, Sherline was back in bed at this time for her post-breakfast nap. Erèz couldn't expect her to disturb her sleep, walk downstairs, and see who was at the door. As Erèz tiptoed on the freshly scrubbed floor to get to the door, the knocks grew more impatient. She opened the door to her immense surprise and joy on Yaya, Benjamin, and little five-year-old Roberto.

Erèz was overjoyed and literally exhaled, "What a shock!" Yaya smiled brightly from ear to ear upon seeing her sister, but also immediately noticed Erèz's red swollen eyes and the tear stains from the hours Erèz had spent crying from what had happened to her the previous night. They embraced and held each other's hands tightly.

Benjamin remained quiet as always and looked very proud and happy with a satisfied smile on his handsome face. He had finally been able to make his wife's dream come true by making the journey from Guinaudée to the city of Jérémie to see her sister.

Yaya, sensing that something was wrong with Erèz, stared at her, scrutinizing her body from head to toes, and relentlessly said in her protective big sister voice, "Erèz why have you been crying so much? Look at you! Are you always crying in this house? Why? What is going on Erèz?"

Erèz half heartedly tried to brush away the questions in the doorway, but at one point, Yaya said, "Look me in the eyes, ti fiy,(little girl)!"

And that was when Erèz couldn't hold her tears any longer and let them run loose down her pretty face to free her soul of all the pain she was carrying from Misyé Noël's violation of her body and Madame's implication in facilitating it.

Erèz, suddenly realizing that the teary reunion was still taking place in the doorway, signaled to Yaya and her husband to go through the alley to the bench in the backyard where they could continue their visit, and that was when they all heard the voice of Madame from inside, "I smell something burning!"

Erèz jumped as she remembered that the stock in the meat for the bouyon had almost been dried up before she answered the door. It must have been burned and ruined by now!

Yaya hesitantly headed toward the alley, keeping her eyes on Erèz for as long as she could before Erèz disappeared behind a door. To Erèz's relief the meat for the bouyon was still salvageable. However, the smell of the slight burn had woken Madame from her mid-morning nap, and that was enough to warrant a sharp punch to Erèz's mouth. Erèz knew her lip had split because she could feel the warmth and taste the iron from her own blood, but she proceeded cooking with her head down, trying not to look at Madame, let alone meet her eyes. She felt too ashamed from yesterday's events, knowing that Madame single-handedly planned the entire crime against her.

When Erèz was able to get away from the kitchen safely, she made her way to the yard, feeling even more mentally drained, depressed, ashamed, and humiliated. She realized that whatever small amount of dignity she had left as a human and a young woman living in this horrible house had completely vanished the night before. She wanted to disappear with each step she took after Madame's punch to her lips as didn't know how she could face Yaya and her family in the backyard.

Yaya scrutinized Erèz from head to toe and pierced through the zombified aura that surrounded and plagued her entire being. As Erèz got closer, little Roberto asked his aunt Erèz in a little peasant's voice, "When are you coming to see us?"

Erèz answered vacantly, "One of these days, pitit mwen."

Yaya didn't want to be overheard, and waited for Erèz to get closer before unloading on her, "Do you know you look like a zombie? You definitely don't look like someone who is living, I will tell you that! You look more like you belong in that cemetery over there than here among the living! Erèz what has happened to you?"

Erèz didn't reply a word back to her big sister to avoid Yaya's feisty temper and she went straight to the large bin full of laundry in front of her with her head still down scrubbing pieces of clothes against each other in the foam, avoiding both Yaya's and Benjamin's stares. She scrubbed away at the rust-colored stains on the dress she'd worn the night before, not knowing what else to say or do. If Andrea had been there, she would have likely remembered to offer Yaya and Benjamin coffee and leftover rolls by now, but Erèz was in no state of mind to think of that mere gesture of hospitality.

After Yaya had questioned her for awhile, and Erèz evaded most of the questions being asked, Yaya gave up. She indicated it was time for them to leave, and Erèz wiped her hands of the soapy white foam and proceeded to empty Benjamin's bag full of African yams. They had brought just enough yams on their long trip by foot to Jérémie from Guinaudée that their weight didn't present too much of a burden to Benjamin, but the offering of fresh food for the household was still generously significant.

Little Roberto asked for some water and suddenly looked very tired from the long journey, although Yaya and Benjamin might have alternated carrying him on their backs or sides. They must have left by dawn, but the sun batted hot at eleven in the morning. It would be a long time before he could rest, as they still had to go to the flea market to buy soap and other household items before heading back to Guinaudée.

As Yaya got up, she looked up above her to meet Madame's eyes staring at them from Sherline's window. Yaya's blood boiled as she looked at the woman who had been abusing and mistreating her sister for the past ten years.

Yaya forced herself through gritted teeth to say loud enough for Man Féfé to hear, "Good afternoon, Man Féfé."

Madame answered casually, "How are you all doing?"

Yaya turned toward Erèz and said, "Look at me in the eyes, Erèz! Can't you come back to Guinaudée? You are old enough to pack up and come back. Look at you and your skinny legs! Even your face is bony. You are a stick! Come home, Erèz!"

Tears started rolling down Erèz's face again. She didn't want to tell her sister how terrible her life had been or the new horror that had unfolded the night before. Erèz just shook her head repeatedly at each of Yaya's commands.

"We are leaving. I don't know when we'll see you again." Yaya left with an aching heart. She had not expected to find her sister in such a deplorable state after all these years. All she wanted to do was to drag Erèz right back to Guinaudée with her. On her way back, Yaya regretted not hauling Erèz off right in front of Madame's cold eyes.

After her sister left, in spite of her feverish body and the pain that she felt all over, Erèz finished cooking the bouyon. She served the dinner, did the dishes and took them back to the kitchen upstairs, and started ironing the clothes she had hand-washed during the day.

It started raining, and Jako screamed as he paced back and forth in his cage: "Man Féfé, la pli, la pli, la pli." Bòs Cyprien burst out laughing, and even Erèz found herself cracking a little smile and chuckling at Jako's interruption of the peaceful afternoon because of the rain. Erèz couldn't laugh long, though, and rushed to gather the clothes she'd already ironed and the ones she hadn't yet touched to finish ironing in the back corner of the living room. That night, her fever spiked, and the pains from her internal and external bruises persisted, stinging even sharper.

Each time she tried closing her eyes that night, she kept seeing Yaya's glance piercing her body. Yaya's deep stares pierced her soul in her dreams deeply, as if she was able to peek through all the things Erèz wished nobody knew about her.

CHAPTER 47
School

The following Sunday afternoon, she went to buy bread as usual for that evening's supper and Monday's breakfast. She was in no mood to laugh at the anecdotes of people waiting in line for their turn to buy bread. On her way back, carrying the tray of bread covered with embroidered white linen, she noticed Marianne standing in front of her house. Erèz quickly looked down and away, hoping Marianne didn't see her.

"What's going on Erèz? Are we no longer friends?" Marianne yelled jokingly from her porch. Man Jan happened to overhear Marianne from her living room and wondered what might have happened between the two. Marianne and Man Jan shared a special bond, and Marianne kept nothing secret from Man Jan. Man Jan's engaged conversations with Marianne usually happened while Marianne sat in front of her on the small bench as Man Jan scratched dandruff flakes off Marianne's scalp, greased each strand of hair with lwil maskreti, and braided her hair in all sorts of beautiful two- and three-stranded twists and braids.

Erèz and Marianne's friendship was never quite the same after Erèz's first rape. The emotional turmoil and intense feelings of shame shattered something in Erèz's soul, and she was never able to be open and forthright with Marianne as she had always been in the past. Where once the two had communicated with open hearts, Erèz found herself retreating into herself more and more. Feelings of inferiority and being less-than plagued her being and consumed her. The rapes continued, referred to by Madam as "massaging Misyé Noël's feet."

When Misyé Noel needed no massage on a Friday night, Erèz stayed busy in the kitchen as long as she could before bringing out plates full of fritay for the men to enjoy. On the Fridays that she didn't have to give private massages, Misyé Noël acted around the table as if he didn't know her. Of course, the sexual comments about her body and perky breasts and the sardonic laughter echoing from the room never ceased. Powerless, Erèz complied with what Madame asked of her every time. The one thing Erèz was thankful for was that the other men seemed to respect that she exclusively was "Misyé Noël's little woman" and Madame showed no interest in making her "massage" any of their "feet." Thus, because they respected the group's male code in a common accord, they didn't actively pursue Erèz through Madame for special massages.

Two weeks after the initial foot massage to Misyé Noel, Madame stood in the doorway of the kitchen while Erèz was cooking and said, "I talked to Madame Salnave, the director of the school for the restavèks, and she said I could send you to school next Monday afternoon."

Erèz couldn't believe she heard Madame right. She had been depressed for the longest time over not being able to go to school, but now that was all about to change. Madame didn't even wait to buy new shoes and fabrics for her plaid uniform. It was as if she was trying to compensate for her evil ways.

Erèz couldn't wait to finally be in school after ten years of being a restavèk in Madame's household. It was actually happening. Madame sent her to a seamstress in town to have her measurements taken and the uniform fitted a few days later. Monday couldn't get there fast enough.

When the day came, she arrived at the school right on time and was directed to the beginners' class where most of the kids' ages ranged from seven to nine. There were a handful of older students, but Erèz was the oldest and tallest. It didn't matter to her, as she was elated that her lifelong dream was finally coming true. She was ready to finally learn the alphabet, and to read and write. She felt that all the trials and hardships she'd gone through leading to that day had finally paid off.

The name of her professor was Mademoiselle Fabienne, and she was a well-respected lady in town. Mademoiselle Fabienne wore a long rose-pink dress with skin-toned tights, and a cream-colored slip that peeked out from underneath the hem of her dress. She didn't take attendance considering how quickly children came and went. New faces were replaced with even newer faces from one week to the next as aristocratic families in town let go of their restavèks and replaced them.

When she noticed Erèz, she asked, "Are you the girl from Man Féfé's?" Erèz smiled and nodded yes.

"How old are you?"

"I don't know, Mademoiselle Fabienne," replied Erèz.

In fact, Erèz wouldn't know her birth date, and thus her exact age, for many years to come. Her birth certificate was safely guarded by Yaya. As the oldest sister, Yaya was entrusted to keep the little plastic bag that contained the family's important documents such as birth certificates, marriage licenses, and their parents' wedding rings.

Some of Erèz's classmates struggled to stay awake after the first fifteen minutes, and Mademoiselle Fabienne grew tired of jolting them awake by saying "Lévé!" ("wake up!") every time one or more students would nod off.

Mademoiselle Fabienne continued writing letters of the alphabet on the large blackboard in the front of the class and said, "Repeat after me…" The students who were still awake and able to pay attention repeated each letter of the alphabet after her.

Mademoiselle Fabienne handed Erèz a brand-new book that was going to be her reading primer to study from and do her homework. Smelling the fresh pages of her new book was a dream come true. Opening the book, she saw the first lesson for her was on the first letter of the alphabet. All the shapes and forms the letter A could take were displayed for her to learn. She was so immediately enthralled at all the shapes that she eagerly focused on grasping the concepts of this amazing letter, A.

As Erèz sat mesmerized by the scent of her new book, Mademoiselle Fabienne noticed an out-of-breath Bòs Cyprien standing in the doorway, staring at her. Mademoiselle Fabienne, seeing that this man very obviously needed something, asked him in Creole to state his business.

Bòs Cyprien's voice snapped Erèz out of her studies, and she knew immediately that she was in trouble. Mademoiselle Fabienne looked at Erèz a bit sadly, and asked her to gather the little notebook she brought with her, her brand-new book, and pencil, and put them in the fabric bag Madame had given her on her way out.

On her way to the house, Bòs Cyprien said, "You forgot to clean the table and fix the chairs before you left. Madame is very unhappy." Erèz became very worried as she recalled having washed the dishes, but had completely forgotten to clean the dining table and tidy the chairs in her rush to get to school on time. She sweated profusely and the stains generated from the sweat started showing around her armpits.

When she reached the end of the hall, she could overhear an agitated and infuriated Madame talking to herself in a frenzy, "I'll show her. That wretched little snob! She'll quit being such a little snob by the time I'm done with her." Erèz's heart palpitated and raced. She knew she was going to get it bad.

As soon as Madame saw Erèz's head poke through the door, she struck her straight in her mouth and split her lip wide open. Blood started dripping down her chin right away.

"You disgusting little zombie. You knew you didn't clean the table, but left anyway!" Madame said with angry, bloodshot eyes. Erèz held a hand to her mouth to keep the blood from falling to the floor and rushed away to finish cleaning what she had started about an hour and a half ago.

Madame followed her and said coldly, "And you can forget about that school thing. You've ruined that, haven't you? That's it for you! You're done."

Hearing that hurt Erèz far more than her bloodied swollen lip. Her heart broke and another piece of her died inside. She wasn't going to be able to wear her brand-new uniform, and the only letters in the alphabet she would recognize were just the A, B, and C she had previously learned from Marianne.

CHAPTER 48
Changes

On September second of that same year, Erèz turned eighteen years old even though she didn't know it. Life was moving for everyone, but hers remained much the same.

Her godmother let her know that Ilèyis had finally found himself a beautiful girl named Sabrina, nicknamed Sèsè. The shy Ilèyis had even worked up the courage to ask for her hand in marriage. Sabrina's parents saw that he was an upstanding young man and a very hard worker. Ilèyis' godparents and Sabrina's parents all happily agreed to the union, and they were married in the church. Erèz wished she could see Ilèyis, but he had no desire to set foot in Madame's house after what Yaya reported back to him about her visit with Erèz.

Yaya started traveling to Jérémie more often to sell her fresh garden harvests and to more easily buy the items her family needed. Yaya never came back to the house of Madame, her cousin, after the last visit, but Erèz knew where to look for her at the flea market on Saturdays. Yaya often gave a gourde or two to Erèz to buy what she needed.

Four months later, around February, Erèz missed her period and a few weeks later, she found herself waking up feeling nauseated on more mornings than not. She even became skinnier as the days went by, and Madame initially thought she might be sick with worms.

In May, Madame came to the kitchen and asked how long ago she'd had her period. Erèz thought back and realized her last period had been back in February.

"Then you must be pregnant?" Madame said, but it wasn't really a question. Erèz just stared blankly at Madame, admitting to herself for the first time that she indeed must be pregnant.

"Well, then you are going to pack up your belongings and get out of my house right this second before you shame and disgrace me and my family in this neighborhood or in this city. Get out now!"

Erèz stood there paralyzed, and her heart started racing. She wasn't sure if it was for real. Was she really being kicked out of the house just like that, after ten years of service? As she stood there with her mind racing, Madame slapped her across the face so hard that one of her front teeth flew right out of her mouth and a thin trail of blood splashed across the room along with it.

She didn't wait for another hit and quickly ran to gather her things. She had no idea what she was going to do next. Where could she go? The only friend she had, or rather used to have, was Marianne, but Marianne was off studying culinary arts at the main technical school in town. Besides, they had become distant since she started being forced to massage Misyé Noël's feet. Now, Erèz was pregnant and carried this baby against her will because it amused Madame to degrade and humiliate her by allowing Misyé Noël use her body as his personal plaything.

As Erèz rapidly made her way to the little room where the sacks of charcoal were kept, Bòs Cyprien noticed her frenzy and urgency and said in a somewhat commanding tone, "Hey, where are you going?"

In response, Erèz vomited right in front of him. Madame, her own cousin, who was still pacing heatedly back and forth in the living room overheard the question and yelled, "Let the woman go!"

Erèz left unceremoniously with the fifty gourdes that she'd managed to save over time and a few belongings in a fabric bag that she had sewn herself. Her bag contained clothes, toothpaste, a piece of soap, a few panties, some bras, a little plastic bottle filled with dark castor oil, and the pair of black shoes she'd kept around. She had those shoes just in case she was ever to attend something special, but that something special never came. For a moment, perhaps in slight delirium, it amused her that these ancient shoes still looked brand-new although they no longer fit her.

As she walked, aimless and confused, everyone who met her in the streets with the plastic bag on her back filled with random things avoided and dismissed her as a crazy vagrant woman that they wanted nothing to do with. That night, after wandering around town trying to make sense of what had just happened, she spent the night sleeping on the porch of the Saint Louis Cathedral.

Erèz was convinced in her heart that all the saints her mother used to pray to wouldn't let her down now in the darkest hours of her life. On that porch, she sobbed the night away, unable to push away the countless emotions that overwhelmed her. Despair was perhaps the heaviest emotion she felt as she had no idea where she would stay or how she would find work to support herself and a baby. She decided she was going to avoid approaching anyone she knew as she didn't want to be shamed or ostracized by people she cared about, as commonly happened to young women like her who gave birth to illegitimate babies. Somehow, she managed to fall asleep staring at the stars flickering in all their splendor, but she was plagued by nightmares. In the darkness of her dreams, she was desperately running away from a slew of hateful voices that laughed and screamed at her for being a depraved woman who should have done better for herself.

Eventually, the clicking of ladies' high-heels woke her from her agitated slumber. It was nearly four in the morning, and mass was about to start. Parishioners who faithfully attended the early morning mass started arriving wearing their well-pressed clothes, shawls, slips, and tights. Teachers, public workers, and some students committed to and involved in church activities made up the core of that dedicated morning worshipers. Erèz woke up with her head throbbing, paralyzed on that cement porch padded with red bricks. Andrea's kind face entered her mind. Despite herself, she felt a hint of a smile spreading on her face as she remembered Andrea. It'd been six years already since Andrea's departure from Madame's house and she didn't have a clue where she lived, but perhaps, she wondered, she could find someone who did.

As she laid on the ground thinking about finding Andrea, Erèz listened to the singing from inside the church, the reading of scriptures in French, and the regular rituals she was familiar with from when she attended the church of Saint Peter in Guinaudée.

Mass ended around six-thirty, just in time for attendants to go back to their respective houses to eat breakfast before heading to their daily activities, school, or work. The parishioners walked quietly through the church as if to not disturb the saints they had just prayed to. As soon as they set foot on the street, however, their voices filled the air as friends and fellow church members engaged in multiple conversations and discussed church activities. Eventually, the street became quiet again as they bid each other au revoir, kissed each other on the cheeks and rushed off in different directions. Some people threw a few gourdes toward at Erèz where she lay on the ground. Helping the less fortunate was part of their duty as faithful servants of God. She laid there unmoving and unable to even acknowledge the parishioners' charity.

Sometime late morning as the blazing sun made its way through the sky, Erèz realized she couldn't remain on the ground any longer as the bricks on the floor became unbearably hot. She managed to get up and pick up her cotton bag with her belongings. As soon as she was up, she felt the earth spin around her, and she vomited what little was left in her stomach from yesterday's breakfast, along with bile. She sat back down on her bag holding her head in one hand hoping she would feel better.

After an hour or so, she felt able enough to try starting walking again. She tried considering where exactly she was going to go when another wave of nausea engulfed her. It was also the same time that Marianne was on her way to culinary school. Her well-pressed pleated khaki skirt and shirt were spotless, and it was obvious she took a great deal of time to carefully iron each pleat. As she walked on the path leading to the church, Marianne noticed a young woman bent over, holding herself up with one hand against a mango tree, vomiting. As she drew closer to the woman, Marianne thought the woman bore a striking similarity to her former best friend, Erèz. After a few more steps, she knew it was, in fact, Erèz. Marianne's eyes grew wide for a moment at this totally unexpected realization, and tears started rolling down her cheeks. Each tear carried with it some of the red talc powder from her cheeks and dripped on the collar of her uniform.

"Erèz, what's happened to you? What is going on?" She rushed to her side with her tearstained face.

Erèz kept her head facing the ground out of shame, not wanting to look straight into Marianne's soft, dark eyes. Erèz let out an involuntary cry and slid to the ground against the mango tree's trunk. She brought her knees close to her body and dropped her head.

Marianne sat down next to her. The acrid smell of vomit filled the air, but she didn't care. Erèz told Marianne everything. It was the first time she'd said anything aloud to anyone about all the horrors she'd experienced living at Man Féfé's. Marianne knew Erèz suffered a great deal, but she had no idea just how bad it was and how much worse it had become once Misyé Noël came into the picture. Marianne held Erèz close to her and cried with her, saying, "pa kriyé sò!" ("don't cry sister!"). There was nothing Marianne could do to help, but the affectionate moments they shared under that tree gave Erèz some feeling of renewed strength. Marianne, with tears still in her eyes, hugged her tightly and kissed her on the cheeks before they eventually parted ways.

Once Erèz found herself alone again, her thoughts revolved back to Andrea as the only person in the world who might be willing to welcome her. She remembered Andrea said she lived in Saint Helens before she quit working for Madame. It struck Erèz how strange it was that even after ten years living in Jérémie, she barely knew anyone besides some of the vendors at the flea market. She sat by the mango tree lost in her thoughts when an older woman approached her and offered a bowl of rice and beans and beef with okra stew. From the rosary hanging around her neck and the gray head scarf, it was clear that she was part of some sort of ministry in the church feeding the poor around town. Erèz realized it was late afternoon and she still hadn't eaten since the previous day. It would take only twenty-some more years for Erèz to find out that that angel's name was Tant Cécile.

That warm and delicious plate of food was a confirmation to her that the saints her mother loved praying to were watching over her.

After the first bite, she realized just how hungry she was. Tant Cécile, stood there watching Erèz with so much pity as she grabbed the food from the plate and desperately shoveled it in her mouth as if she'd never eaten or seen food before. After sitting with Erèz for a while as a sign of compassion, Tant Cécile decided it was time to move on to the next soul in need.

"God, bless you, my daughter," she said kindly, just like Andrea used to do at Man Féfé's house in the afternoons before she left.

Erèz sat under the tree with a full belly and a clearer mind, wishing she knew the directions to Andrea's house. She decided to rest there a little longer and gather some strength, then she would make it her mission to figure out how to get to Saint Helens.

In her quest to find directions to Saint Helens, she made sure to completely avoid the flea market so as not to bump into any of the vendors who knew her, and especially not Tant Tètè who sat in the same area where her godmother regularly sold her fresh goods when she came to Jérémie. Erèz couldn't believe her luck when the first person she asked for directions to Saint Helens was able to help her.

She followed the instructions exactly as they were told to her. The walk took her by the ocean in the heart of the city. Perhaps any other time she would have loved to admire the view, but she held her head down in hopes of inviting fewer degrading comments from passersby who felt it necessary to make cruel remarks about her destitute appearance.

She walked as fast as she could and when she got to where she thought Saint Helens might be, she started asking people if they knew of an Andrea who lived in the neighborhood and where her house might be. No one she spoke to knew Andrea. Erèz began to think she was not in the right place. Perhaps keeping her head down for most of the journey meant that she'd missed a turn somewhere. Soon, it became clear to her why nobody knew Andrea. Andrea worked seven days a week. She left her house and children very early in the morning and didn't return until late in the evening. Other than close neighbors, it was likely most people didn't know Andrea.

Erèz tried to think of ways she might find Andrea. Would she have to wander the streets during the early hours in hopes of finding Andrea on her way to work? How many days or weeks would it take her before she ever found her? Maybe Andrea didn't even live in Saint Helens anymore.

"Erèz? Is that you, Erèz?" Erèz's eyes widened at the sound of her name. At first, she thought she must be hallucinating from exhaustion or despair or both. That voice was none other than Andrea's. There was no mistaking it.

She turned around, unsure if this was real or her mind playing tricks on her. There stood Andrea right in front of her. Erèz smiled with her whole being for the first time in a very long time.

It felt to Erèz as if they'd never been apart. She immediately felt safe, at ease, happy, and comfortable in Andrea's presence as she had from the first day they met at Madame's house.

Andrea let Erèz lead the conversation, waiting for her to reveal what she wanted to reveal when she was ready. She didn't want to ask prying questions that might be too painful to answer. But even before Erèz spit her heart out, Andrea concluded she must have been kicked out of Madame's house.

Erèz didn't hold back and explained everything to Andrea. Andrea's heart broke when Erèz spoke about that first night massaging

Misyè Noël's feet and how it continued to happen on many Friday nights after. Andrea started to cry when Erèz spoke of sleeping on the church's porch after Madame kicked her out upon discovering she was pregnant with Misyè Noël's baby.

"Let's go, my daughter!" said Andrea, as they'd been standing all this time on the side of the street. Andrea knew she was taking a risk by having Erèz at her house. Getting pregnant out of wedlock by a married man was something that made any woman a pariah, regardless of the circumstances leading to the pregnancy. Andrea knew that as Erèz's belly grew, her neighbors would look down on her for fostering a "prostitute" who had gotten tangled up with a married man. Regardless, Andrea couldn't fathom the idea of turning her back on Erèz when she needed her most. Her love for Erèz was too strong, and she would face any criticism that came her way for fostering her at her home.

CHAPTER 49
Andrea

Walking up the little hill leading to Andrea's house was surprisingly difficult for Erèz. Andrea noticed her struggling and grabbed the cotton sack with Erèz's belongings, loading it on her own back. On her other shoulder, Andrea was carrying the small black leather bag with a brass buckle that Man Féfé had given her many years ago. It had already seen many years of use before it was given to Andrea, who hung onto the bag as a token that represented her survival and endurance over the course of years of unending mistreatment and abuse in the household of an aristocratic mulatto family. Even when the bag was falling apart, Andrea carried it as one of her most prized belongings.

When Andrea and Erèz finally made it to the house, Andrea's children ran to Andrea excitedly smiling from ear to ear, "manman, manman." The kids had been waiting an entire day to see their beloved mother. Andrea's two-year-old, Sandra, tugged on Andrea's long black pleated skirt, indicating she wanted her manman to carry her. Andrea obliged by kissing her on the cheek after lifting the child into her arms. Micheline, the middle child, peered shyly at Erèz after hugging her manman, and the eldest, Tania, grabbed the black leather bag from her.

Before Tania turned around to take the bag to Andrea's room, Andrea stopped her and motioned toward Erèz with her head, "Can you say 'bonswa Manmzèl Erèz'?"

Slightly embarrassed and with a small shy smile spreading on her face, Tania said, "Bonswa Manmzèl Erèz."

Erèz wasn't sure she'd ever heard anyone refer to her that way before and replied, "Good evening, my daughter."

Tania turned around and rushed to her mother's room with the black leather bag, digging for the candy that Andrea faithfully brought for each of them every evening.

In just two days, Erèz had traveled between both worlds of social class. She had gone from the opulence of Madame's aristocratic home and lifestyle to Andrea's impoverished home.

An old flannel blowing in the direction of the breeze served as a front door to Andrea's house. There was multiple stitching and several patches sewn throughout to keep it together as one large piece. The floor was slightly better than what Erèz had been used to in Guinaudée. Andrea's house floor would be considered an improved one; it was pasted of dirt in most areas and cemented in a few parts such as the bedrooms. From the front door, one could see straight into the back-yard where construction rocks piled up in the corner of a small latrine. The rocks indicated that Andrea probably intended to cement the entire floor of the house someday. The pieces of flat wood that served as walls to the latrines barely covered half of its side. A strong shove could have taken the whole latrine structure to the ground. There was no running water at Andrea's house like there was at Madame's. Tania had to go to a neighbor's house to fill a gallon jug with water. This made Andrea and the kids very conscious about water consumption, as each gallon cost them five cents.

That night Andrea asked Erèz to sleep in her bed. Erèz refused to do so, knowing that the bed was reserved for adults of the house. Andrea wouldn't accept her excuses.

"You are the guest. I will sleep on the floor with the kids."

That was Erèz's first time sleeping on a bed since she could remember. That night, she struggled to fall asleep. Her mind repeatedly played the scene where Madame coolly kicked her out of the house without so much as a thank you for ten years of hard labor. She felt a mix of emotions, ranging from anger to sadness to shame as she could hear Madame's voice in her head, berating her and accusing her of shaming her family in the eyes of the neighborhood and as far as the entire city. Those words reverberating in Erèz's ears painfully pierced her heart and when she finally fell asleep, she slept more deeply than she ever had in a long time. She slept until ten in the morning, and for the first time in ten years, she slept through the rooster's wake-up call. There was nobody at Andrea's house to delight in throwing water on her if she slept past that first crow. After ten long excruciating years, she was free from a rooster's alarm clock.

That morning before heading to work, Andrea stood at the doorway of the bedroom staring at Erèz sleeping so soundly. Her heart was full of warmth for Erèz, but also so much pity for everything the poor young woman had been through. Andrea didn't want to disturb her, and blessed her with a silent prayer while performing the sign of the cross. While Andrea was gone during the day, a neighbor came by occasionally to check on the two younger girls, but eleven-year-old Micheline did most of the caring for two-year-old Sandra during the better part of the day. That year, Andrea couldn't afford to send both Tania and Micheline to school, and so Micheline stayed home taking care of little Sandra.

When Erèz woke up, it took her a moment to remember where she was and everything that had unfolded to get her to Saint Helens. She spent some time enjoying the fact that she didn't have to do anything for anyone today. Her mind soon refocused on her current living situation, the baby she was carrying, and what her future looked like as a single mother raising a child born out of wedlock. She pulled her toothbrush from the cotton bag she carried, poured some water in a small aluminum pot, brushed her teeth, and made her way to the latrine to wash herself. She changed into her white flowery dress and noticed for the first time that her four-month baby bump was pronounced and undeniable.

Upon coming inside, Micheline pointed and said to her in a voice that conveyed respect for the visitor of the house, "My mother said one of the soups is yours."

Erèz looked to where Micheline pointed. On the one table that stood in the room that served as a living and dining room combined, she saw that Andrea had left two semi-brown bananas and four bowls of bread soup.

"Thank you," said Erèz, smiling at little Micheline, but she didn't feel that she had the appetite for bread soup. Instead, she went back to the backyard, sat herself behind the pile of old rocks by the latrine where the kids couldn't see her, and proceeded to cry her eyes out for the next two hours.

CHAPTER 50
A Spell

O nce Erèz had exhausted her round of tears for the day, she decided to take a walk around the streets of Saint Helens. She was craving smoked herring, and she wanted to get some other ingredients to cook dinner for the kids and for Andrea when she got home. She would definitely not be going to the usual flea market as she didn't want to face any prying questions from the vendors she knew quite well.

As she set foot outside, she took a long look at her surroundings, trying to memorize as much of the street as possible, especially where Andrea's house was located. Neighborhood women that were coming in and out of their homes noticed her and stared, as they'd never seen her before. Though their stares may have been innocent enough, Erèz felt as if they all knew the details of her story and were silently judging her.

Erèz walked, staring at the ground, lifting her head only if she approached someone or if she thought there might be a store where she could purchase the items she ought to buy. Eventually, Erèz followed her nose to a little quincaillerie (neighborhood shop) that sold what she needed. The woman behind the counter, who was also the owner, located the items Erèz asked for while making sure to keep peering back at the strange-looking new girl in her shop.

The owner wrapped the pieces of smoked herring in brown paper. Erèz wished she had cut the pieces of smoked herring a bit bigger for their price, but she kept silent instead of bargaining. The woman handed her the packaged herring, rice, and beans with a quick, "Mèsi."

As Erèz turned to leave with her herring, rice, and beans the woman asked, "Where do you live?"

Erèz responded that she was staying with Andrea just down the road.

The woman shook her head slightly and whispered under her breath, "Well, look at that piece of nothing!"

Erèz felt humiliated at the comment and the judgmental glower, but her low self-esteem impeded any desire to stand up for herself. It was something she was never taught to do or even think about. Erèz returned to Andrea's house with her head hanging a little lower than when she had left.

That afternoon, when Andrea came home from work, the smell of the rice, smoked herring, and bean sauce welcomed her at the door. Erèz had also braided all three of the girls' hair and bathed Tania. Andrea smiled broadly and expressed her appreciation to Erèz for her help. Andrea took the plate that Erèz had set aside for her to her room and invited Erèz to follow her.

To Andrea's surprise, the bed was made and the broken cement and dirt floor had been carefully swept to give a very clean feel to the room. It was something Andrea always intended to do, but never found the time.

Andrea couldn't stop thanking Erèz for the delicious and unexpected dinner between bites. Nobody had cooked for Andrea in years.

Once she finished eating, Andrea said, "You are almost five months pregnant. We really need to get you to a clinic to make sure that you and the baby are healthy."

Erèz had not considered the idea until Andrea brought it to her attention. Erèz didn't think the fifty gourdes she'd managed to save over the past ten years would be nearly enough to pay for any clinic visits. She didn't mention her concerns to Andrea, but she nodded, knowing it was imperative to go to a clinic to care for the baby moving in her belly.

"I am going to talk to Komè Josette to see if she will hire you to do her laundry for a couple of months. You'll need money for yourself and the baby." Erèz was full of gratitude that Andrea embraced her like a mother and was thinking of everything that needed to be done. Erèz no longer felt as alone and abandoned like she had when she'd woken up on the church's porch.

Komè Josette hired Erèz to hand scrub loads of dirty clothes on Thursdays and to iron them on Fridays for ten dollars a month. As a peasant worker for Komè Josette, she was treated as such. It was nothing she wasn't already used to. Her food was served in old chipped bowls, and instead of eating inside with everyone else, she sat in the backyard on a bench, and drank water from cupped hands, or occasionally from an old stained cup. Regardless, she managed to save money and buy items she would need when the baby arrived.

Erèz also greatly helped Andrea with her kids and kept the house tidy. On her days off, she hand-sewed maternity dresses for herself. She learned of several free clinics in town and went to her appointments. Sometimes, Erèz wondered if Madame, her own cousin, ever told Misyé Noël about her pregnancy and the true reason why she was no longer at the house.

One evening during the seventh month of Erèz's pregnancy, Andrea came to the house feeling extremely unwell. Erèz wasn't even sure how she had managed to make it home. She walked through the front door out of breath, lurched to her room without saying hello to the kids, and collapsed on her bed with her bag over her shoulder. Erèz rushed to her room with a wet towel and placed it on her forehead. Andrea was unresponsive and remained so even after Erèz pulled on each of her toes and simultaneously both of her ears, trying to revive her. Erèz changed Andrea out of her work clothes and into the old flannel dress she always wore when she came home in the evenings.

Erèz unlatched the window and opened it to ventilate the room.

"Man Andrea, Man Andrea..." Erèz said non-stop as she tried opening Andrea's eyes with her hands and shaking her awake. Andrea remained semi-lifeless, and Erèz felt the gaze of all the three girls from behind her. She turned around to see the panic and fear in their eyes. All three walked toward the bed holding hands, and little Sandra started crying, sensing that her manman wasn't well.

Tania broke down, putting her head on her mother's chest crying, "Manman, you can't die. You can't leave us now. It's way too early for this!" Upon hearing this, Micheline started hyperventilating and crying at the foot of the bed.

Erèz was just as distraught, but she didn't want to worry the kids further. She tried to calm Sandra down. After two hours of Andrea laying on the bed unresponsive despite Erèz's efforts to revive her, Erèz asked Tania to go call Man Joséphine, the neighbor who used to watch the kids while Andrea was at work.

Man Joséphine rushed over exclaiming, "What has happened? What has happened to Andrea?"

She walked to the bed and called Andrea's name many times. Andrea stretched and turned her body toward the wall as if she was in a deep sleep, unaware that there was a room full of people hovering around her. Man Joséphine turned her on her back, tilted her head, and put a cup of water to her lips. It looked as if Andrea was trying to swallow the water, and that relieved Erèz's heart a little bit.

Man Joséphine moved to the end of the bed and started pulling Andrea's toes one after the other, just as Erèz had done previously. After some time, Andrea looked like she was definitely coming back to life. When she was finally fully conscious, she stared at everyone as if they were complete strangers.

"Who are you? Why are you here in my house?" she said. Everyone was stunned.

Andrea pulled herself into a sitting position in the bed and held her head in her hands. She began rambling and mumbling incoherently. Sandra wanted to be with her manman, but when Erèz tried handing the toddler to her, it was obvious that Andrea still had no idea who the child was.

Erèz spent much of the evening consoling the kids and listening to Andrea's incoherent and senseless ranting. Andrea's condition persisted well into the next day.

Man Joséphine returned very early the next morning and said to Erèz, "I am going to go downtown today to look for someone from Abricot to send for Andrea's aunt, Man Dieula. I'll also make sure to inform the Colonel that she is very ill and can't work today." Erèz was extremely grateful for the help and care of Man Joséphine, who was more like a family member to Andrea than just a neighbor.

Man Dieula arrived two days later, and Andrea was still in the same state. She mumbled incoherent words that no one could make sense of.

Man Dieula thanked Erèz for taking care of Andrea and the children saying, "Thank you, my pitit fi m, (my daughter). God will return you all the favors."

During that time of Andrea's sickness, Erèz couldn't go to Komè Josette's house on Thursdays to do the laundry as she'd been doing every week. Erèz learned from a neighbor that Komè Josette replaced her the very first day that she didn't show up. The news that her income was gone troubled Erèz, especially with the baby arriving soon, but she knew for sure that she wasn't about to abandon Andrea who had been her only source of love, support, and maternal affection for many years.

Man Dieula concluded that by the way Andrea was behaving, she must be interacting with supernatural beings from another world. The senseless conversations she was having with herself were her communicating with those beings no one could see. Clearly, Man Dieula thought, someone had cast a voodoo spell on Andrea.

Man Dieula asked Erèz if she knew of anyone that might wish to harm Andrea. Erèz considered the question carefully, but had no idea who might have taken issue with Andrea. Andrea worked long hours and then came home to her children. When would she have had time to make an enemy who would go so far as to curse her like this?

Man Dieula sat on a little bench right by the back door thinking deeply of what to do next. She cradled a cup of coffee in her hands and sipped it thoughtfully.

"No doctor can heal this ailment. We have to figure out who did this to Andrea. Do you know if maybe Andrea owed money to anyone? You're sure she never mentioned anyone's name to you, who might hate her?"

"No, ma tant, she'd never said anything like that to me." Erèz said, but continued to think pensively. Maybe she'd missed something.

From inside the house they heard Andrea scream, "Leave me alone!"

Man Dieula rushed to the room, and found Andrea engaged in a conversation with an invisible someone or something that was unseen in the physical world. Man Dieula tried to tilt Andrea's head, hoping she would be successful in giving her a few drops of coffee. Her attempt was unsuccessful as Andrea started crying like a baby, turning her head from one side to the other and whining in a toddler-like voice, "I don't want to drink coffee! No, I don't want coffee!"

Saddened, Man Dieula left her alone and went to rejoin Erèz in the backyard.

"I think what I am going to do is head back to Abricot tomorrow morning and find a granmoun ougan (an experienced voodoo priest) who will know how to treat Andrea's malefic sickness. Don't worry! I will be back by the evening," she concluded.

True to her word, Man Dieula came back the following evening with an older man that Erèz identified right away as a ougan. Ougans rarely introduced themselves as voodoo priests, and they hid their religious beliefs from society, but people always knew where to dig one up when their help was needed.

Bòs Polo didn't bother with small talk as he entered the house filling the air with a strong smell of kléren (sugarcane alcohol).

"They sent me." He said simply and enigmatically. He made strange gestures that Erèz didn't understand the purpose of. He bent down almost unnaturally as if to sit on a chair that didn't exist. He repeated this motion several times and then made a 360 degree turn from a standing position with one leg extended forward.

Next, from a leather sheath that hung from the waist of his trousers, he drew a machete with a freshly sharpened edge. He swung the machete around as if he was chopping something unseen. That terrified Erèz, but she didn't move and remained there holding little Sandra.

Bòs Polo headed toward Andrea's room without being told where it was.

"I am here. I am the master of this place!" His loud powerful voice bellowed. Erèz wondered if Bòs Polo was perhaps himself possessed with some malefic spirits or maybe just drunk.

Man Dieula, on the other hand, observed the ritual with a quiet reverence. The only sound and motion she made was to ask Erèz to take the children outside as this was not something they should witness.

As Erèz headed outside with the children, she overheard Bòs Polo loudly commanding spirits to come join him in his healing session. He called some of them by names, and the mere sound of those names struck fear in the hearts of Erèz and the kids. She started reciting prayers she'd learned long ago at Saint Pierre church back in Guinaudée. Although she didn't remember all the French words of the prayers, as she sat on the little bench outside, she started mumbling bits and pieces of them for protection, and reciting repeatedly, "Hail Mary, Mother of God, pray for us poor sinners, amen."

A few minutes later, Andrea walked through the backdoor and headed to the latrine for the first time in two days. She was still lost in her own world and ignored Erèz and the kids. Not long after, she emerged from the latrine mumbling her strange conversations, seemingly still in a trance.

Inside the house, Andrea took notice of Bòs Polo and asked him in a whisper, "Who sent you?"

To Erèz's surprise, Bòs Polo asked Andrea the same question and she suddenly released a terrifying piercing howl. Involuntarily, Erèz burst into tears.

Man Dieula came to her and said, "We are going to take Andrea back to Abricot with us tomorrow morning. She will continue getting treatment, and we may need more help to free her soul from the spirit she's possessed with." Erèz's heart sank hearing this, but she understood.

News spread fast across the neighborhood. One neighbor after the other came by wondering what might have happened to Andrea. Each of them had their own theories on who or what had sent a spell on Andrea. Man Dieuseul wondered if perhaps Andrea hadn't paid Man Paul for the fabrics for the uniform she purchased for Tania. It was known that Man Paul was very impatient when it came to matters of money owed to her.

"Maybe she is the one hitting Andrea with this spell!" Man Dieuseul shared among the curious neighbors that now filled the living and dining room. A few of the women couldn't hold back tears as they returned to the living room from Andrea's room. Seeing their friend and neighbor in that heartbreaking condition wasn't an easy pill to swallow.

Two of the people who showed up that night were Lieutenant Colonel Gérard and his wife. The lieutenant's wife's perfume invaded the room immediately, announcing a rich woman had arrived at the house. Her garments and shoes indicated that she shopped overseas, as nothing like she was wearing in her attire would have been found available in the city of Jérémie.

They both politely and gravely bid everyone good evening as they entered the house. Though they didn't pretend that forcing themselves to speak Creole was beneath them, it was obvious they weren't used to speaking it regularly.

The lieutenant lifted the old piece of flannel in front of Andrea's room and waited for his wife to step in the room before dropping it behind them. Man Dieula walked behind the lieutenant and his wife with an awkward smile on her face. Man Dieula's peasant-like demeanor clearly indicated that she wasn't used to being around high-ranking citizens. Both the lieutenant and his wife tried to communicate with Andrea, but it was no use. She was lost in her own world, mumbling.

Just before they stepped out of the room, the lieutenant's wife folded several bills discreetly and slipped them into Man Dieula's hand. Man Dieula was touched, and thanked her for the unexpected kindness and generosity. She followed them to the front door as they respectfully said their goodbyes to the crowd that filled the living room.

CHAPTER 51
Grief

Man Dieula secured a branka for the journey to Abricot. A branka was a stretcher made of two wooden beams with a canvas in between to carry a disabled or sick person. Man Dieula also made sure to find four men to carry the stretcher, and compensated them with both money and kléren for them to drink during their journey of carrying Andrea to Abricot under the hot sun.

In the morning, Andrea struggled with Man Dieula and the four men, screaming that she didn't want to go to Abricot. Through her ramblings, she revealed that the spirits needed her to be in Jérémie.

When Man Dieula finally left, she blessed Erèz on her way out saying, "God is with you, pitit fi m. Thank you for everything you are doing!" Though she left her with a blessing, she didn't leave Erèz money to care for the kids. At that point, Erèz only had forty gourdes to her name until she gave birth to her baby. This would be all the money she had to continue getting ready for the baby and to take care of herself and the kids with, but turning her back on them wasn't an option.

Erèz did her best to care for the kids and continued sending Tania to school every morning. Andrea's absence weighed especially heavily over the kids on that first night. Tania and Micheline had nightmare after nightmare, and Sandra woke up throughout the night crying. Erèz barely slept that night either.

As days turned into weeks, there were no tidings of Andrea. After three weeks, Man Joséphine, who continued to come check on the kids at the house, finally had some news. She'd met Andrea's cousin, Antoinette, anba la vil Jérémie. Antoinette revealed that sadly Andrea's condition had worsened. Antoinette was planning to stop by the house after vending her goods to see the kids before heading back to Abricot. When Antoinette arrived at the house, she brought with her sugar cane, avocados, African yams, ripe bananas, and a few quenepas. It was a short visit as she had a twenty-kilometer trek back to Abricot.

Andrea passed away two weeks later, and Man Dieula had no time to notify Erèz and the kids about the funeral. Abricot didn't have a morgue where a body might be kept, so Andrea was buried immediately. As soon as Man Dieula stepped through the front door, Erèz immediately knew that Andrea had died. The look on Man Dieula's face and the black dress she wore indicating sorrow and loss of a loved one were enough to convey the bad news. Erèz began crying immediately, and it didn't take long before the whole neighborhood gathered in the living room crying and mourning the passing of their neighbor, Andrea. Tania and Micheline understood that they'd just been orphaned and were completely inconsolable. Little Sandra didn't know what was happening, but the sadness and weeping of everyone around her caused her to cry as well.

That night, the women in the neighborhood brought spiced ginger tea, bread rolls, cassava bread, and empanadas for everyone to eat. The men gathered bottles of kléren to drink as they played dominos at Andrea's wake. Man Dieula warmed up teas and coffees in an old pot for everyone in attendance. Occasionally, someone threw a joke to lighten the mood. A laugh might be heard, and at times, the entire house burst out laughing depending on the joke, but grief and sorrow crept back in immediately. The sounds of Andrea's friends and neighbors sobbing filled the neighborhood that evening. Some cries were much louder than others as a sign of heavy grief over the lost soul they mourned. Erèz spent most of the evening numb, sitting on the ground in a corner seeing her entire life flash in front of her.

The neighbors left around six in the morning. Once they were gone, Man Dieula, Erèz, and the kids fell asleep right away and slept almost all day long. They woke up to a persistent knock on the doorframe sometime in the afternoon. It was Man Joséphine with the most extravagant dinner Erèz had eaten since she left Madame's house. The smell of the food made them realize how hungry they all were. They ate the rice and beans and fish sauce with broiled plantains as if it was their last meal on the face of the earth. Man Dieula expressed how grateful she was to Man Joséphine who responded "Vwazinaj se fanmiy" ("We are all family").

Friends and acquaintances of Andrea came and went by all evening, including vendors in the flea market that Andrea bought from often, who stopped by after vending. Man Dieula let them know she would be clearing out the house as soon as she could possibly gather enough strength to do so. Against her will and avoiding everyone's eyes, she announced she would take the kids as well as Andrea's belongings back to Abricot with her. That news hit Erèz hard. Most of the money she'd saved for her baby's birth was spent on the kids during Andrea's illness. She realized she would once again be out on the streets with nowhere to go, but this time, she would have a baby to care for. Man Dieula noticed the look on Erèz's face and immediately let her know that she was quite welcome to come to Abricot and stay after the baby's birth. Erèz nodded silently, but couldn't shake the overwhelming sadness and worry that consumed her soul and entire being.

That same evening, Man Dieula pulled Erèz aside away from the other neighbors sitting in the living room as a sign of comfort and whispered, "We know who killed Andrea. Bòs Polo communicated with the spirit tormenting Andrea, and the spirit confessed who had sent it to kill Andrea. The person is another servant who worked for Lieutenant Gérard. She is not going to live long after as Bòs Polo will be taking care of her for us. I will make sure to let you know when Ougan Polo retaliates by taking her life." Erèz shivered at the idea of someone else dying because of Andrea's passing and in the name of Bòs Polo acting as a ougan. Knowing that part of the story, Erèz became especially scared at the idea of sleeping in the empty house alone once Man Dieula and the kids moved to Abricot.

Man Dieula left as planned three days later with the kids. It was a tearful event for both Erèz and the kids. She kissed little Sandra on the cheeks while wiping tears out of her little eyes. After the last horse carrying them, their belongings, and Andrea's disappeared in the distance, Erèz remained rooted in the same spot staring at nothing but the emptiness of her life as her world crumbled in front of her eyes. Everything that was close and dear to her heart had just vanished.

Erèz went back inside the house and laid on the thin bedsheet she'd been sleeping on for the past ten years. Countless thoughts came and went in her mind. Some made sense and some didn't, but she wondered what her next steps could possibly be. Man Joséphine had told her that payment for the house would be due soon, and she wouldn't be able to pay. Where would she live? How was she going to care for the baby that was due to arrive in a month? Erèz even started feeling guilty, reflecting on Andrea's sickness, reliving the moments, and wondering if she could have done anything to save Andrea's life. She eventually fell asleep despite her worries and slept all day. A kick from the baby woke her up only to realize she was starving. She decided that in order to sustain herself and stretch out the last ten gourdes she had, she would need to survive on a cassava bread diet. She'd buy it early in the morning and eat it midday so as not to be kept awake by hunger later in the night.

Every morning, she managed to walk up to the little store to buy herself two cassava bread and a small amount of sugar. When she got back to the house she emptied the sugar into an aluminum can, added some water, and proceeded to dip the cassava bread in the sugared water to make it last as long as possible and trick her mind into believing she was eating more food than she actually was. The malnourishment began to show quickly as her face became gaunt and her skin dull and dry. She could no longer afford the prenatal vitamins that the clinic had recommended for her. Toothpaste was also a luxury she now had to forgo, and a dark mold covered some of her teeth and weakened them. The state of her teeth embarrassed her so much that she avoided talking to people and definitely didn't smile. Not that she had much to smile about anyway!

Fortunately for her, Man Joséphine occasionally came by with a plate of food for poor Erèz. Man Joséphine predicted that due to Erèz's belly pointing straight, she would give birth to a girl. Had Erèz's belly been pointing downward more, then she would have predicted a boy. Erèz was happy to hear Man Joséphine predicting her baby to be a girl as she had been hoping in her heart that the baby would be a little girl.

CHAPTER 52
Arrival

The head nurse managing the hospital admissions that morning scrutinized Erèz from head to toe without even trying to hide her disdain. Her dirty braids, the old dress now stained with amniotic fluid, the dry flakes of skin that covered her in patches on her skinny legs made it blaringly obvious that she belonged to the lowest social class of Jérémie. The nurse's hateful stare displayed her feelings openly to Erèz. The nurse couldn't stand those destitute women from the streets who showed up to the hospital unable to even pay for the bed they would occupy during their stay. She also knew the ways of those filthy women she despised so well, begging non-stop for favors and pleading for a longer stay at the hospital for lack of shelter and a place to stay once they got discharged. Sometimes, they would go around the hospital harassing more privileged mothers for food, soaps, and other baby items and once they left the hospital, they would breastfeed their babies in the open air around the city of Jérémie.

Man Joséphine stood next to Erèz like a mother during the process. She noticed the nurse's very evident prejudice, but didn't dare mumble a word, well aware that Erèz's appearance would provoke exactly that type of reaction in the society that fostered such treatments. Although she was way better off than Erèz, she herself belonged in the lower social class of Jérémie. The nurse was also able to easily detect the difference in their financial situations by the quality of the fabric of Man Joséphine's handmade dress and the almost-new pair of handmade leather sandals she wore. The nurse concluded that Man Joséphine was lending a hand to the girl in front of her. Erèz, for once, couldn't care less about what was thought of her and her social class as she was in a great deal of pain. She clutched her belly with one hand and tightly gripped Man Joséphine's arm with the other.

The large and long room they stood in contained multiple beds, some of which had occupants that had just given birth or were about to give birth. To the right, a small hall led to the private rooms where the rich women of the city occupied to deliver and nurse their newborn babies. That group of women was attended to the second they set foot in the hospital. Usually, they arrived with an entire entourage of family members and suitcases filled with carefully hand-embroidered little garments for their soon-to-be-born babies. The nurses always welcomed them with a smile and would usually go out of their way to make their stay at the hospital as comfortable as possible. The women in that group had the luxury of filling out their paperwork in the comfort of their paid private rooms. Unlike these aristocratic women, the ones in Erèz's class who arrived to give birth at the hospital were forced to stand in front of the wooden desk with a nurse sitting behind it, yelling impatiently at them for the information needed for their paperwork because the women didn't know how to read and write. In that nurse's perspective, women like Erèz constituted more of a nuisance than anything else. Man Joséphine stepped up at one point and asked to fill the paperwork on Erèz's behalf. She did so the best that she could and signed it for Erèz instead of settling for the simple X required of illiterate women. The nurse pointed at a bed at the very end in the left corner of the room, and Man Joséphine held Erèz's hands. She could barely lift her feet due to the excruciating labor pain. Once they got to the bed, Man Joséphine helped Erèz get onto the high-rise bed by assisting her to lift her legs while supporting the weight of her pregnant body. She then pulled the small white enamel tub underneath the bed to place it right up front just in case Erèz needed to get up and pee.

A nurse arrived shortly with a gown for Erèz to change into. The nurse then threw a sheet over Erèz and checked how far she was dilated before taking her into the little delivery room where the babies of poor women were delivered. Realizing that Erèz was dilated enough, she pushed her bed toward the delivery room. Man Joséphine followed them, but the nurse matter-of-factly told her that she wouldn't be able to go into the room. Man Joséphine waited on the other side of the door, and not too long after, she heard the sound of a baby crying. With a great sigh of relief, she whispered, "Thank you, Manman Mari, Mary the Mother of Jesus!" She then recited the holy prayer to Mary and thanked her for protecting Erèz and for blessing her with a safe delivery. While on her bed in the delivery room, Erèz too thanked Mary, the Mother of Jesus, for her protection and for gifting her with her first baby. She was overwhelmed with emotion and cried as she held her baby daughter.

The nurse didn't say much to the new mother, but she asked her what she wanted to name the baby so she could complete her paperwork. That was something Erèz hadn't given much thought to since the past nine months of her life had been very turbulent.

"She's a girl," said Erèz absentmindedly as her memory took her back to that afternoon in her brand-new uniform learning about the letter A and all the different shapes of that letter. The nurse, who had shown very little compassion since Erèz stepped foot in the hospital, was losing patience waiting on her.

"Alice. Her name is Alice." The name sounded perfect to her when she said it.

"And the last name?" The nurse asked unimpressed.

"Oscar." She said, giving her own last name.

There was no reason to mention Misyé Noël and potentially create more shame and generate more scandal for her life.

The baby was born anemic, and Erèz was prescribed a list of medicines she couldn't afford. She hoped praying to Mary would keep her baby alive.

After a week in the community room at the hospital, Erèz was released and Man Joséphine walked from Saint Helens to Bordes to pick her up. Man Joséphine brought a brand-new handmade dress for Erèz to wear as a gift, and an umbrella to protect the baby from the sun. The thirty-minute walk turned into two hours as Erèz was still hurting from the delivery, and carrying the baby under the hot sun was a cumbersome task.

When they stepped inside the empty house, the smell of the bush bath that Man Joséphine had prepared welcomed Erèz. Although Erèz knew the bush bath was painful for new mothers, she was grateful Man Joséphine took it upon herself to prepare one for her to cleanse her urinary tract, relieve her body from the stress of giving birth, and stimulate the lactation.

Man Joséphine pulled some of Erèz's clothes from what could be considered the only piece of furniture—Erèz's bag—to set up a makeshift mattress for the baby on the ground. Man Joséphine spread Erèz's thin bedsheet over it, leaving plenty of room for her to lay beside her baby and breastfeed her. She placed baby Alice on the little mattress and supported Erèz to the little backroom to give her the bush bath. Man Joséphine proceeded to list all the leaves in the bush bath so that Erèz could learn about them. In this bath, Man Joséphine said that she put papaya leaves, the number one natural muscle relaxer; soursop leaves; mint; kachiman leaves; sour orange leaves; a few barks of cedar; two slices of burnt sour orange; and a generous amount of coarse salt. Man Joséphine rubbed handfuls of the cooked leaves all over Erèz's body as part of the process to relax her muscles. At one point, Man Joséphine handed her the broken bowl she used to pour the green water over her body and told Erèz to drink it. Though the potion looked repugnant and seemed unappetizing, Erèz knew she couldn't refuse an adult's command. Against her will, she drank the potion as Man Joséphine said, "This will wash down your intestines."

Contrary to rich families, who slaughtered goats and cows to make goat-head soup and cow-feet soup to strengthen the body of the new mother, Man Joséphine provided pitimi (millet) and bean sauce to give Erèz's body the boost she needed to feed her new baby. Man Joséphine brought her a plate every day as that was all she could afford to help care for Erèz as a new mother. Man Joséphine advised that the regimen would treat the baby's anemia. It didn't take Erèz long to feel the difference in her health, and she watched her baby gaining strength and color in her skin.

After three months, Erèz thought of ways she could go about finding a job as a servant with a family in town. The biggest problem was finding someone to watch the baby during the day while she was gone. She thought about asking Man Joséphine but thought better of it as Man Joséphine had complained on multiple occasions about being overcrowded with her children and grandchildren that she cared for at her house. Erèz also feared that no family would allow her to bring her baby to work to distract her from the duties she was hired to perform.

She finally found a job to be a temporary servant to wash and iron clothes for a family who only lived fifteen minutes away and was willing to let her bring the baby along. That job, surprisingly, brought a lot of joy to Erèz's heart. At three months old, the baby was extremely happy, and her daughter's smile wiped away much of the sadness that generally plagued Erèz. That joy was short-lived as, to her big surprise, she found her few belongings outside the house with a new lock installed on the flimsy front door one evening when she got back from her job. She sat on a large rock near the house cradling baby Alice and wondered where she was going to spend the night. She thought about going back to her work asking for a spot to spend the night with the baby, but she knew the only spot that would be offered to someone like her was already occupied by the gason lakou although they had two vacant bedrooms at the house.

People walked up and down the street as it started to get dark. Occasionally, she'd hear a child's voice greet her with a "Bonswa ma tant" as they innocently continued on their way. Other adults glanced at her quickly with pity, but didn't say a word as they looked away. The idea of spending the night in the open air under the stars with her baby frightened her. At least, she knew if she could take her baby to the cathedral's porch, Mary and all the saints would watch over and protect them. With that thought, she found renewed strength and decided she was going to spend the night on the cathedral's porch. Erèz took what was necessary and left the rest in front of the house hoping no one would steal it. With her bag loaded on one shoulder, and Alice propped upon her hip on the other side, she headed to the cathedral's porch for the night. Upon arriving, she was welcomed by an authority of the church who told her that sleeping on the church's porch was forbidden. The man wearing a priest's collar informed her that the poor's presence on the porch every morning was unbecoming for the church.

"To be perfectly honest, many of your ilk are disgusting, dirty, and you smell terrible!" The man told her in no uncertain terms. He then pointed toward the large tree right across from the church as the spot they could use to set up for the night. As she looked over, it appeared that a little group of homeless people just like her had already set up a small camp of sorts.

Realizing that this uncharitable man would likely be patrolling the church all night to keep away anyone who might try to sleep on the premises, she walked over to the small camp. Some of the people were friendly, but Erèz hated to admit that some of them were quite dirty and did indeed emit some foul odors. She tried her best to stay away from those ones and avoided letting them touch baby Alice; however, despite her best efforts she couldn't keep away all the people who wanted to say hello to the baby and play with her.

Baby Alice became ill with diarrhea not too long after. Erèz feared that moment would eventually come considering she had no way of sanitizing the baby's only two bottles by boiling them as she used to when she occupied Andrea's house. There, in the backyard, she would start an open wood fire to boil the baby's bottles and let them dry on a piece of towel. Since she'd been kicked out, all she could do was rinse the bottles with water from random public water fountains or with some that she carried in a recycled gallon jug. At least the cathedral wasn't turning away the poor from fetching water.

After three days of non-stop diarrhea, Erèz decided to take Alice to the hospital. She knew she didn't have enough money, but she hoped that a doctor or nurse would have some pity on her and save her baby's life. Much to her relief, the doctor saw Alice and put her on an IV right away to hydrate her tiny body. The doctor prescribed several medicines that Erèz was unable to afford.

As Erèz waited on the doctor to come back with more information, she looked at her weak little baby. Tears rolled down Erèz's cheeks, and she felt scared she might lose her. She started praying to Mary, asking her to give little Alice one more chance in this life. If the baby survived, she promised Manman Mari that she would pack her things and head back to Guinaudée where she would be welcomed. There, no matter how hard and challenging life was, a piece of bread was always split among everyone to make sure no one ever went to bed hungry.

When the doctor returned, Erèz was told the baby had diphtheria, a severe life-threatening form of diarrhea. Erèz prayed with all her heart and soul for Alice to live through this. Miraculously, the tiny and fragile Alice survived her dangerous illness after three weeks of intense monitoring in the hospital.

Erèz knew in her heart that the best way to ensure that the saints were committed to their protection before embarking on the journey back to Guinaudée was to get the baby baptized. This would protect her from the bad spirits during the journey. She looked for Marianne and asked her the favor to be the godmother of the baby. She did the same by asking Ti Roro to be Alice's godfather. Both Marianne and Ti Roro couldn't believe their eyes on how fast Erèz had grown and matured. They found it an honor to witness to a baby's baptism for the first time and to be the ones who would care for the baby just in case something happened to Erèz. They also knew how crucial it was as fervent Catholics to commit the baby's life to Jesus and the saints. Before Alice's baptism could happen, the first step was to get straight with the church and explain why Erèz hadn't participated in the eucharistic sacrament for so many years.

CHAPTER 53
Guinaudée

Erèz was true to her word to Manman Mari. For the miracle that she had granted of life to baby Alice, Erèz kept her promise to return to Guinaudée. She let the family she worked for know that she wouldn't be returning, and she left early the next day. With a bag containing her most important belongings on her shoulder and baby Alice in her other arm, Erèz headed back home for the first time in eleven years. She paced herself as she walked to make sure she wouldn't grow too tired in the first few hours. When she arrived at the banks of the Guinaudée River, Erèz was amused that it hadn't changed at all from when she crossed it some ten years ago for the first time. She set the baby on the ground on a towel and removed her shoes. Lifting her skirt so it wouldn't get wet, she walked into the river up to her ankles. That simple act brought her so much joy and so she kept going. As she got closer to the middle of the river, the water became deeper, and she made sure that she placed each foot on a solid rock before making the step forward.

Erèz decided to take a drink right there in the middle of the river. After her first sip, she realized she was extremely thirsty and continued to drink cupping her hands. A floating pile of horse manure drifted by her as she was mid drink, making her dry heave. She decided she had enough water. As she continued her journey back home, she ran into her godmother who was heading to the city of Jérémie.

"Erèz, is that you?" called a familiar voice.

"Good morning, marènn! (godmother),"Erèz responded upon seeing who had called out to her.

"Is this what you bring back to us?" The joy on Erèz's face quickly faded from seeing her godmother's face staring at the baby in her arms. Her godmother didn't need to say one more word as the look of disappointment and disapproval in her face spoke volumes. Erèz's godmother didn't even care to take a look at the baby. It finally struck Erèz that readapting to the community she was raised in would be more challenging than she anticipated.

Erèz stood quietly frozen as her godmother lectured and shamed her. At one point, while her godmother was still moralizing her, she gathered enough courage to take her first step to continue on her way with her head bowed saying, "M alé wi marènn (goodbye, godmother),"

As she walked farther away, she overheard her godmother rambling half to herself and half to some of the other Madan Saras:

"She was sent to the city for a better life and to make something of herself, and what does she do? She spreads her legs and comes crawling back to Guinaudée with a bastard baby."

Erèz wished she hadn't heard that coming from her godmother, but knew to be ready for this kind of treatment from other family members once she set foot in the neighborhood she grew up in. Once she got close to the house of her childhood, she felt it getting larger with each step, and noticed her brother Ilèyis step outside. Part of her jumped out of excitement to see her brother for the first time in ten years, but a bigger part of her knew that showing up with a baby in her arms wouldn't seal a kumbaya reunion. Ilèyis saw Erèz approaching and couldn't believe his eyes; he stood in the same spot staring at her until she was only feet away from him.

"What are you doing with this?" He nodded his head at Alice with an expression not too dissimilar from the one her godmother had upon seeing the baby. Erèz bit her tongue so as not to create more hostility for herself. Ilèyis took the opportunity to go on a furious tirade about how she was sent to the city to have a better life and all she did was turn herself into a prostitute.

He continued, "How are you even going to take care of that thing?" Erèz didn't know what to respond to that question as she was hoping her home to be a haven considering the rough years she'd survived. Unexpectedly, Ilèyis vehemently slapped her across the face with all his might. The stinging slap startled her and terrified baby Alice who immediately started wailing.

Ilèyis turned to go back in the house without even looking at baby Alice. To him, Erèz was just proof of the shame and disgrace that Erèz had brought upon herself and her family.

She waited a few minutes trying to calm her daughter before stepping into the house. She didn't expect Sabrina, Ilèyis's wife, to be such a beautiful dark-skinned woman with long puffy hair like her mother's. From the way Sabrina looked, Erèz suspected she was educated and likely had served as a house attendant to a rich family in the city. Erèz's mind couldn't comprehend how a quiet, strange, and uneducated Ilèyis managed to land such an accomplished beauty.

Sabrina, nicknamed Ti Sè, tried to lighten the mood by breaking the awkward silence with the, "I can tell the baby didn't care for the way her uncle welcomed her." Erèz released half a smile.

From the other room, Erèz heard another baby crying. She'd had no idea that Ilèyis fathered a baby too.

"Oh look, our little one has her own way of welcoming her cousin," Ti Sè smiled as she crossed over to check on her own baby. In spite of her humiliations, Erèz was relieved at Ti Sè being so kind and welcoming and that made her extremely grateful to her. She became hopeful that others might be less bashful than her brother.

Ilèyis had done a great job with the house in the time that Erèz had been gone. The floor was all cemented and the front door had been redone along with the main side door that opened up to the kitchen in the backyard. The kitchen's roof was still covered in coconut leaves, but it is obvious that it had also been redone. The kitchen looked sturdier now and would be more functional when it rained compared to how it used to get easily flooded in the past. The finished work looked professional and it was obvious that some money was invested in hiring someone who knew what they were doing to rebuild it.

As Erèz admired the new look of the house, a powerful migraine hit her, and she became slightly dizzy and wavered. Ti Sè, noticing that Erèz must not be feeling well, placed a bamboo mat on the ground where she could lie down with the baby.

"Here, just rest a while. You've had a very long journey," Ti Sè said in a compassionate tone.

While Erèz and baby Alice slept, Ti Sè cooked plantains with salted cod sauce and made sure to save her a plate. When Erèz finally woke up four hours later, she was famished. She hungrily ate everything in her plate and wished she could wash the delicious food down with some icy limeade as she used to at Man Féfé's house. She then fed little Alice, who had started getting fussy.

As she fed Alice, she thought about how her godmother and brother welcomed her. Although the way both treated her couldn't be compared to what she'd endured at Man Féfé's house, it still made her feel sick to her stomach. She decided in her heart to keep the details of the circumstances under which she became pregnant a secret. The memories of her pregnancy were too painful and too demeaning, but her family and people in the community might still judge her and blame her for having attracted her fate by luring a married man in. On the other hand, she wondered if they would be more sympathetic to her if they found out what she'd been through. At the end of the day, she decided neither way mattered and that was her story to keep to herself, and she would face the church's condemnation and the community's judgment as it came.

The following morning, Erèz woke up and helped around the house by sweeping the floors in each room, the front and backyard, the kitchen, and the front porch. She also walked several miles to fetch water. Carrying heavy buckets full of water was going to take some getting used to as she hadn't done that in eleven or so years.

Ilèyis had still not spoken to Erèz, but his nasty glares shredded her to pieces whenever she caught them. In truth, Ilèyis was happy to have his sister home even when she'd dishonored herself and the whole family, but he would never admit it to her . He didn't understand why Erèz couldn't save herself and wait to find herself a nice young man in the city of Jérémie to marry.

Yaya treated Erèz even more brutally than her godmother and Ilèyis. A few days after her arrival, Erèz gathered all the strength she could before facing Yaya's hot temper. She took baby Alice to visit her aunt and meet her young cousin Roberto. While Erèz wasn't expecting for Yaya to welcome her with open arms, she could never have imagined Yaya shutting the door in her face when she showed up, stating, "We don't allow people like you in this house." It was a stab to Erèz's heart, and she turned away devastated and distraught over Yaya's humiliation.

That Sunday, she wore her best dress to church with Alice in her arms, and just as she expected, everyone looked down on her. Not a single one of her childhood friends had approached her as the news of her being back to the village with a baby born out of wedlock had spread like wildfire during the week. Some of them intentionally whispered to each other as they stared and pointed at her to belittle her. Upon her return from mass that Sunday, she noticed that Alice's powdered baby formula was running extremely low. She started feeding Alice black bean sauce with mashed plantains and breastfed her regularly to make the milk last longer. Erèz knew she had to look for some work to generate money. She proposed to Ilèyis to sell produce from his garden at the flea market and Ilèyis agreed.

Every Wednesday, just like she used to do with her mother when she was a little girl, Erèz loaded her basket with fresh goodies such as green plantains, soursops, sugar cane, quenepa, and anything that was in season on her head while carrying baby Alice on her side. The ten-mile walk with Alice was arduous for Erèz, but the trip was worth it. Other days, like Tuesdays and Thursdays, she sold the provisions she was able to harvest at the smaller markets closer to the house.

One day, upon returning home from the market, Erèz overheard Ilèyis in a heated discussion with Ti Sè about how they couldn't let her stay at the house any longer. She quietly stopped to listen and Ti Sè was adamant that they'd done more than their fair share for Erèz, who had now become more of a burden with the baby. Ti Sè had grown tired of her presence and wanted her gone. Ilèyis pleaded for her to stay, saying he couldn't let his sister wander in the streets, but Ti Sè wouldn't hear of his excuses. Erèz decided she would disappear the following day and never set foot in their house again. She didn't sleep at all that night, wondering how she would handle what would come her way next.

CHAPTER 54
Man Rebecca

Erèz decided she was going to go back to the Maché Guinaudée to see if one of the Madan Saras she was friendly with would hire her and take her on with her baby. Fortunately for her, it was a Wednesday and she took on the journey to the flea market. Her first thought was to talk to Man Rebecca, who sold textiles and also was Erèz's best mango customer. Usually, when Erèz brought mangoes to sell, Man Rebecca would immediately buy all of what she had and compliment her on the quality of her produce. Out of pure miraculous coincidence, it happened that Man Rebecca had indeed been looking for a servant for the past two weeks. That very day, Man Rebecca took her and baby Alice home with her to the city of Jérémie.

Man Rebecca was a single woman with no children. It wasn't until Erèz made it to her house in Jérémie that she realized that Man Rebecca, besides being a textile wholesaler, was also a renowned seamstress in the city of Jérémie. It briefly crossed her mind that Man Féfé might show up one day to have gowns sewn for her by Man Rebecca, but she promptly brushed that idea off as she decided it was probably unlikely Madame would show up, and hoped she was right.

Man Rebecca treated baby Alice like the daughter she never had. She not only made beautiful dresses for Alice, but she also spent her own money to buy her shoes, socks, and ribbons to match the dresses she sewed. She also treated Erèz with great kindness and respect for the way she ran her house. Many nights, as Erèz prepared supper, Man Rebecca would play with Alice and sometimes they would fall asleep together on their sofa. When young Alice could finally mumble a few words and talk, she referred to Man Rebecca as "Tant Rebecca" out of respect.

Baby Alice enjoyed a great deal of stability with Man Rebecca loving on and providing for her. She went to school when she turned four years old, and Man Rebecca sewed her little uniform, a pleated skirt and plaid blue marine shirt. She wore a new pair of black shoes and carried a brand-new leather handbag that Man Rebecca had made for her. Alice didn't especially excel when it came to academics, but she was very talented when it came to painting, embroidery, and most tactile skills.

During the time she lived with Man Rebecca, Erèz went back to visit Ilèyis many times, and she explained why she'd left the way she did that day. She didn't wish to stir up strife in his marriage or stay longer than she should where she wasn't fully welcome. Erèz was also able to mend her broken relationship with Yaya. Yaya's rejection had hurt her deeply. Yaya slamming the door in her face left a sour and indelible mark in her heart. Despite Erèz's moldy teeth, her newly found life at Man Rebecca boosted her self-esteem, and with her salary she was able to afford most of what she needed as a young woman. She was very pleased that she could put the hurts of her past behind her and could visit her sister, brother-in-law Benjamin, and nephew Roberto, who had grown to be very handsome. Not long after, Yaya became pregnant with her second child, a little girl that she would name Micheline. When Erèz visited Yaya, she brought her provisions like Palmolive soaps, laundry soaps, toothpaste, and everything she could, and Yaya respected her for how she was able to turn her life around.

It was also during that time, much to Erèz's surprise, that Misyé Noël began sending her money. He didn't make direct contact with her or try to see Alice, but he apparently wanted to take some responsibility for the child he fathered. Erèz didn't know that he was even aware of Alice's existence, but in the city of Jérémie word traveled and gossip and rumors spread quickly. It would have probably been more surprising if Misyé Noël didn't somehow find out about Alice. Perhaps his conscience nagged at him considering how he stole Erèz's virginity and the role he took in Erèz's life by playing with her innocence and getting her pregnant at such a young age. It was very possible that Madame let loose of her feelings and let him know what happened, but no matter how he found out about the birth of Alice, it didn't move Erèz either way at that point.

CHAPTER 55
Carnival

When Alice was seven years old, Erèz would grease her scalp and comb her hair on Sundays for school the following day. Alice spent those Sunday evenings peeking from the balcony window that faced the street, observing neighbors and people passing up and down. Erèz, on the other hand, after combing Alice's hair, would lie on the bed, relaxing a bit and letting Alice in on her thoughts. Occasionally, Erèz glanced toward Alice's direction through the veil of the white linen drapes that were beautifully hemmed over some mismatched pieces of costly leftover lace that Man Rebecca had used for the expensive wedding gown of a dignitary's daughter.

That Sunday was different. Rara bands headed anba la vil for the start of carnival festivities that would last three days. The rara bands wore different uniforms, and the men carried their bamboo instruments in their chambray shirts, half-rolled khaki or brown pants, and with their cross-body bags made of crisscrossed bamboo leaves. Apparently, the bags look empty as part of the band's uniform, but often one of the musicians would pull a bottle full of kléren for a shot of alcohol under the blatant sun and heat. The women in the bands, some barefoot, went at the head of their group. They wore white bandanas on their heads and danced while holding the bottom of their skirts to reveal a sparkling white slit. Other times, the entire band choreographed moves created spontaneously to match the rhythm of an engaged musical piece. The women bent their back going in circle around the men carrying the shiny polyester blue, red, and the Haitian flag hooked on the high pole. People following the band along with the ones dancing to the music on their porches clapped out of excitement removing their sandals to move their bodies

Some of the men had red or blue polyester bandanas tied by the handle of the bags. This indicated that they were the band leader, or that they knew the mystic world, or were healers. In some bands, the women danced as if they were possessed by something supernatural that overpowered their beings, making their bodies swirl like a fish without bones. Sometimes the bands stopped and stood in front of houses when the residents stood in front and cheered on the music and live dancing. Out of the blue, the bands put on a whole show, playing tunes and sounds they had carefully selected and rehearsed for this specific house, anticipating some gratification from the owner. Man Rebecca always kept her door closed during carnival season to prevent scenarios like these from happening. Alice enjoyed the scenes of whatever she could from the carnival festivities happening on the street from the balcony. Her heart jottled a bit each time a Madi Gra or masked man in his accoutrement passed by or chased a little girl from her front porch as the family laughed and joked candidly. Alice was always amused by Carole, the crazy lady on the street who always pretended playing an aristocrat woman by wearing a piece of colorful fabric around her neck as her necklace with two empty cans as the pendant to the necklace. Carole always spotted traces of charcoal around her eyes as her eyeliner. Carole followed the band that she liked carrying an old white bag with a golden buckle a woman might have given to her.

The band's stops happened less frequently than they had when Erèz was a child, but she always remained mesmerized by the loud rhythms that the talented men produced with their bamboo instruments, tambourines, and graj (an instrument consisting of a long aluminum grater and a piece of iron), as well as the dance moves of the ladies dressed in chambray and all sorts of colorful fabrics and scarves.

CHAPTER 56
Ghost From The Past

One afternoon, as Erèz walked back from the flea market she turned a corner and literally bumped into a man.

"Excuse me! I'm so sorry," he said. They both stared at each other in a bit of shock as they both recognized each other. That was Bòs Latou, the womanizer and alcoholic, who had just run into her.

"Erèz, this can't be!" A smile spread across his face.

Erèz wasn't sure how she felt, seeing him. The sight of him brought back a slew of bad memories.

"Bonswa Bòs Latou," she said and hurriedly tried to get around him and continue on her way. He called after her and followed her down the street, trying to get her to talk to him, but she made it clear she wasn't interested in entertaining what he had to say, thinking that he might still perceive her as that innocent young girl at Man Féfé's house that married men drooled over.

Bòs Latou wasn't one to be deterred so easily. He followed her at a distance long enough to note the house she went into and considered that information victory enough. Now that Bòs Latou knew where Erèz lived, he would have plenty of opportunity to bait and pursue her. Sleeping with three other women at that time didn't stop him from pursuing Erèz as he'd been longing for her since his eyes first landed on her. Maybe now he would finally have her. Sometimes at night before heading to one of his mistresses' houses, Bòs Latou would catch a glimpse of Erèz on the balcony as she innocently watched people passing up and down the street. Bòs Latou tried to catch her attention by waving and shouting up to her, but she'd roll her eyes, roll down her blinds, and go inside. Other days, he stalked her and followed her on her way to and from the flea market.

"Aren't you an adult, Bòs Latou? Why are you following me around like a little boy?" Erèz would angrily shout at him to leave her alone.

After two years of relentlessly pursuing her, Erèz finally gave in and became involved in a relationship with Bòs Latou. Their usual place to meet was in the exterior corridor of Man Rebecca's house after she'd gone to bed at night. Most nights, they stayed up late talking and laughing in hushed tones. Eventually, the talking ceased and gave way to soft moans as their naked bodies intertwined, and they each hungrily took what was needed from the other.

Bòs Latou simply couldn't get enough of Erèz. He had spent years eyeing her and now it was as if he couldn't get his fill. He saw her as often as she would let him, and most of their encounters happened when Man Rebecca was out during the day and Alice was at school in addition to their nightly exploits.

Sometimes, Bòs Latou would happily take breaks from his work in the mechanic shop that he owned to come spend hours at Man Rebecca's house with Erèz. One Wednesday, they were almost caught. Man Rebecca skipped the market because she wasn't feeling well. Bòs Latou, who had no idea Man Rebecca was home resting that day, came to meet Erèz as usual. Bòs Latou started whistling in their usual meeting spot, and Erèz madly dashed toward where he stood to ask him to stop before Man Rebecca came down to discover him there. He left disappointed that day, but they managed to keep their relationship secret from Man Rebecca.

Word of their relationship eventually did get out, and sometimes Erèz would bump into one of the other women with whom Bòs Latou was also involved. They often threatened her and told her to stay away from Bòs Latou if she didn't want to get beaten on the street one of these days. One time, a woman screamed at her from an upstairs window, "You really think Bòs Latou prefers you over me? Is that what you think? Keep walking skinny bony legs with your flat butt!" Erèz ignored the angry jealous woman and continued on her way. Those angry mistresses' harassment got to a point where Erèz became numb to it.

Erèz became pregnant with her second baby a year after her first sexual escapade in the dark corridor with Bòs Latou. When Erèz informed her that she was pregnant with Bòs Latou's baby, Man Rebecca's eyes filled with tears. It broke her heart, but she told Erèz she was going to have to let her go peacefully so that the rumors that would ensue wouldn't stain her spotless reputation in the city. Erèz knew she would need to find somewhere else to stay before her belly started showing.

Erèz shared the news of her pregnancy with Bòs Latou who replied that he wasn't the kind of man to run away from his responsibilities. He promised Erèz that he would find her a place of her own so that she could be at peace while taking care of Alice and carrying her pregnancy. Knowing his reputation for doing exactly the opposite of what he'd just promised, Erèz didn't actually believe him. Much to her surprise, a couple weeks later Bòs Latou announced to Erèz that he had found her the perfect place in Saint Helens and invited her to go see it. Erèz couldn't believe her eyes. The house was on the same street as Andrea's old house. It was bittersweet, but she was very pleased to have a place to call her own for the first time in her life. It also made her happy to know that if any of her family in Guinaudée wanted to spend the night in Jérémie, they now had a place to stay to do so.

Alice turned ten years old that September, and the baby was born the following month. Bòs Latou and Erèz decided to call the baby Bernadie. Alice loved her new little sister and was ecstatic to be able to help her mother with tending to her sister's needs. She often asked her mother to feed the baby and told her that she would like to have more sisters. Erèz would laugh and often responded, "If God and Mary, the Mother of Jesus, want me to, then I will."

Over time, Bòs Latou became more and more distant with Erèz. His visits became less frequent, but every two to three months he would stop by to visit Erèz, Alice, and the baby, and bring them money. One day during one of his random visits, Erèz could tell something was off with him. He decided to spend the night, which was something he hadn't done in a long time. Erèz soon learned this was because he had something quite difficult to discuss with her. His wife knew about baby Bernadie and wanted to adopt her. If Erèz agreed, she would be welcome to visit the baby and she realized this was the best option. She hadn't been working after giving birth, and the small amount of money that Bòs Latou gave her sporadically didn't cover much of their needs. It was going to break her heart, giving up baby Bernadie to Bòs Latou's wife, and it would devastate Alice's heart, but the decision truly was the best for the moment.

When Erèz explained what was going to happen with baby Bernadie, Alice threw the biggest tantrum, just as Erèz expected. Erèz gently explained to her that the adoption was the best thing for her sister. Alice didn't care and hated what was happening, but she knew that her mother had already made up her mind and there was nothing she could do to convince her otherwise. Baby Bernadie would be going to her new home that Sunday.

Sunday arrived too quickly. Bòs Latou came to pick them up that morning and make the trip back to his home. Man Latou, Bòs Latou's wife, was a bit intimidating at first, as she was much taller than Erèz and built broadly. As they spoke, Erèz learned that she already had three kids of her own, the youngest being four years old. On top of that, she'd adopted many of her husband's kids who were born out of his extra-marital affairs.

Because baby Bernadie already carried Bòs Latou's last name, Latour, no formalities were necessary for this adoption to take place. Alice was extremely distraught when they left Bòs Latou's house that Sunday and took some time adjusting to the house without baby Bernadie. Erèz made sure to take Alice to Man Latou's house every Sunday to visit and hold the baby, but she always cried when they left.

CHAPTER 57
Bòs Luc

Shortly after Bernadie's adoption, Erèz obtained a job right across the street from her house with a bachelor preacher named Bòs Luc. He was a committed evangelist in the Methodist church in town and a carpenter at the Rehabilitation Project Gébeau located five kilometers from his house in Saint Helens. He lived alone with his son Luckner.

Erèz cooked, cleaned, and hand-washed and ironed their clothes. Luckner attended Lycée Alexandre Pétion, which was a forty-five minute walk from Saint Helens.

A year into the job as a maid and servant to Bòs Luc, Erèz became pregnant with Bòs Latou's second child, Guirlaine. Because Bòs Latou wasn't present at the delivery room for this second baby, and Guirlaine contrarily to Bernadie carried Erèz's last name, Oscar. Bòs Latou's presence became very scarce after Baby Guirlaine was born.

Erèz went back to attending Bòs Luc and Luckner three weeks after delivering baby Guirlaine. Both Bòs Luc and Luckner were relieved she was back as they both missed not only her delicious food but also her warm and subtle feminine energy, which filled the house with a motherly presence. Erèz, also enjoying their company, would often go back to Bòs Luc's house in the evenings to make hot chocolate or plantain porridge for them to dip fresh pieces of buttery bread into for supper. Bòs Luc found himself dreading the times when Erèz wasn't around. He realized he was always happier when she was in close proximity and felt like something was missing whenever she was gone for the day. He found himself fantasizing about what it would be like if Erèz was his wife and she would never have to leave. Bòs Luc vainly tried to push away those thoughts, but his feelings grew stronger for her and this idea of asking Erèz to marry him wouldn't leave his thoughts. As a committed Christian preacher, Bòs Luc convinced himself that his strong feelings and desires toward Erèz were only carnal and he somewhat convinced himself that he could pray his way out of his emotions.

Three years later, making peace with himself that his feelings were deeper than simple physical attraction, and that marrying Erèz must be God's will for his life, Bòs Luc decided to openly confess his feelings to Erèz. Amusingly, Erèz had no idea that he even looked at her in this way, as Bòs Luc was the most disciplined, meticulous, studious, and focused man she knew. Erèz always smiled with amusement at the thought of Bòs Lik—as she called him instead of "Luc" due to her limitation of pronouncing his name in French—ever entertaining ideas that might distract him from his faith. Every night, he would sit at the small wooden dining room table, reading his Bible and preparing his sermon for the following Sunday. When Erèz left for the day and called out, "M alé wi, I am taking off. I will see you tomorrow, God willing," Bòs Luc would barely lift his nose from his Bible to somewhat absent-mindedly reply, "Alé ak la pè" ("Go with God's peace").

One night, he gathered enough strength to tell Erèz that he would like to set up a time to talk to her about something.

"Okay, I look forward to it," Erèz responded somewhat amused and not thinking much of whatever this special chat with her boss was going to be about, but later that night, as she laid on her bed trying to sleep, sequences from her traumatic past resurfaced and all sorts of anxious thoughts crossed her mind. She worried that Bòs Lik wanted to let her go, and then what would she do? It didn't help that that same week, Man Rebecca died. Both Erèz and Alice were heartbroken. When they attended her funeral at Cathedral Saint Louis, Erèz and Alice sat in the back of the church where people of her social class regularly sat, as they needed to leave ample room for the rich folks and dignitaries who arrived late to mass. Erèz noticed Man Féfé and Mét Féfé sitting up front in the third row of the last column on the right from where she was sitting. She didn't realize how raw the wounds from her past life were until her eyes landed on them. She glanced away from them and tried to push away the flood of memories and emotion that was triggered at the sight of them. As soon as the funeral was over, she took Alice's hand and made sure they were the first to step outside. She decided it would be better to skip the procession to the cemetery for the official burial of Man Rebecca so they could avoid bumping into Man and Mèt Féfé.

CHAPTER 58
Proposal

The day had finally come for Bòs Luc to have the conversation with Erèz.

"I want to marry you," he said simply and resolutely, catching her completely off guard. Erèz looked at him coyly with just a hint of a smirk inching at the corners of her mouth.

"This is not how you would say something like that," she mused while trying to also hide how nervous she felt.

"I am serious. I want to marry you."

"You know that I don't know how to read and write, right?" She said unsurely, looking at him carefully for any reaction.

Of course, a man who loved her so deeply could never be dissuaded so easily. Bòs Luc replied that such a thing was not difficult to fix. He could easily teach and help her with literacy. What truly mattered was that he saw in her an amazing mother for his future children and an ideal wife. The conversation was brief and somewhat awkward. Neither of them knew how to move forward from there with the employer-employee aspect of the relationship. What they knew for sure was that it was the beginning of a beautiful relationship.

Not long after, Bòs Luc and Erèz became pregnant with their baby girl, Elsy. Though a joyous occasion, it was crucial that the two marry before the pregnancy became a scandal and ruined Bòs Luc's reputation as a devout preacher. Bòs Luc contacted the main pastor of the Methodist church right away so that he could finally marry this woman he'd loved for so long. Pastor Alain Rocourt's only requirement was that Erèz must renounce her Catholic faith and her worship of Mary, the Mother of Jesus. She was to accept Jesus as her true and only personal savior and gave up on praying to the saints. Erèz agreed to this and understood that she would attend classes to learn the doctrines of the Methodist church before becoming an official member of the church.

Prior to the wedding ceremony, the pastor met with them separately to counsel each of them regarding the great commitment they were both undertaking in the sacrament of marriage. Furthermore, the pastor required that Erèz be baptized prior to the ceremony. During her baptism, Erèz repeated lines of prayers after the pastor reading from a little black liturgic book to publicly solidify her commitment to her newfound Christian faith. After the baptismal ceremony, the pastor made it known to Bòs Luc and Erèz that the wedding wouldn't be held in the main sanctuary of the church due to Erèz's pregnancy. Instead, it would be held in the pastor's presbytery since they'd already engaged in premarital sex.

Yaya, who was now pregnant with her fourth child, traveled with her husband and their three children from Guinaudée to Jérémie to attend the wedding. Marianne was also in attendance with her handsome husband and their two beautiful mulatto babies. Erèz's god-mother and Ti Roro came in loving support as well. Since none of Erèz's friends and acquaintances were members of the Protestant church, Bòs Luc asked two of his co-workers from the Project of Rehabilitation of Gébeau to stand as witnesses to their wedding.

Afterwards, they moved to a beautiful two-story house in the suburb of Bordes in Jérémie. This was a great contrast from the slums of Saint Helens. Bòs Luc had been saving for years as he bided his time and waited patiently for the right woman to enter his life. He could easily afford the annual rent of that house with his salary. There was enough room for Alice and Guirlaine and Bernadie—when she visited—as well as Luckner and the new baby. They even set up a spare room to host family members from the countryside when they traveled to the city and wanted to visit and rest before heading back to their homes. Bòs Luc's brother, Ernest, visited from Marfranc often, while their sisters, Bertha, Rolande, and Christienne, traveled from Ravine-à-Charles. Friends also stopped in to see them on their travels from Port-au-Prince during the holidays before hopping on a bus to the countryside.

CHAPTER 59
Reconciliation

Bòs Luc, after much thought and consideration, came to the conclusion that if Erèz was ever to start healing from the years of abuse, instability, and trauma from her past, she needed to face the pain of revisiting them, and reconciling and making peace with them.

For one thing, Bòs Luc wanted to open his home to Misyé Noël and Bòs Latou to visit their children whenever they wished. He loved and cared for Erèz's children as if they were his own, and he definitely didn't need the money both those men occasionally sent for their care. Regardless, the kids' biological fathers should have the option to remain connected with them as they grew up. In his grand reconciliation plan, Bòs Luc wanted to approach Mèt Féfé to see how he could bring the entire family for a visit to their house and pay their respect to Man Féfé. This was his great opportunity to prove to that woman, Man

Féfé, that despite everything she'd put Erèz through, Erèz had come out bright and shining on the other side of life. Not too long after Elsy's birth, Bòs Luc shared the plan with Erèz that he would be talking to Misyé Noël, Mèt Féfé, and Bòs Latou and his wife. Erèz didn't argue with her husband's plan although she didn't think she could successfully face those people, especially Man Féfé.

Before they knocked on Man Féfé 's door that day, Bòs Luc had brand-new outfits made for Erèz and the girls, and he also lectured the girls to be on their best behavior. He even paid to have a lady, Man Françoise, who later would become one of Erèz's best friends, come to the house to flat-iron Erèz's hair. By that point, Bòs Luc had also trained himself to address Erèz as Man Luc, giving her the respect she deserved as a married woman and his wife instead of addressing her by her maiden name.

When they knocked on Man Féfé's door, she welcomed them in the living room with an unguarded smile on her face. Her facial expression seemed lighter. Was it possible she'd grown some compassion or humility during the fourteen years since Erèz had last seen her? Or perhaps she just felt too ashamed to be disrespectful to the well-dressed family standing in her living room.

"Is this you, Erèz?" she asked as she looked at Erèz in disbelief.

"Oui, Madame," was Erèz's simple response, said with the French accent of a peasant who still bowed before her former abuser.

Bòs Luc sat proudly and solemnly in his suit on one of the vaulted wooden chairs. His attire and rigidity of his straight spine suggested how seriously he took this moment. One might think that he was going to a wedding, a funeral, or possibly to preach a sermon at one of the churches he'd started in the countryside around the city; maybe even to deliver someone from a demonic spirit as he was accustomed to.

He didn't say much for a long time. He and Mèt Féfé sat quietly and listened to Man Féfé and Man Luc talking about anything and everything as they got caught up about their children. That first meeting was short, but it was long enough that Erèz could at least start to reconcile her painful and chaotic past with her peaceful present. That visit freed a piece of Erèz's soul, but still couldn't fully heal her from the years of trauma that resulted from living within those walls. Thanks to Bòs Luc, her family was now welcomed with respect and dignity at that house. As she and her family rested their backs on those large plastic-wrapped sofas that she had cleaned countless times but was never allowed to sit on, she celebrated the victory of gaining her respect back as a human being in front of Man Féfé.

Bòs and Man Latou both chose to be more actively engaged in the life of Guirlaine after Bòs Luc officially reached out to them. Man Latou welcomed Bòs Luc's initiative with open arms as she looked forward to meeting Bernadie's younger sister.

The plan for reconciliation didn't go quite as smoothly with Misyé Noël, as his wife took two years to accept the fact that he'd had a child out of wedlock with a restavèk-turned-servant; however, she eventually came around to becoming a part of Alice's life.

CHAPTER 60
The Good Life

Erèz's family members never stopped praising and admiring all the positive changes that happened in her life after she married Bòs Luc. Erèz was grateful to have married a man who helped her forget the atrocities she'd lived through. Her marriage was one filled with respect, love, support, and an abundance of stability. With Bòs Luc, Erèz discovered the true meaning of love and for the first time in her life, she stopped worrying about an uncertain future. Erèz constantly showed her love and respect for her husband as she attended to his needs and ran the house as the perfect mother and wife he'd seen in her. In turn, that made him love her even more. At church, they were inseparable and nicknamed "Roméo et Juliette." With Bòs Luc's encouragement, Erèz became deeply involved in various church ministries including the Women's Ministry and the Jails Ministry. As a member of the Women's Ministry, she joined the group every third

Sunday to sing in front of the church. Everyone in the assembly could see Erèz didn't know the words to the song. She looked up and down from the hymn book she was holding, pretending to read them. Being illiterate didn't stop Erèz, who continued to actively participate in the Women's Ministry's meetings on Friday afternoons and sing her heart out on Women's Ministry Sundays.

During the 1980s, the perfect time for Erèz to finally learn how to read and write presented itself when President Jean Claude Duvalier announced his administration's National Alphabetization Program for adults. Until that time, the few letters Erèz knew from the alphabet were the handful she'd picked up from Marianne's book when she was little. Erèz joined thousands of adults in the city of Jérémie to go to school every afternoon. She beamed with pride as she attended class daily. There wasn't a single day that she was too tired to study and complete her homework in her book titled *Zonbi Gouté Sèl* (*When A Zombie Tastes Salt*). She mastered reading and writing, kept track of people's names who purchased bread and peanut butter on credit from her, and managed to not make a fool out of herself when she read the words to the songs in her hymn book, especially the ones in Creole.

AFTERWORD

Despite all the suffering and misery of her earlier years, my mother had a very happy life with my father. Looking back as her daughter, I realize my sisters and I have each inherited part of her psychological trauma. I also realize that despite all of her activities, both entrepreneurial and spiritual, my mother carried a deeply melancholic soul due to the events of her childhood.

The idea of seeking psychological help was a completely foreign concept to us Haitians when we were growing up. Seeking help from a psychologist would have required our family to already have the awareness that we could actually benefit from what a psychologist could potentially offer. Moreover, expressing the desire to seek help from a psychologist was highly stigmatized. Society would have immediately looked down upon the family because of this desire for mental help, and we would have been perceived as "being crazy." I am sure my parents never considered the possibility of meeting with a mental health professional. Instead, my mother dealt silently with her pain as best she could, and despite all her hardships, both my father and she provided for us and were able to put us through the most reputable schools in Jérémie.

Although the Haitian government is working diligently to establish laws that would protect restavèks, much more immediate and tangible changes need to be made. Haiti has a long way to go before it has completely abolished this system, which is directly rooted in the widespread lack of opportunities for families living in the countryside. Many of these struggling families, like my mother's parents, don't have the means to care and provide for their children. Thus, they feel the need to give them away to strangers or rich family members in hopes of providing their beloved children with greater opportunities in life. However, the reality is that many of the privileged families choose to treat these innocent children inhumanely and cruelly.